ANN JACOBS

Sex, Love and a bit of Magic

ELLORA'S CAVE
ROMANTICA®
WWW.ELLORASCAVE.COM

COMMITMENT

"No promises, no pain" is Gaelen Reston's mantra. But her longtime lover, Brent d'Angelo, wants a woman to cherish for a lifetime. He just has to persuade Gaelen that a real-life commitment doesn't mean the end of their fiery fantasies.

ILLUSIONS

Master magician Drake Conover is dark, dangerous and irresistible to women. But a terrorist? Agent Erienne Duval doesn't think so, but it's her job to find out—by any means necessary.

Including seduction...

COLORS OF LOVE

On the run for his life...

All he wanted was a chance to live long enough to testify against the mob. Tampa architect Zachary Lang comes to magic practitioner Selena Cross looking for a place to hide from the people out to keep him from his day in court. Instead, he discovers a submissive soulmate.

Looking to find the love of her life...

Although Zach doubts his lover's colorful magic stones and incantations can shield him from harm, he's in for a surprise. She tells him to trust the stones and follow his heart, and he discovers she's right. The stones are magic after all. And their love has magic all its own.

COLORS OF MAGIC

Sex makes the magic stronger.

Bounty hunter Garrett Bryant's soul is as battered as his body. All he wants is to get his ex-wife Elaine out of his mind so he can heal and move on. But now their daughter is missing, and Elaine wants his help.

A white witch gives him two talismanic stones to lead him in his search. She tells him to follow his heart, and his instincts. And that love has a magic all its own...

An Ellora's Cave Publication

www.ellorascave.com

Sex, Love and a Bit of Magic

ISBN 9781419964404
ALL RIGHTS RESERVED.
Commitment Copyright © 2002 Ann Jacobs
Illusions Copyright © 2002 Ann Jacobs
Colors of Love Copyright © 2004 Ann Jacobs
Colors of Magic Copyright © 2003 Ann Jacobs
Edited by Martha Punches.
Cover art by Syneca.

Trade paperback publication 2011

With the exception of quotes used in reviews, this book may not be reproduced or used in whole or in part by any means existing without written permission from the publisher, Ellora's Cave Publishing, Inc.® 1056 Home Avenue, Akron OH 44310-3502.

Warning: The unauthorized reproduction or distribution of this copyrighted work is illegal. Criminal copyright infringement, including infringement without monetary gain, is investigated by the FBI and is punishable by up to 5 years in federal prison and a fine of $250,000.
(http://www.fbi.gov/ipr/)

This book is a work of fiction and any resemblance to persons, living or dead, or places, events or locales is purely coincidental. The characters are productions of the author's imagination and used fictitiously.

SEX, LOVE AND A BIT OF MAGIC
Ann Jacobs

ఴ

COMMITMENT
~9~

ILLUSIONS
~75~

COLORS OF LOVE
~159~

COLORS OF MAGIC
~243~

COMMITMENT
ಙ

Chapter One

She wanted him now. In the flesh, not as a husky, sexy voice coming to her over the phone from across the Potomac River.

He was in Alexandria, less than an hour away from her Georgetown apartment, but he might as well be on Mars.

"Touch yourself, Gaelen. Stroke your silky skin the way I wish I could. Remember when we made love under that covered bridge in Amish country?"

How could she forget?

Brent had started it in his Jaguar sedan on I-495, just north of Baltimore, when he rested a hand on the inside of her bare thigh, stroked her with lightly callused fingers.

Warmth had starting building the minute he'd touched her, spreading and intensifying with each suggestive motion of his hand. She cautioned him to pay attention to his driving when he started edging through heavy traffic toward an exit.

"I'd made reservations at a bed and breakfast my nurse had told me about. One with all the luxuries and the kind of absolute privacy I wanted for us that weekend."

Hearing his voice made her picture his dark, smiling eyes, the sensual lips that made her long to taste him. "I like you, Brent. Anywhere."

"Remember how I got you hot while we drove down that road beside the stream?"

Gaelen stroked the inside of her upper thigh the way he'd done that day last spring, imagined it was Brent who was pleasuring her now. "If those Amish farmers in their buggies had seen what you were doing, they'd have been scandalized, d'Angelo."

"They'd have been more shocked if they'd happened to watch us fucking under that covered bridge."

"You asked for it, darling." She moved her hand higher, slipped a finger under the edge of her bikini panties and massaged her aching clit the way he'd done that day in the car. If only he were here!

What he'd done to her with that skilled finger felt so good, it should have been illegal. Her fingers itched to cup him, feel the instant response that always gave her a sense of feminine power.

"I couldn't wait to have you inside me."

"No, and after you unzipped me and took my cock in your mouth, I couldn't wait, either." He laughed, a low-pitched rumble that came from deep within his muscular chest.

"I wanted all eight beautiful inches of you, and I didn't want to wait." He hadn't been able to hide the fact he needed her, too.

"Think of yourself all hot and wet with me inside you. Imagine my tongue on your clit, lapping up your honey. Want me to come over and spend the night?" His husky whisper conjured up an image in her mind of him here, now, fulfilling her every fantasy.

God, she did. She ached to feel his long, thick penis stretching her, filling the emptiness inside her. She cursed the rule she'd made at the start of their affair that they'd avoid invading each other's private space.

Damn the reasons she'd insisted on so much autonomy.

"No. But keep talking, darling."

"Remember how you went down on me? It was all I could do to hold it in until I found that bridge."

She pictured herself stroking the satiny length of him, snaking her tongue out and sampling the pearl of moisture at the tip of his hard, hot sex. Drawing him into her mouth and swirling her tongue along his shaft while he clenched the steering wheel and alternated between ordering her to stop and begging her to keep it up.

When she'd felt the car roll to a stop and looked up from her sensual feast, it had been dark. "Thank God nobody decided to go through that bridge while we were there."

He laughed again, reminded her how sex with him was always fun. "An army couldn't have stopped me, not as hot as you had me by then. You were on fire, too. The fear of being caught turned you on. Didn't it?"

"I'd never had sex in a car before. Or in public anywhere, for that matter. Yes, it turned me on to think about somebody happening by, seeing me riding your…"

He'd tease her, she knew, but she couldn't say it over the phone, even when she was burning to have him thrust that delightful part of himself inside her now.

"My cock? Don't tell me you're still afraid to say the word after all you've done with it over the years."

His chuckle made her smile through a haze of sexual frustration.

"Is it hard now?"

"Like a rock, sweetheart. The way it was that day, when you rode me in the front seat of my car. You were hot and wet for me then. Are you now?"

"Oh, yes." She was wet for him now, aching and needy.

The slapping sounds and musky smell of sex, mingled with the scent of glove-soft leather upholstery, flooded her memory, surrounded her in the silence of her lonely bed. She lifted her head, whispered a command so raw she wouldn't say the words out loud, not even to him. The same command she'd whispered that day under the covered bridge.

"What did you do with that present I got you?"

"It's in the top drawer of my nightstand, right where you told me to put it."

"Open the drawer, Gaelen."

She reached for the nightstand, drew back. "No."

"Yes. Unless you want me to come over there—"

"All right." She fumbled for the pink gel dildo that was a sorry excuse for him.

"It's cold," she said, complaining.

"Warm it in your hands, the way I'm warming my cock in mine. Then put it inside you and pretend it's me."

When she did, she pictured him lifting her, impaling her. Raising her up and slamming her down on him, over and over, harder and faster, the way she was trying to move the dildo.

"Yes, Brent. Oh God, yes."

Her climax took her voice away then, but she heard his corresponding groans and pictured the look of fulfillment washing over his handsome face. It took little effort to imagine, because it was the same look she'd seen countless times during the fantasy weekends they'd been sharing for nearly five years.

The satisfied face of her lover.

She loved watching him after he came, knowing she'd been the one to put that satisfied look in his dark eyes. Watching the corners of his sensual lips curve upward in a heart-stealing grin made her want to do it all over again.

Maybe she didn't tell him often enough. "I love making love with you, even if it's only in our heads. I'm starting my month of vacation next week. And our anniversary's coming up. Let's do something really special to celebrate five years together."

"I've arranged to have two weeks off starting this Friday. What do you have in mind?" he asked, his deep voice relaxed now that he'd apparently taken the edge off his sexual tension.

"Anything you want, darling."

"I want the whole two weeks. I want to spend every moment of it with you. Sleeping, waking, making love..."

She could almost hear him smile, and imagining the sleepy, contented glint in his deep brown eyes made her go warm inside. Brent d'Angelo was her gift from the gods—the fantasy lover who made her life complete while giving her all the space she needed.

"It's your turn to pick a place. Where would you like for us to go? St. Croix? Martinique? Paris, maybe?" The idea of sharing a long sexual feast with Brent in some exotic, romantic place made Gaelen's heart beat faster.

"My place, Gaelen."

Brent wanted to spend two weeks, playing house with her? A slice of real life instead of another erotic encounter fueled by fantasy?

Memories best forgotten flooded Gaelen's mind, fed the terror his words evoked. She wanted to scream no, but her voice caught in her throat.

Brent smiled when he heard her swift intake of breath. "You said, 'Anything you want, darling.' Well, I want to spend our anniversary here. In my bed, my home. With you."

"But Brent—"

"You said anything."

"But...but we agreed to keep out of each other's private space. Keep our affair apart from our real lives." She sounded distraught, as though the idea of invading his territory terrified her beyond reason.

It had suited Brent five years ago to go along with Gaelen's wish to keep their real worlds out of their relationship. But he hadn't anticipated that their affair would go on all this time.

If anybody had tried to tell him five years ago that he'd still want Gaelen Reston as desperately as he had the day they met, Brent would have suspected insanity. But he did. He wanted her more each day.

At first he'd seen her as his blonde princess, the walking, talking proof he'd risen above his blue-collar roots. A stylish, sophisticated status symbol to flaunt before his colleagues. A cool, feminine beauty who didn't need his skill as a cosmetic surgeon to gain the look of perfection so many sought but couldn't attain, with the added bonus of brains and business acumen.

But then he'd fallen in lust.

So had she. He'd never had reason to doubt that she desired him as much as he did her. She trembled in his arms every time they came together, held onto him as though she'd never let him go.

Brent rolled to his side, switching the phone to his other ear as he imagined waking up to the sight of her blonde hair spread across his dark green pillowcase.

"I know," he told her. "But I believe we can move into the real world and still keep the fantasy we've created over the past five years alive. I want to try."

It had begun to bother Brent that Gaelen limited their weekday contact to phone calls except for the business social events they attended together by mutual consent. The fact that she wouldn't often grant him the intimacy of an all-night session of loving annoyed him, and her insistence that their encounters be on neutral ground made him uncomfortable.

"No, Brent."

He wasn't going to give in. "Yes. You promised. I'll pick you up Friday after work, and we'll come here. Pack whatever you think you'll need. We'll shop in Old Town, so don't worry if you forget something."

"You're not being fair."

"All's fair in love and war, sweetheart, and I'm beginning to believe I love you. I owe it to myself to find out—and so do you."

"All right. But I'll be doing this under protest—and I warn you, don't get the idea cohabitation's going to become a habit, because it's not."

How like Gaelen to get her hackles up.

"I plan to love you so well, fulfill every fantasy we've ever talked about so completely that you'll never want to leave. Keep that in mind while you're trying to think up ways to weasel out."

"What fantasies, Brent?"

He chuckled. "Whipped cream. Honey. Hot tubs and Jacuzzi jets. We'll give each other body shaves if the idea still turns you. Hell, I'll even go to the triple-X store and buy every kind of sex toy I've ever heard of. Maybe even some gadgets neither of us has even imagined. We won't stop until we've tried them all."

"Tempting me, aren't you?"

"I'm trying." He figured sex with Gaelen would never get boring, as long as they kept coming up with new, titillating games to keep their mutual lust at a fever pitch.

And he intended to do his part.

"Well, you've succeeded. But you'd better get some sleep now. What are you doing first thing in the morning? Another face-lift?"

He recalled grousing when he'd first called Gaelen today about being bored from the routine of back-to-back rhytidectomies he'd done today on a senator, a diplomat's wife, an aging actress, and a high-level business executive.

"A post-mastectomy breast reconstruction," he told her after mentally reviewing tomorrow's OR schedule. "Want me to call you in the morning?"

"Your workday begins way too early for me, Dr. d'Angelo. Let me go so you can get some sleep. Your patient deserves to have you rested and wide awake."

"Until Friday, Gaelen. I can't wait to wake up in my bed and see your gorgeous face. Make love with you before breakfast. Look at you over that first cup of coffee. If I weren't going to be on vacation, I'd kiss you good-bye each morning before leaving for work."

She sighed. "Sounds too much like domesticity to me, darling. Let's not spoil what we've got going. It's too good."

"I bet we could make it even better." If she'd give living with him a shot.

But Brent should have known that wasn't in the cards. It wasn't as if Gaelen hadn't always rejected domesticity on any level.

"Hang up now. I'm not going to be responsible for you going into surgery ragged out."

"Okay. We start our celebration Friday. Six o'clock."

"A holiday, trying out domestic bliss, right?"

"Right. And don't forget, we're going to be fulfilling all those fantasies. Two weeks, Gaelen, twenty-four, seven. G'night, sweetheart."

As he lay in the dark watching shadows play on the tall, narrow windows of his third floor bedroom suite, Brent wondered if Gaelen would ever let their relationship move along to a deeper, more serious plane. A level where she'd made it clear from the beginning that she wasn't about to go.

A level he hadn't wanted, either, when they'd defined the boundaries of their relationship.

But he hadn't imagined then that he'd ever long to settle down the way he did now, each time he watched one of his colleagues hurrying home to the kind of family he'd once thought was too routine to interest him. It hadn't crossed his mind five years ago that he'd ever fantasize about little boys with Gaelen's deep blue eyes, or dark-haired little girls who looked a lot like him.

Gaelen had been up front with him from the beginning. She wasn't into commitment. Over the years he'd begun to understand why, piecing together the bits of her past she'd shared with him in rare reflective moments.

The product of an apparently unhappy marriage that had ended with her mother's suicide, Gaelen had also observed her sister's disastrous marriage and acrimonious divorce. With her family history, she had reasons for shying away from permanent relationships.

Good reasons. Changing her mind now might be the hardest task Brent had ever set for himself.

Still, he took heart when he thought of the way they meshed, and not just in bed—though he couldn't imagine finding a better sex partner. Yes, Gaelen was his soul mate as well as the only woman he'd wanted in his bed for the past five years.

He wasn't about to let her go.

Chapter Two

Gaelen should have walked away, ended the relationship. But she hadn't been able to do it, even when she recalled disturbing little things Brent had said over the past few months that made her think he no longer was satisfied with their fantasy love affair. Suggestions that she see where he lived and worked, invitations to meet his family, pleas to get together on weeknights at her place or his.

So here she was, about to do what she'd sworn she never would do—spend not an hour, not a day, but two entire weeks with Brent d'Angelo on his own turf.

As the sun started to set on Friday, Gaelen stared out the window of Brent's Jaguar at his whitewashed brick townhouse. In the fashionable Old Town district of Alexandria, it was so close to the Potomac River that a damp, slightly fishy smelling breeze reminded her the boat dock lay just down the street.

While Brent walked around to open her door, she gave in to her fear and trembled. Sure, she'd seen his place before when they drove past it on the way to the marina where he docked his restored Lightning class sailboat. But she'd never been inside.

She'd never committed herself before to spending two whole weeks with Brent anywhere, much less in the home he'd bought two years ago.

It scared her more when she realized he'd kept her up to date about every step he took to renovate the historical landmark and give it his personal stamp. And solicited a lot of her advice.

From the outside, the place reminded her of the house where she'd lived as a child. Its traditional facade, the venerable brick walkway and the tidy beds of flowers on each side of the front door would welcome most visitors.

Not her. They reminded her of screaming arguments between her parents that had punctuated nearly every evening in her memory. Of the awful quiet in that house after her mother's death.

Gaelen shook harder.

Death. The final escape. Her mother must have been in terrible pain to have ended her life the way she had.

Would echoes from those times haunt her when she went inside Brent's home?

She wouldn't let them.

Swinging her legs around to the ground, she shot a hesitant smile Brent's way. Determined to guard her heart, she resolved to hold onto the fantasy, keep the real world from encroaching upon them, no matter where they might be.

A brilliant smile lit Brent's face, made her glad she'd given in on this. She'd let him think she was giving him the reality he wanted—reality in the arms of his dream lover.

He opened the front door, stepped back to let her inside a small foyer furnished only with a long, narrow refectory table. "Want a tour?"

"Later. Right now I want you."

He laughed. "Impatient, are you?"

"Yes."

"Then let's go upstairs."

He practically dragged her up the three flights of stairs, and they came together in a frenzy, as though each moment were the last they'd be allowed to share. Afterward, Gaelen lay on Brent's bed and looked around. The room, along with the adjoining bath where he'd disappeared to shave, occupied the entire third floor of the townhouse.

She liked the restful cream-colored walls, and the way they contrasted with forest green sheets and the hand-woven wool comforter that served as a bedspread. A lush, pale green carpet picked up the lighter color of the geometric design on dark green pillows they'd tossed from the bed onto the floor.

Their taste in decorating apparently shared the same accord as their sex drives.

She'd chosen cream and green for her bedroom, too, although she added touches of yellow in the floral pattern on her chaise lounge and the matching swags that flanked cream Austrian shades.

Brent's windows, long and narrow, were naked but for forest green shutters, now folded back to let in a breathtaking view of the sun that soon would disappear beyond the Potomac.

Pleasantly sated, Gaelen rose and stretched. She'd shower now, make herself ready for the sexual feast Brent had promised moments ago, following his apology for the impatient coupling neither of them had been able to wait for or prolong.

Sex with him never failed to heat her blood. But he made the raunchiest acts fun.

Brent had a way of never taking himself too seriously, despite having the kind of looks that made women drool and a glamorous, demanding career that had made him rich and famous years before he celebrated his thirty-fifth birthday last month.

They fit together like two puzzle pieces. And his easy grin brightened her world.

When she opened the bathroom door and looked at him, she yearned to run her fingers through his glossy dark brown hair, mussed now but still bearing evidence of his stylist's skill at taming its stubborn tendency to curl. She'd often said his tanned face would have been pretty if he'd been female, only to have him tell her with the authority of his profession that he had too prominent a nose and too square a jaw ever to pass for pretty no matter what his gender.

She loved the look but not the feel of the heavy five o'clock shadow he was mowing down with a blade instead of the electric shaver he kept in his car and had used during the weekend jaunts they'd enjoyed in the past.

"Need some help?" she asked when she stepped inside the bathroom. As always, the sight of his hard, naked body made her go hot and liquid inside.

"Maybe later, sweetheart. Go on, let me finish here and I'll join you in the shower." The suggestive look in his dark eyes held a world of promise.

* * * * *

Brent tried to gauge Gaelen's reaction to being in his personal space while he scraped off the heavy shadow of a beard that plagued him by this time every day. He watched her slip silently into the shower stall, hardened immediately when he anticipated joining her there.

He was going to enjoy every minute, making her whispered fantasies come to life.

She stood in the shower, her shadowy image enticing him in the mirror through the frosted glass of the door. Watching her fondle her nipples with soapy fingers had him aching for her again, though it hadn't been an hour since they'd made love.

The steamy fragrance, so like the one that always lingered on her skin, filled the air and aroused him more. He listened to the water splash onto her satiny skin, imagined droplets pooling in the hollow of her navel, slithering down a path he itched to follow with his tongue.

His gaze riveted on the view in the mirror, he set the razor down, ran a hand across his jaws and cheeks. She reached and took down the shower nozzle, her breasts swaying with the smooth, languid motion. He forgot to breathe when, in enticing slow motion, she braced one leg on the built-in seat and directed the spray between them.

Hearing her soft sigh made his cock twitch. Damn, if she wasn't the sexiest woman he'd ever known. Anticipation had him rock-hard and throbbing, and he hadn't touched her yet.

Pussy-whipped. That he was, and he loved it.

He loved Gaelen.

Seeking by feel alone, for he couldn't drag his gaze away, he dug with one hand in the woven basket on the vanity and curled his fingers around a small rectangular box.

The spring-operated lid popped open, the snapping sound it made momentarily obscuring Gaelen's moans as she very slowly rubbed her soapy fingers along the pouting lips of her pussy, spread herself to let the water needles massage her pretty pink clit. His mouth watered with anticipation at the prospect of tasting her there.

Brent drew out a pair of surgical steel spheres from the box, rolled them back and forth in his hand. His cock twitched harder.

Toys. The spheres weren't the only ones he'd brought home from the store. Maybe he ought to clamp down his unruly sex, ensure he'd last long enough to drive Gaelen wild.

The idea of putting on a cock ring made him wince. They were way down on his list of favored gadgets. Hard as it would be, he'd try for self-control.

Palming the spheres, he held them under hot water until they warmed. Then he set the basket by the shower door, opened it, stepped under the warm spray, and went down on his knees.

"Stay right where you are, sweetheart. I've got something for you."

The pulsing spray stung his cheek as he nuzzled her clit with his lips and tongue. The taste and smell of her, clean and sweet-salty, made him want to dispense with the foreplay and

Commitment

get right on to the main event. But he wanted her crazy with wanting him, first.

She whined when he pulled away, thrust her pelvis his way while he inserted the spheres.

"Are you practicing GYN exams, Doctor?" she asked, her voice a sexy purr above the rush of water onto his head and neck when he looked up to meet her gaze.

"Feel." With both hands, he rotated her hips slightly, just enough to set the ben-wei balls in motion. Her smile lit the steamy enclosure, made him swell and harden even more. He should have put on the damn cock ring.

"Sit down."

She did, right at the edge of the seat the way he wanted her. "My God, Brent."

"They get you hot, don't they, sweetheart?"

"Mmmmm. What do these have inside them? Oooh, they're...They feel...incredible. Like little tongues darting around inside."

"They're filled with mercury." And the motion of the heavy metal inside the spheres had to be arousing as hell. "Remember when you said you thought you'd like to go to work with ben-wei balls inside you, reminding you there's something down there that needs this." He rose on his knees, rubbed the head of his cock along her silky slit.

"Uh-huh. But I'm not at work. And you're right here." She squirmed, as though to suck him inside. "I need you inside me, now."

"Not yet." Sinking onto his haunches, he bent and flicked her with his tongue.

She grabbed his head, dug her fingers into his sopping hair. "Please. Do something." Writhing, she slid even farther off the edge of the seat, opened herself wider.

He took her clit in his mouth and sucked, gently at first, then harder. God, how he loved tasting her, experiencing the wild response in her that made him feel like twice the man he was.

He slid one hand up her body. Her skin reminded him of warm, wet velvet, and her nipple stabbed his palm. Gathering it between his thumb and forefinger, he stroked the tip, then pinched the elongated nub.

Letting go of his head, she slid her hands to his waist. "Fuck me. I'm dying."

He paused, blew lightly on her trembling flesh as he wrapped his free arm around her, slid her nearly off the seat and draped her thighs over his shoulders. "Not yet, sweetheart. You're not as hot as I want you."

Her swollen inner lips glistened, drew his lips and tongue. He thrust two fingers inside her, found her wet and trembling there. Her shrieks of pleasure when he opened and closed them as he flailed her clitoris with his tongue damn near made him come.

He wasn't going to last much longer. One by one, he fished out the ben-wei balls and set them on the shower seat. Frantic to fuck her, he lifted her and braced her back against the shower wall. Beyond any effort at finesse, he wrapped her long silky legs around his waist and thrust home.

Her moans fed his need, and the way she clenched him with tight, hot inner muscles shattered the last of his control even before he felt the tremors of her climax fade away. Taking her with him, he collapsed on the seat and hoped the warm spray would restore his strength.

"Sorry, sweetheart," he muttered when he regained the ability to speak. "Next time I'll put on the ring. Maybe then I can last longer than your average horny fifteen-year-old."

"A ring?"

Apparently it was that word that had made her muscles go tense before she pulled away and shot him a panicky look. Her resolve never to risk loving had to go deeper than he'd thought, if the mere mention of anything that reminded her of commitment sent her retreating to a spot deep in her mind. A spot he couldn't reach.

The last thing he wanted was to spook her, spoil the time he intended to use to change her mind. He made himself smile, kept his tone casual.

"Not a ring ring, Gaelen. The cock ring I bought when I went shopping last night for toys. It just may let me last long enough so we can fulfill some of the fantasies we've whispered about."

She burrowed her fingers into the thick bush that cushioned his sex, gave a few hairs near the base of his penis a tug.

"Ouch."

Her eyes sparkled, and her expression turned mischievous. "Better not use one of those unless you want me to give you that body shave we talked about."

"If I get a shave, sweetheart, so do you," he said, his tone as threatening as he could make it and still imagine her soft as a baby all over, warm and wet, incredibly smooth and sweet to taste.

She ran a hand over the hair on his chest. "I don't mind. Think how touching each other will feel without this in the way. Besides, you've got a lot more to lose than I do."

Damn, he never should have commented to his Muslim colleague about that Yemeni princess's lack of body hair while they'd been performing liposuction on various portions of her ample anatomy. If he hadn't, he wouldn't have learned that Muslims, male and female, removed every trace of their hair except for what grew on their heads.

And if he hadn't known, he couldn't have passed that information along to Gaelen during one of their midnight sessions of phone sex. He also wouldn't be contemplating the choice he'd soon face, between shaving not just his face but his entire body every day and living through weeks of itching while the hair grew out again.

On the other hand, if he hadn't planted the notion in Gaelen's mind, he wouldn't be getting another hard-on now, at the prospect of spreading honey over her silky-smooth pussy and licking it off drop by drop.

Playing out their shaving fantasy suddenly appealed to Brent, for in addition to seducing his senses with pure sexual heat, it would distract Gaelen, quell the uneasiness he still sensed whenever he saw her look around his home.

Brent didn't like seeing fear in her expressive dark blue eyes. Fear he imagined came along with the realization that she'd stepped over some invisible line. The one she'd apparently drawn to limit the degree of real intimacy she'd risk with him.

"I'll go first."

Suddenly eager to feel the buzz of electric clippers, the cold blade of a razor against his skin, Brent stepped out of the shower. "Come on, dry me off. Pretend I'm some desert sheikh and you're my handmaiden, making me ready for whatever concubine I've chosen for the night."

* * * * *

Stretched out on a huge forest green bath sheet in the empty tub after Gaelen finished shaving his backside, Brett seemed totally relaxed but for the jutting flesh that tempted her to straddle him and ride. He practically purred when she ran a cordless clipper over the supple olive skin on his chest, arms, and legs. When she reached the top of his muscular thighs, nudged them apart, and carefully clipped away his pubic hair, the purr morphed into a low groan of delight.

"Don't stop, sweetheart. It feels good. I understand now why the Muslims haven't given up on this particular ritual."

She understood, too. Nothing in her memory exceeded the tactile pleasure she'd experienced against her palms and fingers moments ago, when she stroked his satiny butt cheeks to make certain she hadn't missed a spot.

His hairless skin showcased the rock-hard muscle and sinew beneath. Sheer male beauty, unobscured by subterfuge. Seeing him, feeling him like this was a gift he made to her. No one else.

"You remind me of a big lazy jungle cat, the way you're stretching and purring." Gaelen lifted a steaming towel from his front and began spreading fragrant shaving gel over his body again. "Spread your legs, darling."

"Your wish is my command." He squirmed when she coated his crotch with the gel, and his penis swelled and nudged her hands as though to remind her it was ready for whatever she had in mind.

She bent and licked away the pearl of moisture at its tip. "When I finish making the rest of you as velvety as this, I'd like to cover you up with whipped cream and lick it off you. Everywhere."

"Everywhere?"

"Yes. Even here." With one finger she applied the gel around his anus.

Was that a blush on his olive cheeks? She wasn't certain, but there was no mistaking that his penis liked the idea, even if his mind wasn't so certain.

Very carefully she shaved him. The razor glided over firm flesh, revealed glistening skin over hard male sinew. Her mouth went dry, and her sex grew hot and wet.

Gaelen followed the razor with her fingers, checking each denuded inch of him from neck to toe, until she had him feeling as smooth to the touch as the finest satin. Then she rubbed oil into his skin.

Its fragrance hung in the steamy bathroom, took her breath away as she surveyed her handiwork.

Brent took her breath away. A burnished bronze god, vibrantly alive. Every motion defined by rippling muscles no longer cloaked by a pelt of fine black hair. Nothing to distract her from worshiping the sheer maleness of him. She stared, her mouth dry, her fingers itching to touch this man of her dreams.

He stood, lay a fresh towel in the tub before bending and retrieving a thick rubber ring from his basket of toys. "I want to make you as smooth as a newborn before we start playing again. And I won't last to get the job done without some help. Here, sweetheart. Put this on me."

She looked at the ring, then at his swollen sex. "How?"

He stretched the ring, then handed it to her. "Slide it all the way down my cock, then stretch it and work my testicles through, one at the time. It won't work unless it's tight."

She winced. "I don't want to hurt you."

"And I don't want to disappoint you. If you're squeamish, I'll do it."

Once he had the ring positioned, his sex jutted straight out from his body, gleaming and pulsing strongly against the wicked-looking restraint. Without hair down there, he looked different. Bigger, yet strangely vulnerable. Gaelen couldn't resist touching him, sliding her palm along his velvety length until he groaned.

Then she took the spot he'd vacated in the tub and smiled. "I think I'll pretend you're some classic statue, darling. Here. Do me, and then we can both imagine we're that erotic sculpture you pointed out at that gallery show last month."

Chapter Three

More blood surged to Brent's groin when he recalled that particular piece of art, the provocative position in which some god and goddess had been captured making love in a shallow forest pool. He winced at the bite of the ring as he finished running the clippers over Gaelen's creamy white torso.

"Want it that way, do you?"

"Do you?"

Hell, yes, he wanted her every way, every place, in every position he could imagine. She was his addiction. And he was in misery.

She might as well suffer too. Deliberately, he tweaked her clitoris until it throbbed against his fingers before spreading gel between her legs.

"Ooh. That feels good. Don't stop."

He picked up a straight razor and carefully plied it over her tender skin.

"You're lucky," he said, only half kidding. "The only place you're going to itch while your hair's growing out is down here. I'll be scratching myself all over."

"Maybe I won't itch at all. Maybe I'll keep myself smooth down there, just for you."

Blood rushed to his groin. The ring cut into his flesh, reminded him why it was there. "If you want, I'll take care of it for you permanently. I've been meaning to practice with that new laser electrolysis unit we just got at the office."

She laughed. "I doubt I can afford your services, Doc."

"I couldn't charge you. It wouldn't be right, since I'd be enjoying the benefits, too." He spread her outer lips a little wider, shaved first one and then the other.

"You've got a steady hand. I'd never dare to use a straight razor."

"It's not much different from a scalpel. I get lots of practice, precision cutting." He ran the blade across her skin one more time, followed it first with his fingers, then his tongue. "There. You're softer than a newborn's cheek."

"So are you." She stroked his chest, her fingers making lazy circles around his left nipple before drifting downward, lightly squeezing his aching cock and balls.

White-hot need shot through him like wildfire. He lifted her, drew her into his arms, and deposited her in the swirling hot tub in the corner. About to burst, he lost no time joining her there.

* * * * *

He positioned her hands on the bench at the edge of the hot tub, spread her legs apart as he massaged her buttocks. When he moved close behind her, his body kissed hers with naked flesh that reminded her of fine old satin.

Everywhere he touched her, she burned. And he was everywhere. His mouth suckling the sensitive nape of her neck, his hands kneading her breasts, long fingers teasing her nipples into fiery points of sensation.

"You mentioned that sculpture we saw."

She pushed her torso backward, needing more contact. "Yes."

His muscular arms surrounded her, secured the length of her back to the smooth, sinewed expanse of his chest and belly. His huge, naked sex sought her. Found her. Sank deep, deeper, until the tip of his penis found her womb and his velvety scrotum rested within her sensitized outer lips.

"The couple in it looked like this," he said, his deep whisper silky, as smooth as their joined bodies.

He remained still, except for the tremor that hinted his body wasn't enjoying its enforced stillness. When he spoke, he sounded as though he were in agony.

"I sure as hell don't feel like we're that statue, sweetheart. Hold on, I'm going to take you for a hard, fast ride."

All Gaelen could see were the lush tropical plants that ringed the tub, blocked the view through a glass wall. And the foaming water that whirled about her widespread legs, splashed their bodies and released the clove-scented fragrance of the oil she'd used to burnish his smoothly shaven torso.

She closed her eyes and concentrated on the sensations Brent sent through her body. He tugged her nipples with his talented fingers, stroking their tips with a touch as light as that of a feather—the feather he'd taken from his Robin Hood hat and tormented her with after the masquerade party they'd attended last Halloween.

The delicious pleasure-pain of him filling her, retreating, thrusting deep, hard. Deeper and harder, until her world burst in a kaleidoscope of sensation. Until she heard him shout out her name, flood her sex with hot bursts of his seed. Her body clenched his, joined him in another celebration of life.

As she lay in his arms later and felt his heart beating strong and steady against her ear, Gaelen realized they'd shared more than killer sex. Sex alone, not even the mind-boggling sex Brent always gave, couldn't have made her feel this way. It took something more to give her this sense of completeness.

Something that felt suspiciously like love.

* * * * *

Sunlight streamed through his bedroom window, made Brent blink at the sudden light.

Then he saw her. Gaelen, her hair a delightful tangle of pale silk against his pillow. He'd dreamed of waking up like this, sharing lazy mornings.

Sharing all their mornings.

Reality made the dream pale by comparison. He reached out, smoothed a wayward strand of her hair between his fingers.

His cock stirred lazily against her backside.

She sighed, wiggled toward him until their bodies fit together like spoons and she had him nestled between her silky thighs.

"Gaelen?"

No answer. She could sleep like the dead, he recalled from the weekends they'd shared over the years. And no question about it, this morning she needed her rest. Brent lay there a few more minutes, savored the closeness.

"You deserve breakfast in bed, sweetheart," he whispered as he moved away, careful not to wake her.

Gaelen rolled over, opened one eye long enough to see Brent disappear down the stairs. She should get up, fix her hair, put on her face. But she didn't have the energy to move. Pleasantly sore, she sat up, stretched, and burrowed under the covers again. This wasn't one of their fantasy weekends, and it was Brent who had insisted on this touch of reality. He might as well get a taste of what she looked like on a "normal" morning.

Soft instrumental music wafted up the stairs, along with a delicious smell of coffee mingling with something sweet and spicy. Could Brent actually be cooking at this time of the morning?

She guessed he could when she recalled him mentioning that he started operating on patients at the ungodly hour of seven AM.

Whatever. Nature called, so she stumbled to the bathroom. Bath sheets littered cream tiles marbled with deep green that matched the sleek fixtures. Water still bubbled in the recessed hot tub set in a glass-walled corner and surrounded by tropical plants that gave the room a sensuous outdoor feel. Fragrant steam filled the air.

Gaelen would never think of Brent again without remembering this. Reality? Fantasy come true was more like what had happened in here last night. She steeled herself against confusing tenderness and caring for love, wanting what she could never risk.

Footsteps on the stairs drew her from her sober thoughts. Running a brush quickly through her tangled hair, she shrugged into a terry robe and pasted on a smile.

There was Brent, his hair adorably mussed, his feet bare. His smile reminded Gaelen of the Cheshire Cat in Alice In Wonderland until she looked into his eyes and saw devotion shining there. The aroma of coffee and sweet rolls tickled her taste buds, lured her to the round table in front of the window where he'd set down a big wicker bed tray.

"I'd planned to feed you in bed, sweetheart. Did my banging around downstairs wake you?"

Gaelen shook her head. "The music did. I didn't know you were into classical. I enjoyed it, knowing you were down there listening, too."

"Yeah. I like to wake up to Mozart and Beethoven. There's a passion there that you don't find so much in modern music. Makes me think of you. Of making love." He held a chair for her, bent and kissed the back of her neck after she sat down. "This is my favorite time of day. When everything outside's coming alive."

They might be compatible lovers, but Brent's morning cheeriness definitely would take some getting used to. He didn't seem to mind looking at her at her worst, though, and that had to be a plus.

Determined to figure out what Brent found so invigorating about early morning, Gaelen blinked, then looked outside. A pair of fat gray squirrels chased each other along a limb at her eye level. "Look, Brent."

"They do that nearly every morning. When I first saw them, I worried that they'd fall, but they seem to have all the skill of high-wire artists." He sat and took her hand. "This morning, I'd rather look at you."

Suddenly Gaelen realized how awful she must look. "Oh, no."

"Oh, yes. I like seeing you with your hair mussed, your cheek creased from sleeping on my pillow. Here, try a muffin." Brent laid back the napkin, handed her a warm bran muffin. "It's full of raisins and walnuts and all sorts of good things."

"And I'm hungry." She took a bite. "It's delicious."

"Glad you like it. I figured you'd worked up an appetite last night. I know I did."

Heat flooded her cheeks, which surprised her considering all they'd done to each other to stimulate her hunger—and not only for the fresh fruit, muffins, and coffee that they were quickly reducing to a handful of crumbs and a lonely raspberry left in a crystal serving bowl.

"Want that last bite?" she asked.

He smiled, picked up the berry between his thumb and forefinger. "Eat. Doctor's orders."

Leaning across the table, Gaelen sucked the berry into her mouth. "Bossy, aren't you?"

"I want you to keep up your strength. I've got plans for you."

"And what have you got in mind?"

"Guess."

His lascivious look made her muscles clench in anticipation. "I don't know if I'm up to two weeks' worth of activity like we enjoyed last night."

"But you're game to try?"

She was. "Darling, I came more times last night than I can count. Yes, I'm game for anything."

Suspicious that what she was feeling now for Brent was as much love as passion, Gaelen sought to prove the opposite. "Right now I want..." She stood, knelt at his feet, slid his robe off his shoulders. "...dessert." With that, she took him in her mouth and laved him with her tongue.

Already half-hard, he swelled and hardened the instant she cupped him and gently rolled his testicles between her fingers. His clean-shaven groin felt like satin, made her yearn to feel it against her own naked sex. He smelled and tasted like cloves and musk and man.

Her robe abraded her nipples, so she paused long enough to shrug it off, then rubbed the aching nubs against his muscular calves. She took him deeper in her throat, swallowed.

"My God, sweetheart. No more. Stop." He took her head between his hands, lifted her head. "Ride me."

Her mouth felt desolate at the loss, but she scrambled to her feet because she needed him inside her, too. Straddling his lap, she took his throbbing length inside her. When she licked her lips, she tasted him there.

"Slow and easy?" she whispered, her tongue snaking out to bathe his earlobe as she rubbed her nipples back and forth against his smooth, muscular chest.

He bucked. "Hard and fast. God, sweetheart, I love you."

I love you.

What he meant, she told herself, was that he loved making love with her.

"Me, too." She moved, harder, faster, until they slumped against each other, sated on each other for the moment.

* * * * *

Gaelen practically purred when Brent blotted her dry after they showered a few minutes later. "I do, you know," he mentioned casually.

"What?" She lifted his hand, pressed a kiss on his palm.

"I love you."

"Don't, Brent."

"Why not? It's not just your gorgeous body, sweetheart. Or the fact you make every fantasy I ever had come true in bed. Come on, admit it. You must care, too, otherwise we never would have lasted five years and still be as hot for each other as we were the first time—"

"That's why it has lasted. We haven't let reality intrude. We agreed. Surely you remember?" She met his gaze, her eyes as wide as if she'd just encountered a vicious jungle beast.

"Yeah, I remember. You offered me every young man's fondest wish-uninhibited sex with a woman I could take anywhere and be proud of. No expectations. No commitment."

"That was what I wanted then. What I still want, Brent."

He sensed her doubt, for though she held his gaze, her voice wavered. "Are you sure, sweetheart?"

"Yes." She trembled in his arms, made him realize now wasn't the time to push.

Chapter Four

෨

He kissed her briefly, then clasped her shoulders. "Okay. What say we get dressed? I'll show you around the house, and then we can take a walk around Old Town. I'd like to get your opinion on a watercolor I thought might look good in the dining room."

He'd given her a reprieve.

Not a long enough one, Gaelen feared as she followed Brent through each nook and cranny of his beautifully restored old house.

Uncanny. She saw nothing she'd change if she lived here, too. Cream textured walls, natural wood moldings, modern furnishings with simple lines and soft suede upholstery made a comfortable backdrop for a few spectacular pieces of art, some boldly patterned accent pieces. The state-of-the art kitchen shared a modern, sybaritic elegance with his master bath.

Old and new, coexisting in harmony. She'd have expected nothing less, if she'd ever considered how a man like Brent would choose to live.

But she hadn't. She'd looked at the outside of his venerable townhouse, pictured it filled with museum pieces or quality reproductions like the place where she'd grown up. She shuddered.

Had memories of her childhood prejudiced her against Brent as well as the place where he lived? Part of Gaelen wanted to take a chance that not all families tore each other apart the way hers had. That she was as wrong about fearing commitment as she'd been about guessing how Brent lived in the real world.

In her head she knew that not all families were as dysfunctional as hers had been. But her fear that history might repeat itself wouldn't let her bridge the gap. Fantasy worked. Fantasy was perfect. Gaelen wasn't willing to risk trading the joy for a reality that was at best uncertain.

"You're awfully quiet, sweetheart," he said as they stepped outside and began to stroll toward King Street.

She smiled. "I'm impressed, to tell the truth. I'd imagined your house would be decorated the way it probably was two hundred years ago. Did you use a decorator, or do you get the credit for putting your place together?"

"I did it, with a bit of help from my mom on the kitchen. You shouldn't be surprised. After all, I make my living making human beings look good. Why shouldn't I enjoy doing the same with the place I live?"

"You've got a point. Speaking of making your living, how did you manage to wangle two weeks off at one time?"

"Careful scheduling. And letting a couple of lucrative jobs slip through my fingers because the potential patients wouldn't agree to make their schedules mesh with mine."

"Out-of-towners?"

"Yeah. An actor and a CEO from Houston, each wanting to use their own time off to get rid of time's ravages. One of my colleagues fit them in." He squeezed her hand, then gestured toward a group of plants that took her breath away. "Look. Do you know what variety of hostas those are?"

Variegated green leaves hugged the walkway that led to a pale blue townhouse. Exotic looking sprays of pale blue flowers sprouted from the center of each plant. "I guess they're hybrids. I've never seen flowers exactly that color before."

"They'd look good next to the brick walkway in my courtyard, don't you think?"

"Yes." Another love she'd never have guessed she and Brent might share was a mutual love for gardening. Her fingers had itched to dig right in when he'd showed off what new specimens he'd planted this spring. And her mind had hummed, picturing how she might help him make his already-impressive courtyard a showcase of native plants and flowers.

There was something cozy about strolling around Old Town hand in hand with Brent, an aura of permanence Gaelen guessed must emanate from beautifully preserved old homes, quaint shops, cobblestone streets. Clean air.

She perceived permanence in every discreet bronze historical marker, each window box and decorator pot that brimmed with annual flowers in hues that rivaled a rainbow, every colorful wreath that hung on entry doors along the streets. The pride she sensed as they walked along had little to do with the fact that only the affluent could afford to live behind these inviting doors.

Warmth flooded her heart when Brent stopped at a shop window, pointed out a handcrafted pine rocking chair with delicate scrollwork on its curved headrest. "My mom has a chair almost like that one. Rocked every one of us in it, or so she said. Last time I went home, she was rocking away, lulling Tony's youngest to sleep."

"I envy you your happy memories." She also envied him for his brash confidence, his willingness to meet new challenges head-on.

And she liked what he'd shown her of himself. He wasn't just the fantasy lover she'd known for five years, he was a good man. One she'd love to spend her life loving, if she weren't terrified that day-to-day reality would tarnish their perfect relationship.

Still, Gaelen wondered. Could Brent show her the way to a reality unlike any she'd experienced or even observed up close? Did such a reality really exist?

* * * * *

Brent couldn't wait to get Gaelen home. The breeze off the Potomac ruffled her hair, gave her a carefree look he sensed was more than a facade. If his arms hadn't been otherwise occupied, he'd have pulled her close, shared the warmth that made him hope her feelings ran deeper than she'd admit.

It had been uncanny. When they'd stepped into the gallery, she'd headed straight for the framed watercolor, reacted the same way he had when he'd first seen the abstract still life with its muted tones of green, purple, blue, and gold. He recalled her obvious approval of the eclectic way he'd furnished his place, their mutual enjoyment of sailing and hiking. Her enthusiasm when he let her know he enjoyed doing his own gardening, and using his big, well-equipped kitchen to concoct healthy gourmet fare.

Not to mention their compatibility in bed—and wherever else they felt the urge for a wild, mind-boggling fuck. He couldn't have found a woman more attuned to him if he'd have taken out an ad in the personal section of the Washington Post.

Silk kissed his swelling cock, tickled his naked scrotum. Unbelievable. He shifted the wrapped frame to conceal his untimely erection from passersby. The package wasn't particularly heavy, but its flat rectangular shape made it awkward to hold.

Neither he nor Gaelen had been willing to wait for the gallery owner to deliver it, and when he'd suggested a cab, they'd agreed the unseasonably cool late May day was too nice not to walk, package or no.

Another sign they were meant for each other.

The picture could wait to be hung, he decided as they climbed the steps to his front door. He couldn't wait to be fucked.

* * * * *

"Aren't we going to hang the watercolor?" Gaelen asked when he leaned the package against the dining room wall, then practically dragged her to the kitchen. Late afternoon sunlight streamed through unshuttered windows that overlooked the courtyard, lent the room a pale golden glow.

"Later. Right now I want to eat." His eyes, always dark, looked almost black as they devoured her. His smile held a world of sensual promise, and his nimble fingers seared her with their heat when he slid her loose cotton sundress off her shoulders and down, over her aching nipples, her belly, her sex.

Quickly he rid her of her pale green silk g-string bikinis and lifted her onto the counter. Naked, she shivered at the feel of cold, hard marble against her bottom. But when she stretched out toward Brent for warmth, he moved out of her reach.

"Darling, I'm cold," she protested, but before she could say more, he'd come back, two rounded ice cubes in hand.

He bent, nipped suggestively at her erect nipples as he urged her forward, worked the ice cubes up inside her. "I don't want you to get too hot, too fast," he said when he straightened and backed away.

"Come back here, Brent." The ice made her squirm, and the squirming made her impossibly hot.

He smiled, shook his head.

As if he'd willed it, music started playing. Not a soothing classic. No. A piece with a hard-driving, grinding beat that smacked of sex. Down and dirty, unbridled sex. Stripper music.

She'd once whispered her fantasy about seeing a man do a striptease. Apparently Brent remembered. Ice melted inside her, sent rivulets of water along her naked sex. Cold turned to heat when he began to move, his lean hips pumping in time with the raucous drumbeat.

She willed him to hurry, fulfill her fantasy and ease the yearning he'd already primed to a fever pitch. But he was apparently in no hurry.

His motions smooth, leisurely, he tackled the buttons on his pale blue oxford cloth shirt one by one, never missing a beat though it was building, driving harder now. His hands went to his belt.

Her breath caught. He thrust his hips toward her, then backed away. Offering. Then depriving her. He toed off his loafers, kicked them away.

Unable to stop herself, she slid closer to the edge of the counter, spread her legs. Inviting. Enticing him.

He held her gaze as he moved further out of her reach, compelled her to watch each deliberate motion he made. His brown leather belt slid sinuously through its loops, undulated when he held it toward her before draping it around his neck. His shirt came off at a touch of his hands, drifted to the floor.

His hairless chest took on the room's golden glow. Muscles rippled, caught the light. The music paused. Drums rolled. Her mouth watered.

Strip for me.

"Tell me to take it off, babe."

"Take your clothes off. Please, darling, don't make me wait." Her whole body ached from this delicious torture.

He unsnapped his slacks. The drums rolled again. The rasp of his zipper opening filled scant seconds of silence before the music began again. A slower, harder rhythm now, as though to mimic the grinding of his hips, the rippling of his triceps and biceps as he slid conservative tan khaki down and off, catching his socks on the way.

Black silk boxers. His big, mouth-watering penis strained at the gaping fly. What she wanted inside her now, throbbing in time with the music.

"Take them off."

"Like what you see, sweetheart?" He thrust forward, gyrated. She reached out to touch him, but he ground his hips backward. Just beyond her reach.

Why was he torturing her so? Every cell in her body burned for him. "You know I like it." From the fine sheen of sweat that gleamed on his gorgeous body and the look of barely restrained lust on his face, she guessed he'd come close to his own limit of self-control.

"Then let me see it all, darling," she said in her most seductive voice. "Strip for me. I want you to."

He cupped himself, never missing a beat as he thrust his hips forward, rotated them, retreated. "You want to see this?"

"Oh, yes."

"Are you willing to pay my price?"

"How much?" She couldn't imagine any cost that would make her balk, not now, when her whole body throbbed with wanting him.

He slid the boxers down, no more than an inch. His six-pack abs rippled.

"How much are you willing to give me?

Her inner muscles clenched as she slid her legs wider apart, gave him an unimpeded view of her hungry sex. "This. Any way you want it," she murmured.

He lowered the boxers another inch. And another. A bump and thrust. Retreat. When she met his gaze, he let them slither to the floor.

Her heart beat faster. His pulse throbbed in his neck, in the distended veins of his hard-muscled arms. His abdominal muscles quivered as he moved between her legs, his swollen penis visibly throbbing beneath a g-string of sheer black silk.

A deep-throated drum beat out its cadence, dominated the keyboard and guitars and their more subtle, sexual message. In. Out. His hips drove forward and back like a piston, grazing her aching clit before withdrawing beyond her reach.

Then the song ended and he stood before her, silent. Still. Hot. Sweaty. Powerfully, magnificently aroused. The music began to play again, so softly now that she had to struggle to hear.

"Touch me." His voice was velvet over steel.

So was he. She leaned forward, lapped salty sweat off his glistening chest, nipped at his nipples. Slowly, she slid her hands down his torso, felt the sensual undulations of hard, powerful muscles as he kept his hips moving. Undaunted, she sought her prize.

She splayed her fingers along his inner thighs.

He groaned. "Tease."

"Uh-huh." With both hands she ringed his sex, held him to her while she worked the g-string off. "I'm hungry, now."

"Have some honey."

"Honey?"

"As in bees and wildflowers." He leaned over her, got a jar from the cabinet, and set it on the counter beside her left hip.

Amber honey from the squat jar clung to Brent's finger when he held it to her lips.

She snaked her tongue out, sampled the thick, sweet stuff. "Sweet."

"It'll taste sweeter if I lick it off you here." He smeared the rest of the honey from his finger onto the hardened nubs of her nipples, sent a shiver of delight down her spine. "Give you any ideas?" he asked before drawing one nipple into his mouth and flailing it with his tongue.

She dipped her finger into the honey pot, drizzled the thick honey over his sex. When she bent to taste him, their heads collided.

"Oops. This isn't going to work."

Chapter Five

Brent let her nipple go, sucked the honey from its aching mate.

Then he laughed. "Time to get horizontal, sweetheart."

"Past time."

"You grab the honey."

She did. She also tweaked his nipples with her sticky fingers, and that sent a shockwave straight to his cock. Why had his nipples suddenly gotten so sensitive? Brent breathed deeply, wondered how long he'd last under her sensual assault.

"Hold on." He clasped her at the waist, drew them both down onto the thick braided rug in front of the kitchen sink.

As soon as he lay down, she straddled him, licked away the fine line of honey she'd drizzled over his sex and followed the path it had taken along his scrotum and down his inner thigh. He started mentally declining Latin nouns as he drizzled honey between her legs and settled in to feast.

Suddenly cool air bathed his cock.

"More honey," she murmured, opening herself further to his seeking tongue. Then she smeared him with more of the sticky sweet honey and took him in her mouth again.

She squirmed when he licked hot, sweet honey off her, and when he closed his lips around her hard little clit, she came apart. He flailed her with his tongue, at the same time reaching up to tug at her nipples.

Her moans of pleasure reverberated against his cock. Her breath tickled his clean-shaven balls as she sucked harder, took him deeper in her throat.

He could hardly remember his own name, much less a dead language. He was losing control.

The taste of her, all hot sex and sweet honey, seduced him. He couldn't stop tasting her, couldn't bear the thought of leaving her. Not even for the split second it would take to turn her around and…

She sucked him down her throat, swallowed. He felt it coming. Couldn't hold back. Brent ground his face into her pussy. Once he started coming, he couldn't stop. While his cock still spasmed in her throat, he tongued her clit and made her come again.

* * * * *

They lay on the kitchen rug, a tangle of arms and legs, laughing and kissing and lapping drops of honey off each other.

"Watch out, you're going to get me horny again," Brent warned Gaelen when she straddled him and bathed his silky soft groin with her tongue.

He blew on her sex, snaked his tongue out to flick at her clitoris. "Turnabout's fair play."

Opening her mouth wide, she sucked at his scrotum until first one and then both of his testicles popped into her mouth. Velvety, soft, unbelievably sensual. Tasty, sweet yet salty. His penis hardened again, grew thick and long against the outside of her cheek.

Fantasy. This was pure fantasy, yet Brent managed to make her every sexual dream come true. She couldn't get enough.

"You're going to get it now." He lifted her, lay her on her back, and knelt between her legs.

"So you say."

He rubbed the broad, blunt tip of his erection against her swollen clit. "Yeah. Put your legs over my shoulders. I want you to feel me clear to your throat."

When he sank inside her, she felt complete. Connected. Full. As though they were no longer two, but one. With each slow, deep thrust, the pressure built inside her until she came again, the sheer joy of her climax overwhelming her when she felt him shudder with his own release.

* * * * *

Brent's muscular chest rose and fell with each breath, the sleek golden expanse of his skin catching the faint glow from a floodlight that lit the backyard garden. Asleep now, he reminded Gaelen of a Botticelli angel.

While they'd soaked in the hot tub, he'd asked her to stay after this idyllic time was over.

She'd said no. But maybe heaven wouldn't turn to hell if she stayed. Maybe…

What was she thinking?

Gaelen sat up in bed, aghast. Was she falling in love with Brent in spite of all the promises she'd made to herself? Was she thinking about ignoring the vows she'd made, never to place her happiness in anyone's hands except her own?

She couldn't. She had to concentrate on the fantasies they shared, remind herself nothing this good could last.

She moved her hand over her baby-smooth crotch. They'd shaved each other again tonight, the way she'd fantasized about for months. She'd never imagined the reality could approach her dream, but it did. The sleek sensation of satin against silk, skin against skin with nothing in between eclipsed her wildest imaginings.

She was warm and wet. Even now, she wanted him again.

But he slept soundly, a sated smile on his full, sensual lips. His penis, pale and looking strangely vulnerable denuded of its dark nest of hair, lay at rest against one hard-muscled golden thigh.

Gaelen reached out to caress him, then drew back her hand and slid from the bed.

She had to have some space. Had to think rationally. Had to gather the strength to tell Brent no again, to tell herself she didn't want to love him and risk leaving both of them with broken hearts and broken lives.

* * * * *

Pulling on Brent's robe, Gaelen tiptoed from the room and made her way toward the kitchen.

A crashing noise from the lowest level of the townhouse made her stop in her tracks. Should she wake Brent?

No. He'd set the security system when they had gotten back from their walk. If anyone had broken in, the alarm would have sounded. Something must have fallen. Maybe one of Brent's free weights?

She'd take a look. Carefully, she made her way down the angled stairs, past the main living level to the bottom floor where Brent had a fully-equipped home gym.

When she pressed the light switch, she stifled a scream. Someone had gotten inside, and he lay face down on the ceramic tile floor, his head in a growing pool of blood.

"Brent!" she yelled.

The stranger groaned, then rolled over. "Not Brent. I'm Mark."

"You're Brent's brother?" Gaelen didn't really need to ask, because Mark was a dead ringer for Brent—a little wirier, less muscular, the way she imagined Brent must have been before he'd matured.

"Yeah." He blinked, then wiped a hand across his bloody forehead. "Shit. Must've bumped my head when I fell down."

"You okay, sweetheart?" Brent wrapped an arm around Gaelen, then eyed his brother's bloody face. "What the hell?"

"Got drunk out tonight, Brent. Thought I'd sleep it off here, take the train to the folks' place in the morning. Must have whacked myself on one of your benches. You gonna have to sew me up?"

"From the amount of blood I'm seeing on you and on the floor, that's a fair guess." He turned back to Mark. "Didn't I tell you my place was off limits for the next couple of weeks?"

"Yeah, but I couldn't go home. Mom would've killed me."

"What makes you think I won't? Come on, you're going to have to get your miserable butt up to the kitchen where I can see how bad a number you did on your face."

"Can I help?" Gaelen asked a few minutes later as she watched Brent clean away the blood from his brother's face.

"You can look on the top shelf of the cabinet next to the refrigerator and get my first aid kit."

Mark groaned when Brent pushed him none too gently onto the long kitchen table and told him to be still.

"If you're lucky, there will be a suture set in there, because you need about a dozen stitches. What were you thinking, coming here and sneaking around downstairs without turning on a light? It would serve you right if I sent you home this way."

"Celebrated. Got straight A's this term." Mark's words were slurred, his grin goofy.

"Congratulations. You might want to stay alive long enough to benefit from your hard work. Lie back on the table and be quiet." Brent didn't sound altogether amused.

Gaelen stifled a laugh. She'd never have imagined Brent could pull off the horrified big-brother act. Smiling, she set the large white plastic box on the table.

"Want me to open it?"

"Please." He rattled off a list of items he'd need, and Gaelen pulled out the ones she recognized.

"Is there a package of six-oh nylon sutures? If not, five-oh or even four-ohs will do. Mark won't sue me if he ends up with a scar."

Gaelen sifted through the contents again, handed Brent two very different looking packages. "Here. Both of these are marked six-oh."

"Good. Can you hand me that needle, sweetheart?"

"No needles." Mark sounded like a terrified kid about to have a tetanus shot.

Brent laughed. "I don't think you managed to anesthetize yourself enough to tolerate being sewed up without xylocaine. Gaelen, hold my cowardly brother's hand while I numb his forehead."

Gaelen squinted into the bright light and held Mark's hand while Brent bent over his head, wearing nothing but a pair of black silk boxer shorts, a paper mask, and plastic gloves as he stitched up the gash in his brother's head. A funny picture, though Brent's sure hands and expression of total concentration gave her a hint of how seriously he took his work.

Somehow she'd never thought much about what Brent did for a living, except for realizing he made a good living from making people look their best. From watching him tend his brother's wound, Gaelen got the impression of a caring and thoughtful physician, not the hotshot cosmetic surgeon she'd visualized after listening to his patients' praise at cocktail parties they'd attended.

*\ *\ *\ *\ *

After they'd settled Mark, more sober now and neatly sewn back together, into the bed in Brent's guest room, Gaelen and Brent went back upstairs.

"You don't have to send your brother home on the train," Gaelen said as she slid into bed and rested her head on Brent's shoulder.

"Oh? What are you suggesting?"

"That you drive him home. From what Mark said while you were patching him up, it sounds as though I've been keeping you from spending the time you should with your family."

"My choice, sweetheart. Trust me, spending time with you is a lot more fun."

"Still—"

"I'll drive him home if you'll go with me."

"Okay."

"I'll hold you to that."

"Did you and Mark plan this, Brent?" She circled the base of his cock with one finger, then traced gently around first one testicle and then the other.

"No. Stop that unless you want to pay the price."

"I'm terrified." She laughed but kept up the teasing motion.

When he pulled her head against his chest, her silky hair tickled him, reminded him she was warm and willing and really here. Suddenly he was hard again. "Wanna play some more?"

She nipped his shoulder, then licked away the gentle bite. "Always."

"It's your turn to pick a toy." He reached onto the floor, set the basket onto the bed.

She picked up a string of anal beads and a butt plug, twirled the beads around on her wrist. "Where do you put these?"

"Here." He cupped her bottom, ran a finger around the puckered opening of her anus. "Not at the same time. Unless you want to use one of them on me."

"Hmmm." She stared at the plug, smiled.

Involuntarily, his abs tensed. The idea of anal stimulation had never turned him on. Still, if that was what she wanted...

When she dropped it and the beads back into the basket, he let out his breath, relieved.

She stroked his chest, circled his navel with a finger. "All I want tonight is you."

"You've got me, sweetheart." Nuzzling the soft skin at the nape of her neck, Brent set the basket on the floor. "Tell me exactly how you want me."

"Inside me. Now. I want to feel your big, velvety penis stretching me until I can't take any more. I want your tongue in my mouth, your hard, gorgeous body on mine. I want you to make us both see stars."

So she wanted reality tonight. Plain vanilla sex, not the embodiment of her wildest fantasies. Lovemaking? Brent let himself imagine she'd finally offered him more than pleasure, more than the transient satisfaction of sexual stimulus and climax.

He rolled Gaelen onto her back and nudged her legs apart. "Sounds good to me, sweetheart," he whispered against her lips before he thrust his tongue in her mouth and his cock into her hot, wet pussy.

Bare skin to bare skin damp with each other's earthy sweat, they moved in perfect accord. Her heart beat against his chest as if to dictate the rhythm. Slow. Steady. The hard nubs of her rosy nipples abraded his chest, reminded him of his own rigid cock moving deep within her body. Made him want to lose himself in her, so deep neither of them could tell where one ended and the other began.

Her climax went on and on. He tried, but couldn't hold off his own release as she clenched him as though she'd never let him go.

"Damn it, Gaelen. I love you and I'm not going to pretend anymore that I don't," Brent whispered as they lay, still joined in body the way he hoped that, one day soon, she'd let them bind their minds and hearts.

*****

Last night he'd said it again. The words Gaelen had never wanted to hear. The words that made her shiver with fear. The words that rang in her ears now, as they approached Brent's childhood home.

I love you.

He'd said it in the aftermath of passion, but she believed he meant each of those three terrifying words.

What scared her most was the nagging voice inside her head that said she'd gone and fallen head over heels in love with him, too. That it was a whole lot more than great sex, a gorgeous body, and an arresting face that had kept her wanting Brent d'Angelo for five wonderful years.

Gaelen stared out the car window, tuning out Brent's sporadic attempts at conversation with Mark who sprawled across the backseat, apparently still hung over from his excesses of the night before.

Her satin g-string felt cool against flesh still hot and damp and quivering from Brent's attention in the shower an hour earlier. The matching slip she wore beneath a crinkled cotton wraparound dress softly abraded her torso. It rubbed against her nipples, sending shockwaves through her. Lacy tops of silky thigh-high stockings brushed the outer lips of her sex when she crossed her legs. Her clitoris swelled, its sensitive tip brushing the strip of fabric that barely covered it.

She tried not to think about how his tongue had felt like warm, wet velvet when he'd knelt between her legs and soothed away the razor's sting—or about the sure but gentle touch of his long, talented fingertips as he'd checked to be certain that not a single bit of stubble remained to mar the skin that now felt smooth as her satin undies—yet damp and hot and wanting.

Her gaze settled on his crotch, and she couldn't help imagining how arousing it would be to lay her head on his lap and bathe his freshly shaved penis and scrotum with her tongue. That satiny flesh that gave her so much pleasure shouldn't taunt her as it did now, its length and thickness outlined even though concealed beneath the zipper of beige linen slacks. She reached out to caress him, then remembered their audience in the backseat and drew her hand back.

His grin, when he captured her errant hand and rested it against his thigh, spoke volumes. "Later, sweetheart. We're almost there, and I'm not up to facing my mom with a hard-on."

"Brent!" What would Mark think?

He glanced at the rearview mirror, then at Gaelen. "It would take a cannon to wake my hung-over sibling. Home was everything but quiet—still is, for that matter."

When Brent maneuvered past half-a-dozen cars into the front yard of a modest brick row house, Gaelen tensed. He might only be taking his youngest brother home, but she was stepping over the line she'd drawn in their relationship—a barrier she'd sworn never to cross.

Chapter Six

Gaelen made all the right moves and said all the right things, but the look in her eyes told Brent she was nowhere near at ease. That disappointed him, because he'd hoped his big, loving family might heal some of the wounds her own quarrelsome parents had inflicted on her.

But his description of his family as anything but quiet had proven an understatement. The noise level inside his boyhood home had already escalated beyond what might be termed politely as exuberant.

His father toasted everybody in sight with red wine and blustered about Gaelen's beauty. His mom speculated as to what her unborn grandchildren might look like, while his sisters and sisters-in-law put in their two cents' worth about what a milestone it was to see Brent bring a woman home for his family's inspection.

Only his two older brothers acted halfway normal, and that was because their attention was riveted on the baseball game on TV. Mark, who'd have been with them if not for the hangover, had fallen asleep in their dad's lounge chair almost the minute they'd arrived.

Brent glanced over toward the sagging couch where his female relatives had Gaelen trapped and saw his mom flip open what he feared was the first of many photo albums.

It was past time for a rescue. "Put those away, Ma," he said as he dragged Gaelen to her feet and wrapped a protective arm around her waist. "I want you to see my old room."

"Don't take too long. The roast is just about done," Mom yelled after them as they escaped up stairs scuffed by hordes of d'Angelo feet for more than forty years.

Inside the small attic room where he'd studied, slept, and dreamed for the first twenty-two years of his life, Brent pulled Gaelen into his arms, let the aura of her surround him. "Sorry if they're ganging up on you, sweetheart."

With a none too steady hand, she stroked his cheek. "It's okay. Just… different from what I've seen of family interaction."

"Yeah, we're loud. Pushy. But I haven't a doubt that those folks downstairs love me and have what they consider my best interests at heart."

"I know. I just feel…overwhelmed."

"And not too comfortable, if I read you right." Brent stroked Gaelen's silky hair. "This is where I come from. Who I am, under the fancy office, surgical scrubs and all the trappings that go along with them."

"I like who you are. Never think I don't."

It wasn't the time or place for serious conversation. "I won't. You know, I always wanted to sneak my girlfriend up here and—"

"Have your wicked way with her?"

"Yeah." He caught her skirt in one fist and drew it up, rubbing his knuckles against her silky pussy along the way. "Are you horny?"

Gaelen laughed. "Always. Except I think I hear your mother calling us to dinner."

"Okay, Mom, we're coming," Brent bellowed. Then he lowered his voice as he slipped a finger beneath her skimpy undies and tweaked her warm, moist pussy. "I'll save this for dessert."

* * * * *

Gaelen sat on the porch with Brent's two sisters, polishing off a sinfully rich hunk of chocolate cake. His mother had refused to believe she couldn't make room for the confection on top of a meal that had already packed at least five pounds onto her hips.

She'd be exercising off her indulgence for weeks, she thought as she downed the last luscious bite. Brent, she noticed, was already working off the results of his own gluttony by roughhousing in the small, neatly manicured backyard with his brother Tony's sons.

"Brent's good with kids. I can't wait 'til he has half a dozen of his own."

"Me, either. Gaelen, when are you two going to—"

"We haven't talked about marriage or children." She forced a smile she hoped would soften her terse reply.

"You don't like kids?" Sophia hugged her curly-haired baby girl, shot Gaelen a dirty look.

"Of course I like children." And she'd love to have a couple, if only she weren't afraid she'd provide them with a dysfunctional home like the one where she'd grown up. History, Gaelen reminded herself, had a habit of repeating itself.

"Then you don't like Brent?" His younger sister Teresa sounded as though that thought was too ridiculous to comprehend.

"Yes, I like him. A lot." Gaelen's gaze settled on Brent, who was headed her way, a laughing little boy perched on his shoulders.

If only she could believe she and Brent could have the kind of life together that his parents and siblings had achieved. If only she weren't terrified that reality would spoil their fantasy love affair. If only she could trust herself as much as she trusted him. If only...

* * * * *

"Let's get married. You're the love of my life, the lover of my dreams."

Soft classical music punctuated Brent's softly spoken words. A golden moon lit his features, lent a softness to his expression that Gaelen had never noticed before. Silence cloaked them in his bed as she savored the aftermath of their lovemaking, the warmth of his big body next to hers. A heady musk of honest sweat and sex filled her nostrils.

Until she'd seen him with his family today, Gaelen hadn't understood why her perfect lover might yearn for hearth and home. She'd never considered that he might love children in more than the abstract way all adults react to little ones. She hadn't realized she, too, had deeply buried yearnings for commitment.

Oh, how she wanted to say yes.

But she couldn't. Not with the memories she carried like an albatross around her heart.

While she'd be tempted to take a chance if it were only herself she'd risk, Gaelen couldn't chance destroying Brent and any children they might have, the way her parents had destroyed each other and warped their children.

"Sweetheart?"

"No, Brent. We agreed five years ago, no strings and no promises."

He frowned, as though deep in thought. Then he laid a lightly callused hand over her lower abdomen. "Needs change. I've changed. I believe you have, too. I want to know I'm yours and you're mine."

"You know that already, darling."

"I want to go to sleep with you in my arms and look at you over the breakfast table, every night and every day. I want to feel my baby growing inside you."

Panic rose in Gaelen's throat, made speaking almost impossible. "No."

"Why not? Nothing much would have to change."

"We agreed fantasy was what we wanted. A world of our making where none of the pressures of living would interfere. I don't want us to lose that." Gaelen traced along the ridges of muscle on Brent's stomach, then took him in her hand and gently squeezed.

Her skin tingled where he slid his hand up and traced along the undersides of her breasts with a lazy motion of his fingertips.

"M-mmm," she murmured, and she nibbled at the tender skin along his freshly shaven jaw.

"We can keep the dream alive. But don't you want the ultimate fantasy, sweetheart?"

"Something more mind-boggling than the honey and the hot tub and the toys?"

"Yeah." His hand drifted down, resumed its lazy circling of her belly. "Going to sleep doing this. Waking up, seeing each other's sleepy grins. Maybe making slow, sweet love to start the day off right, or just holding each other close if that's all we're up for after the past night's loving."

He'd stopped stroking her and splayed his fingers wide, as though he knew somehow that she'd suddenly chilled. The heat of his lightly callused palm warmed her from the inside out, chased away the cold. Slowly his touch, possessive yet gentle, sent its warmth through her body. In slow motion, he rolled her to her back and covered her.

He captured her gaze and held it, his own dark eyes filled with need — and more. Then he slid inside her slowly, so slowly she wanted to beg him for more until the tip of his long, thick penis pushed against the tip of her empty womb.

When he spoke, his voice sounded ragged. "I want to come inside you when you're off the pill. Plant my seed and watch it grow. See our baby born, watch him or her grow up with the kind of love we've found in each other. Marvel in the fact that our fantastic loving can create new life."

Gaelen shook her head until he captured her lips in a soft kiss and began to move inside her. Slowly. Deeply. Conventionally.

No props or toys or exotic settings to titillate and enhance the feelings. Just her and the man who loved her, coming together in the most basic act of love and life.

The ultimate fantasy. The one she could never risk becoming real.

For the moment, Gaelen didn't care. Caught up in the magic, she let herself imagine what could never be, allowed herself the indulgence of loving the man of her dreams without fear or reservation.

When she lay in Brent's arms after the sweetest climax of her life and told him no, she cried. But not before admitting she loved him, too.

*****

Brent stared out his kitchen window the next morning, a mug of coffee in hand and a hard-on in his workout sweats. He wanted nothing more than to go back upstairs and join Gaelen, but he'd warned her there'd be no more sex until she agreed to deepen their relationship—live together, at least, if she wasn't ready to commit to marriage.

A vow he knew he couldn't keep unless he kept his distance. A promise that, if it worked, would be worth the discomfort it was causing him for the moment.

Four more days. That was all he had left to persuade her they belonged together for the rest of their lives, before she'd take herself back to Georgetown and start rebuilding barriers he'd spent their time together here, trying to tear down.

In his head, he understood the reasons she wouldn't commit to him.

She certainly had seen the downside of relationships. He didn't need a shrink to tell him growing up around a suicidal mom and alcoholic father would make anybody wary of jumping into marriage. Or to figure out that witnessing her sister's abusive marriage had reinforced her already deeply seated fears.

Her determination not to bring children into a world that could include such heartbreak made sense in light of all she'd gone through.

But Brent's heart ached. Deep down, he believed the five years he and Gaelen had shared and the love that had grown strong between them should have persuaded her their relationship could weather any storm.

He sighed, set down his mug, and headed for the weight room. Maybe a good, tough workout would dull the desire he couldn't seem to quench — and take his mind off Gaelen, if only for a little while.

* * * * *

Brent only thought he was going to deprive her of his body until she agreed to move in with him.

Clad in nothing but tiny gold nipple rings she seldom wore now that the piercings she'd cajoled Brent into giving her a year ago her had fully healed, and a satin g-string beneath a translucent negligee of the sheerest silk, Gaelen made her way toward the sound of metal on metal that reverberated up the stairs from the weight room on the ground level of his townhouse.

Her mouth turned dry when she came into the room and saw him. Sweat glistened on his sleek golden chest and arms as he lay on a bench and pressed the bar of the machine up and down to the slow, sensual beat of a rock song on the radio. His legs were spread, his canvas-clad feet braced on the floor. Taut thigh muscles drew her gaze upward, above the ragged edge of the cutoff black sweat pants that clearly outlined his dormant sex.

Obviously he hadn't noticed her yet. When he did, Gaelen had no doubt that muscle group would come to immediate attention. Smiling, she stepped between his legs and murmured his name.

"Damn it, go away." He steeled himself, refused to let his gaze wander lower than her face.

She wouldn't let him get away with ignoring her. Bending, she bent and brushed her breasts against his sweat-dampened chest. "No."

He closed his eyes. But he couldn't get her nipples, hard and inviting where they jutted out from those gold rings, out of his mind. His mouth watered at the thought of catching the rings with his tongue, driving her crazy. Her flowery musk mingled with the smell of his sweat. Blood surged to his cock, made him feel lightheaded.

Damn. She knew how to tempt him. He wouldn't give in. Grunting with the effort, he forced the bar up, controlled its descent by sheer force of will. Unfortunately his willpower didn't extend far enough to let him block out her distracting presence. Or the gentle friction of fleece brushing his lower abdomen.

His waistband settled across the front of his upper thighs. Her warm, moist breath bathed his cock. Created heat, white-hot, that started there and suffused his body with need.

When she cradled his balls in her hand, he groaned. Then she closed her lips around him and bathed him with her tongue, and he abandoned all pretense of ignoring her.

"Have your way, sweetheart. You're not getting any, though," he ground out through clenched teeth as he set the bar on its rack.

"M-mmm."

Her non-reply reverberated against his cock, made his balls harden more against her palm. He clenched his fists against the need to bury his fingers in her silky hair, urge her to take more of him, go faster.

His abs tightened. He began to sweat again. His breath came in ragged gasps and his pulse raced. He felt as if he'd burst if he held on for one more minute. Then she pulled away.

"No you don't," she said, giving his balls a final squeeze. "When you come, it's not going to be a solo act."

Then she stood and stretched her luscious body over his, taunted him with a fleeting kiss. A brush of her distended nipples against his own. A caress to his cock with the silky confection that cloaked her sex.

"Want me?"

Brent reminded himself no one had ever died from sexual deprivation. "Not unless you're ready to give in and live with me the way you know you want to."

Her smile was feral as she stripped off the negligee. "Bet I can change your mind."

Not if he had any control at all, which he began to doubt the moment she turned and straddled him, her scantily clad pussy directly in his line of vision. Her musky scent, her wetness, lured his tongue.

She caught his swollen cock between her breasts, milked him, then took him in her mouth again. He tried without much success to concentrate on a bead of sweat as it made a lazy trail along his brow and settled in his hair.

How could any man withstand such temptation? Brent gave in, lifted his head, tasted the musk and the honey Gaelen offered so calculatingly. Though he'd sworn he wouldn't, he found her clit and lashed it with his tongue.

He'd stop in a minute. Deny her the release she demanded.

Sure he would.

Moments later he exploded, but not until he'd heard her moan with ecstasy.

Chapter Seven

She'd beaten him at his own game. Proved she could make him forget his vow, lose himself in her body.

So why did she feel as though she was the loser?

Gaelen looked out from the upstairs patio at Brent, who'd jerked his sweats up to his waist and stomped outside the moment he'd regained control and was trimming a vine in the garden as though his life depended on it.

Trimming? What he was doing to that poor jasmine looked more like scalping. The pile of clippings grew to the point Gaelen thought Brent might bury himself in them.

The sound of the phone drew her back inside, but the urgent sound of the woman on the line had her running to give Brent the phone.

"I've got to go," he said, wiping his hands on his sweats as he headed inside. "Come with me. I've got to evaluate a newborn. We'll eat out afterward."

As they dressed, he apologized for the interruption of their vacation. Though she didn't understand why his partners couldn't cover this emergency as well as any others that might have cropped up over the past ten days, Gaelen assured Brent she didn't mind tagging along.

Gaelen let Brent drag her through time-worn halls of Alexandria's public hospital to the newborn nursery. At his insistence, she donned scrubs and joined him as he examined a tiny baby with soft brown hair and big, sad eyes. A baby whose mouth and nose mingled in a hideous, reddened mass.

She couldn't hold back the sob that came up in her throat as she watched Brent examine the deformity.

He spoke softly, first to the baby and then to her. "He has a bilateral cleft lip and palate. It's fixable, though it's going to take some time." Brent took a metal chart from a slot on the plastic bassinet and scribbled something on a blank page.

"Brent, can you really fix that baby's face?" she asked as they left the nursery.

He squeezed her hand. "He's going to need multiple surgeries. Eventually, he should be able to breathe and eat normally."

"But how will he look?"

"Hopefully, fairly normal when all the repair is done. I need to speak to the baby's mom."

Brent left her in the nurses' lounge with a promise to return as soon as he could. Gaelen sat in a corner feeling superfluous, taking in the tired-looking institutional furniture and a grungy coffeepot that sat half-full on a warmer in front of the only window. That baby's face kept flashing in her mind, made her wonder if she'd had a false impression of the kind of medicine Brent really practiced.

"Want some coffee?"

Gaelen looked up at a pretty, round-faced nurse. "No, thanks. I'm just waiting for Dr. d'Angelo."

"I know. And I just wanted to get a look at the lady who took that gorgeous man out of circulation a few years back. I'm Doris Wilson. I'm in charge of the newborn nursery here."

"I'm Gaelen Reston. Does Dr. d'Angelo come here often?"

"Every time we call him, thanks be to God. Busy as he is, he always finds time for our babies who have facial deformities."

Gaelen watched Ms. Wilson shake her head. "Why wouldn't any doctor want to help children like that?"

"Money. Most big-name plastic surgeons run the other way from charity cases, especially ones like this that will require ongoing care for years to come. But Dr. d'Angelo never says no."

"Oh."

"You've got yourself a good one, ma'am. Better hold onto him." The nurse babbled on about how Brent should have a houseful of his own kids, but Gaelen had little success when she tried to tune Doris out.

"Doris, you're scaring my lady," Brent said when he came back a few minutes later. "Come on, sweetheart, I'm finished here for now."

Did Gaelen's discomfort show that clearly? She stood and smiled, murmured her farewell to Brent's one-woman cheering section, and walked out with him.

The warmth of his hand, the strength of his touch made her remember how gently he'd handled that little boy, how highly Doris Wilson thought of him for his willingness to help babies unable to help themselves.

Memories flooded Gaelen's mind. Her parents, using her and her sister as weapons in their constant verbal battles—battles that had gone on until her mother found escape in death. Her sister, escaping sooner from her own brutal husband. Her own life, made complete by loving Brent.

He'd never intentionally hurt her. Could she let go her fear, let him love and protect her until the end of time?

* * * * *

Gaelen didn't say much as they ate on the patio later that day. Neither did he. Brent missed their provocative conversations over dinner, the heated looks and arousing touches they usually shared. Had he lost her by pushing too hard?

No. He couldn't let that happen. Losing her would be like cutting off a vital part of himself.

"Sweetheart, we'll do it your way," he said, willing her to stop staring at the chirping sparrows on a limb above them and look at him.

She met his gaze, her eyes glistening with unshed tears. "Why?"

"Because I love you too much to walk away. Want you too much to do without—"

"Without this?"

As though frantic to connect with him the only way she'd allow, she slid one hand up his thigh, cupped him while she used the other to drag his hand between her legs.

Her touch scalded him. She felt hot and wet against his fingers. Irresistible. He increased the pressure of his palm against her clit.

"Yeah." He couldn't do without this—this fiery fantasy come true that lay at the heart of their relationship.

"I don't want to do without this, either." She gave him a playful squeeze that brought a hot surge of blood into his cock.

"Witch."

She squirmed against his seeking fingers, sighed. Her warm breath mingled with the cool, dry breeze, beckoned him to taste her velvet lips, sample her nectar.

Her tongue slid along the seam of his lips, then slipped inside his mouth. Thought vanished, but for the primitive drive to mate.

He scooped her up, strode inside and up the stairs. Once in his bedroom, he set her down, stripped off her clothes and his. No time for niceties. Not now. Not with her stroking him with eager hands, enveloping him in the smell of sweet perfume and hot, needy sex.

It was only when he collapsed at her side, still trembling from the ferocity of their joining, that he reflected on the reality of their fantasy love, his unrealized fantasy of building a real life with his fantasy lover.

* * * * *

Morning sunshine bathed Gaelen's face, warmed her cheeks. Brent's steady breathing penetrated the silence, and the weight of his hand on her breast made its ringed nipple pucker and harden with anticipation.

For five years now, he'd given her joy, helped her realize her every sensual fantasy. But he'd done more. He'd wormed his way so deeply into her heart that she could never let him go.

She traced a finger along his prickly jaw, recalled the concern she'd read in his expression as he'd examined the baby yesterday. The passion that scorched her each time they made love. The honest enjoyment she'd seen there when they'd spent time with his family. The soft look of love in his gorgeous dark eyes when he'd asked her to be his wife. The obvious pain there when she'd said no.

Brent's not my father. Or the jerk my sister married. And I'm not the weak woman my mother was.

Gaelen's thoughts echoed in her head and drove home her own need as they mocked her fear. How could she turn her back on a future with the man she loved, a future that promised so much joy?

She couldn't. As though a weight had been suddenly been lifted off her chest, Gaelen rose, her spirit soaring.

* * * * *

Brent couldn't read Gaelen's mood. Pensive, then playful, she seemed to be searching for a way to tell him—what?

Anticipation was a two-sided sword, he thought as he shaved carefully in response to her whispered suggestion that she'd like him to feel perfectly smooth tonight—all over. He imagined her doing the same in the guest bathroom across the hall.

While his cock throbbed at the prospects for sensual pleasure that her request had engendered, his brain sent dire warnings that she might be setting him up for a farewell fantasy. After all, their vacation was quickly coming to an end.

He set the razor down and ran his fingers over his chin, chest, and groin. His cock was already hard, and the spray of cold water from the shower nozzle did little to dampen its enthusiasm. Neither did the leather ring she'd given him to strap around his freshly shaven sex as soon as he'd dried off.

As she'd ordered, Brent settled, naked but for the thick black leather cock ring, onto the club chair by his bedroom window. Eyes closed, hands braced on the arms of the chair, he concentrated on the heavy pressure on his penis and scrotum in an effort to ignore the fear that hung heavy in his gut.

Sweet, pungent incense stung his nostrils, aroused him almost beyond enduring while a soft melody lulled away the urgency and left behind a heady, throbbing, slowly accelerating anticipation.

Her footsteps barely registered, but he sensed her presence before she touched him, felt her kneel between his thighs. Her warm, damp breath bathed his clean-shaven sex.

Something silky grazed first one arm and then the other, tethered them securely to the chair arms. Her pebbled nipples and the warm, gold rings that adorned them pressed against his belly, then slid lower to graze his aching cock.

She molded her breasts around him, warmed him.

"I want to touch you, too." He strained against his silken bonds.

"No." Her tongue circled the slit at the tip of his cock, while she cradled his aching balls between both palms. "I love this. Love you."

"You're killing me."

"M-mmm."

After she took his cock deep in her mouth, she opened the ring, set his tortured flesh free. It was all he could do to hold back, make himself endure the delicious pain of waiting. Of feeling her wet, satiny mouth on him, sucking. Loving the neediest part of him.

He couldn't hold it for long. Just as he was about to explode, she shifted and sank onto him. She gloved him, squeezed him, cradled his head against her breasts as he came in fierce bursts of pleasure that seemed they'd never end.

Gaelen released Brent's silken bonds and held him. How had she ever thought she could let him go? She absorbed the aftershocks that reverberated through his big body, took the aftermath of his fulfillment within herself.

His olive skin reflected the setting sun, looked as satiny as if felt against her breasts, her swollen sex. She tasted him, savored the not unpleasant taste of salty sweat that lingered on her lips.

"Brent?" she said later when she felt his sex stir to life again inside her.

He dug his fingers into her hair, drew her back until their gazes met and held.

"I love you."

"So you've said."

She stroked his cheek, his neck, his muscular shoulder and arm. Then she took his right hand and drew it to her left breast. "I want you to marry me. Be the love of my life as well as the lover of my dreams. Live the fantasy of loving you every day, every night."

His dark eyes grew bright, and a smile lit the face that starred in all her dreams.

"You mean it?" He slid the first knuckle of his little finger through her nipple ring, rubbed the pebbled nub.

Her heart pounded so hard, he must certainly feel its beat beneath his hand. She felt his blood surge, too, deep inside her body.

"Yes. I'm very certain now."

He cupped her left breast, then gave both gold adornments a playful tug. "You're ready for another ring, then?"

His mischievous little-boy grin made her laugh. "I think the next one had better go on my finger," she told him, though what he was doing to her nipples with those rings sent a message of heated sexual need straight through her.

"Or here?" He flexed his hips, drove hard and deep again, as hard as though he hadn't just come moments earlier.

The idea of him piercing his beautiful penis made her shudder. "No. I like you just the way you are."

"Good. Hold on."

She did, and he stood. Bodies still joined, they sank together onto the bed. He loved her slow and gentle, fast and hard. With talented fingers and tongue, he brought her pleasure more intense than any she'd ever known. Pleasure born of commitment, she thought in the aftermath as she lay quietly in his arms.

Commitment. She tried out the word, found it brought no more panic. No more fear.

When they said the vows that made it official a few weeks later, Gaelen set aside the last of her worry and turned her gaze to the future.

A future with Brent, filled with fantasy as well as the newly discovered reality of loving each other until the end of time.

ILLUSIONS

Chapter One

The press said he attracted women in much the same way as flowers drew honeybees.

Master magician Drake Conover doubted at the moment that this was a good thing.

He'd just finished a three-week gig in New York City and pocketed a cool mil. And he had two voluptuous blondes in bed with him in his luxury hotel suite, doing things that should have wiped every trace of ennui from his brain, replacing it with mindless lust. He should have come at the sight of them shaving each other's pussies, his prerequisite for giving them tongue.

But Drake was having trouble getting into the action.

Sure, his own clean-shaven cock was rock-hard in Deirdre's wet, warm pussy. And his tongue was doing its thing on Marlys's swollen clit while she played with her cousin's surgically enhanced tits.

But his heart wasn't in the game.

Maybe that was the problem.

Maybe his heart was back home in western Pennsylvania, where he'd agreed to do a benefit performance this weekend for the stroke rehab unit at a Pittsburgh hospital—over his agent's loud objections.

Or maybe he didn't have a heart at all since crying it out that long-ago day when his mother walked out on him and his dad.

It probably didn't matter.

For now, he had two ladies who wanted satisfaction. And he didn't intend to break his years-long string of sexual triumphs by letting them down.

He lifted his hands, clamped them onto Marlys's breasts. Her nipples poked into his palms, begging to be pinched and tugged on.

Marlys liked a little pain with her pleasure, or so her cousin Deirdre had told him when she brought Marlys along to join their sexual games.

Drake nipped her clit with his teeth, gently at first, then harder. He pinched her nipples and tugged on the little gold barbells that pierced them.

"More," she gasped, her hands working Deirdre's big, round tits while Deirdre bounced up and down on Drake's cock with increasing fervor.

What more could he do? Sleight-of-hand could only go so far. Drake had just one cock and Deirdre had it well and truly occupied.

"My ass," Marlys suggested as though she'd guessed his mental dilemma.

Never tell a lady no. Though it wasn't his favorite form of sex play, Drake gave her left nipple one last hard squeeze and lowered his hand between her widespread butt cheeks.

He worked in one finger, then two. Marlys mustn't have been a stranger to anal sex, because it took three fingers and some enthusiastic reaming for her to convulse around his busy tongue and scream out his name before rolling over and collapsing, her carnal appetite apparently satisfied for the moment.

Now Deirdre needed gratification. She liked straight up, simple pound-me sex, his cock reaming her pussy until he stole her self-control and sent her flying. Deirdre was a one-come woman, for which Drake in his present blue funk was eternally grateful.

"Roll over and hold on, baby," he growled, his hands at her waist when he flipped her onto her back. "We're gonna do this together."

Drake liked it best this way. Missionary position with his lover's legs twined like vines around his waist and hips. He liked controlling the action, doing the fucking as opposed to being fucked.

Deirdre clamped her pussy hard onto his cock and milked him. It was close, that mindless state where nothing mattered but the friction, the heat, the rush of spurting his load into a warm, willing female body.

Or rather into the condom Deirdre had rolled on him before she mounted up.

Then Marlys slid between his outstretched legs. His cock in Deirdre to its hilt, Drake paused when Marlys spread his ass cheeks and worked something wet and chilly up his ass. Not her fingers but something bigger.

A dildo?

It hurt like hell, but it was damn arousing, too, not that he needed any more arousing to get the job done now. Experimenting, he withdrew, then thrust into Deirdre again. Marlys's hair and nipple rings tickled his bare back as she rocked back and forth, working the thing in and out in parody of his own rhythm.

Deirdre grabbed him by the hair, brought their mouths together. Her tongue stabbed his lips, forcing them open. Her pussy spasmed around his cock. Marlys's fingers scissored the nubs of his nipples while she reamed his ass. Assaulted in nearly every orifice in his body, Drake let go and let the waves of his climax sweep him into mental and physical oblivion.

Later, after he'd sent the voluptuous cousins on their way, he showered and crawled back into the big bed he'd been sleeping in since coming to New York.

He guessed he was just an old-fashioned country boy at heart, because he felt vaguely soiled from the debauchery he'd just enjoyed.

Quite possibly he hadn't enjoyed it much at all.

* * * * *

While Drake mentally dissected his lifestyle in a New York City luxury hotel, CIA operative Erienne Duval rushed around in a Pittsburgh hotel room, setting up her cover for the covert surveillance she was to initiate on the master magician.

Since her partner Rob died, her job had become her life. For the past year she'd lived and breathed covert operations, her determination fueled with resentment for having lost the man she loved to an Islamic radical fanatic's automatic rifle assault in Karachi.

She'd never refused an assignment since that awful day. No job was too dangerous, no order too intrusive on her privacy. She'd always hated fanatics who destroyed innocent lives in the name of religious or political zealotry, but since Rob's death that hatred had taken on a very personal meaning. She'd do whatever it took to win the war on terror.

Her cover was the volunteer job she'd taken as a PR specialist for a Pittsburgh hospital's community relations department. In that capacity, she'd be Drake Conover's liaison when he set up and did a benefit show to raise money for the hospital's stroke rehabilitation unit.

It boggled her mind, looking at a glossy promo photo of the famous magician, that such a gorgeous man might in fact be a spy. Especially since he donated a lot of his time and energy to good causes like this one.

But according to her bosses, he could be. Traversing the Atlantic as he did several dozen times a year, Conover could very easily be the traitor carrying stolen classified materials and selling them to the highest bidders among the international purveyors of terror. Several recent drops of classified material had happened while he performed in Hamburg and Madrid, well-known as European hotbeds for terrorist activity.

Erienne had to get close to him, find out one way or another whether Drake Conover was what he seemed — or, like the tricks he performed onstage, a treacherous illusion.

She'd seen his photos, and if he looked anything like them, getting up close and personal would pose no hardship. None at all. She was a healthy woman in her sexual prime at thirty, and she hadn't had a lover now for over a year, since the night before Rob had walked into a terrorist's gunsights.

Her nipples beaded when she ran her hand over the soft cashmere of her sweater. Her pussy softened.

Yes, job or no job, it was past time for her to satisfy her body's needs.

Tall, dark, and dangerous. That's how the press described Drake Conover, the thirty-six-year-old magician from a small coal mining community not far from here, who performed his tricks around the world for the rich, the famous, and the infamous. They weren't far off the mark.

Erienne stared at the photo, sensing it didn't hold a candle to the man himself. Some would say he was classically pretty-boy handsome, but he wasn't, at least not to her. His features had a ruggedness she thought suggested physical strength and unapologetic male machismo. Those qualities seemed somehow incongruous with his career choice as a performer. She was especially drawn to his eyes, more for the intelligence she saw there than for the unusual jade-green color gossip columnists insisted came from colored contact lenses.

She had a job to do, and it wasn't to drool over Drake Conover's photo. She had to seduce the man himself and learn his deepest secrets. With a lot of luck, to get herself invited to tag along on his next European gigs — he had shows scheduled in Hamburg and Brussels following his benefit performance here—and capture him if he was selling out his country.

Seducing him might prove impossible. From all she'd read, it seemed Conover had a string of women constantly at his heels. Beautiful, rich, famous women—all of which Erienne was not.

Tall, long-legged women with long, lustrous hair and voluptuous bodies.

But who knew? Like Rob, he might get turned on by her short-cropped hair and the compact body she honed daily with weights and karate practice.

Whatever. She'd get him into bed somehow. After all, not many of the man's globe-trotting lovers would be likely to join him in provincial Pittsburgh, where the glitz was minimal and coal dust hung in the air on hazy days. And she'd come loaded for bear.

She'd bought new sexy, sensual underwear that showed off her best attributes. Had her pubes waxed clean and her cap of glossy reddish-brown hair clipped even shorter, to where it left her nape bare for a man's attentions. She'd even adopted the persona of a hot-blooded sex kitten with short, tight skirts, easy-to-open silky blouses, and spike-heeled shoes that showed off her well-toned thighs and calves.

With luck the master of illusion would want to work his magic on her, if only to alleviate the boredom he was certain to experience away from the bright lights of Broadway and the pleasure capitals of the world. Maybe he'd even welcome a stand-in lover who didn't have bleached-blonde big hair and forty double-D boobs, she thought when she remembered seeing a recent photo of porn star Deirdre Dee hanging on his arm.

* * * * *

The next day as his plane descended, Drake dutifully raised his seat back to its original upright and locked position and enjoyed the anonymity afforded in the otherwise empty first-class cabin. He glanced at his PDA, refreshing his memory as to the name of the woman the hospital's community relations director had said would meet his flight.

Erienne Duval. Supposedly a volunteer worker.

Classy name.

It produced a mental image of a cool, tall blonde with horn-rimmed glasses and a business suit she wore like armor. A woman with a pedigree and three generations of family money.

The sort of snooty broad the mine owner's daughter who'd turned up her nose at him when they were kids had probably become.

Hell, it had been twenty years since he got up the balls to ask heartless little Cindy Moran to the junior prom only to have her laugh in his face. Why did he suddenly recall his humiliation as vividly as if it had happened yesterday?

The rough landing jarred him a bit, took his mind off the brush-off. What did he care who chauffeured him around for the next three days? Hadn't he decided to take a sabbatical from sex for the foreseeable future? Or at least for the next few days?

That vow went out the window when he spied the woman holding up a sign with his name on it. She was no ice princess.

No, unless Drake missed his guess, Ms. Erienne Duval was one hot chick. And from the lascivious look on her face, he had the flint that would spark her into flames.

So much for the sabbatical from sex.

When he waved at her, she dropped the sign and joined him at the baggage carousel.

Her mouth was too wide for beauty—but just the right size to take his cock. And her legs! Long and sleek for such a little thing. Bare beneath a short tight skirt now, they'd feel like heaven locked around his waist. Or tossed over his shoulders while he fucked her with his tongue. Eyes that reminded him of a summer sky glittered as though her thoughts were taking that same direction.

God, he hoped they were. It had been years since looking at a fully-clothed woman gave him an instant hard-on. Good thing his trench coat covered his crotch, or he might be on the way to jail for public indecency.

"Mr. Conover?"

Her husky voice, pitched low for a woman, poured over him like honey. "That's me," he said, his gaze on her instead of the luggage that rumbled by on the conveyor belts.

"I'm Erienne Duval. Your right-hand woman while you're here for the benefit performance."

The corners of her generous mouth curled upward, revealing straight white teeth Drake imagined scraping him ever so gently when she gave him head.

He stifled a groan when more blood rushed into his already swollen cock.

Skin the color of pale pink roses that grew in a tangle of weeds outside the cabin where he'd grown up made him want to touch her cheek, see if it felt as satiny as it looked. He guessed her glossy, very short hair—he thought it was even shorter than his own—would be called auburn, but it reminded him of a sleek cap the color of burnished mahogany. His fingers itched to burrow beneath it and cradle her neat, smooth skull, holding her to her task of swallowing all his come.

She smelled like woman and dark, sensual sex, her scent accentuating the knowing seductiveness in her gaze. Drake had to force himself to look away and search along the carousel for the weekender and garment bag he'd been persuaded to check instead of carrying on.

"What color are your bags?" she asked.

"Black. Like almost every other one on the belt." Served him right, going for unobtrusive rather than distinctive.

"There. They're coming now," he said, having spied the silver tags his agent had given him after they spent an hour in the baggage claim area at LAX, looking as she'd said for "a particular pair of plain black wing-tips at the airport on Friday afternoon."

His luggage in hand, Drake followed Erienne to her car, a nondescript sedan of indeterminate age. As she drove to his hotel, all he thought about was getting her to stay and prove she was really his woman for the duration of his Pittsburgh stay.

Chapter Two

ஐ

Sex appeal oozed out of every pore on Drake Conover's long, lean body. His tangy cologne tickled Erienne's nostrils, conjuring a picture in her mind of tropical islands, coconut palms, and tangy citrus fruits all mingled with the smell of hot, horny male.

Reminding herself as she rode the elevator with him to the thirtieth-floor suite where he'd be staying that her job was surveillance and capture, she tried to ignore the sexual pull she'd felt the moment she met his hot gaze at the baggage carousels.

She couldn't afford to get tied up in knots over the man. Not when she had a job to do. She hadn't expected to look particularly forward to the job of seducing him.

But there was something, completely apart from the sleight-of-hand he apparently performed so well—something about Drake Conover that fueled a flame she'd thought died along with Rob.

She found it easy to conjure up a sexy smile when she gave him a visual once-over. Or to lower her voice to a husky, seductive purr. "Would you like for me to come in now so we can go over your schedule?"

"Yes." His deep, honeyed assent conveyed a world of promise. Sensual sex and something more.

His hand steady, he inserted a key card into the door. Large with short, well-kept fingernails, it was a capable-looking hand, tanned and lean like she imagined the rest of him would be. He stepped back, gestured for her to go inside.

She imagined the accommodations were far below his usual standards. After all, according to her boss, he'd been staying at one of the costliest suites at the Plaza for the three weeks his sold-out show played on Broadway.

This suite, booked by her temporary employers, looked typical of businessmen's suites in mid-range hotels across the country. Sand-colored carpeting and off-white walls. Two large abstract prints that echoed the blacks, browns, and ivories in the upholstery of a sofa, loveseat, and reclining chair arranged conventionally around a dark wood coffee table. A matching desk with telephone and laptop hookup took up the wall opposite a small bar that had two padded stools and held a four-cup Mr. Coffee machine.

"It's not the Plaza," Erienne said apologetically when she stuck her head inside the bedroom door and took a look. Not much imagination had gone into the decor.

His warm breath on her neck sent shards of electricity straight to her pussy. "The bed looks comfortable enough."

The sensations he caused by resting his hands on her shoulders turned her heat up further. "Don't you think that's all that really matters?" he asked.

"Yes." The queen-size bed stood high—crotch high. Or mouth-high if you were on your knees beside it. Its puffy duvet cover matched the upholstery on the furniture in the other room. That bed looked inviting, though not as tempting as Drake himself. "Can I help you unpack?"

"I'll just hang up the garment bag. I'm used to living from suitcases." He unzipped the bag and spread several garments—all black, Erienne noticed—along the rod.

"Speaking of baggage, the director told me to let you know your equipment cases arrived earlier today at the theater. I'm looking forward to seeing your show."

"You like magic?"

Erienne was certain she'd like the magic they'd make in that bed. "Uh-huh. I hear you're the best."

"Not only at making illusions, Ms. Duval."

His voice held a world of sensual invitation. So did his touch when he kneaded her shoulders with those big, capable hands. Suddenly Erienne panicked.

She was supposed to be seducing *him*. And seducing him was supposed to be her job, not her pleasure.

"The schedule. We should go over your schedule," she said in her best professional sounding voice.

Or what passed for it, considering her pussy was dripping, her nerve endings tingling. Her pulse raced out of control.

"Getting to know each other should be our first concern, shouldn't it?"

With a sure, knowing touch he cupped her breasts through the thin silk of her blouse, then chuckled. "Yes, I believe that's definitely the first order of business," he added when he lightly pinched the nipples he couldn't help realizing had turned hard and needy at his touch.

She wanted him.

And Drake wanted Erienne with a fervor he hadn't known for years — if ever. His balls drew up, his mouth grew dry. His cock rose, nudging the rounded firmness of buttocks encased in a snug, short skirt.

He had to taste those full, coral-colored lips, the hard buttons of her nipples that responded so enthusiastically to his touch. He had to drag off that skirt and find for himself whether her pussy tasted as good as she smelled.

She had potent magic, more powerful than any of the tricks he performed onstage. That magic drew him in, made him want to sample more.

More what?

He didn't know.

But his cock was eager to find out.

"Erienne?"

"Yes?"

The husky tone of her voice and elusive, darkly sensual smell of her perfume turned him on. And he loved the softness of her bare nape and the prickle of her shaved hairline beneath his seeking tongue.

"Fuck with me."

"Oh, yes."

Not a hint of outrage or maidenly reluctance. Just "Oh, yes." Drake liked that. Liked her.

Her hands met his when she lifted them to tackle the buttons that held the flimsy silk together. "Calluses?" he asked when he rubbed his thumbs over them.

"Martial arts."

So she could protect herself. Good. He hated helpless females. Anxious to fondle her small, sensitive breasts, he helped her slide the blouse off her shoulders and tossed it to the floor.

His mouth went dry. Her bra was lace and barely there, a scrap of midnight blue against her ivory skin. Cutouts left the hard, reddened nubs of her nipples and soft rosy areolas exposed. He tugged gently on them, watched them swell and darken.

"Convenient," he murmured, chafing the delectable nubs with one hand while he splayed the other over her concave belly. "Have you more delicious surprises for me?"

"Wait and see. "

"I guess I'll just have to make this skirt disappear," he said, grasping the stretchy material and tugging it down around her ankles.

Her thighs were as firm as he'd imagined, her skin satin-soft and pale ivory against a tiny triangle of dark, flimsy lace. If he didn't miss his guess, her pussy would be silky-smooth as well, because he didn't see a hint of pubic hair showing around that eye-catching lace on her mound—just pink, plump flesh glistening with moisture he couldn't wait to taste.

"You like the packaging?" she asked, turning and spreading her legs apart so he got a better view.

"Oh, yeah." On closer examination he noticed the minuscule bikini had no crotch. It didn't even have to come off for him to insert his fingers or tongue—or cock.

Like her short helmet of glossy hair, Erienne's body was compact, made for efficiency of motion. Martial-arts hard. Different from Deirdre and Marlys and the other overblown Playboy playmates who usually shared his bed.

Vive la différence.

Drake tore off his clothes, revealing a buff, tanned body dusted lightly with soft, dark hair—and a rose-colored, fully aroused penis, long and thick, curling slightly inward.

A beautiful penis whose circumcised head rose to meet washboard abs. And large testicles drawn tight inside a dark, velvety looking scrotum. Like hers, his sex was devoid of hair. Seeing him so obviously ready to put that impressive tool to use made Erienne gasp.

Was it with terror or anticipation? She wasn't certain.

Yes she was. Her mouth watered at the thought of tasting him, and her pussy was dripping wet.

When she watched him roll a condom over his erection, she realized Rob hadn't been as well-endowed as she'd once thought he was.

Drake's gaze reminded her of emerald fire, licking out and scorching her nipples, her belly—her dripping pussy. She throbbed there, as if her pussy was saying it wanted his big, beautiful penis buried inside it, thrusting and retreating until she convulsed with long-denied pleasure.

"I can't wait."

The words seemed torn from deep in his massive chest as he closed the distance between them, lifted her, and rammed himself inside her. "Wrap your legs around me, Erienne," he said as he braced her back against an empty wall and grasped her head between his hands.

The rays from the setting sun cast him in muted orange shadow, lending a surrealistic aura to the scene. When their lips met, his tongue demanded entry.

This might-be-a-traitor took her breath away. Well-developed muscles dancing beneath the satiny skin of his chest stimulated her nipples. His fingers, never still, dug beneath her hair to massage her scalp.

The two of them smelled of her musky perfume, his cologne, and sex. Hot, wild sex that was about to carry her over the edge. She opened her mouth, tasted the sweat that had gathered where his muscular shoulders joined his neck.

Harder. Faster. He withdrew, then rammed himself back in deeper with every practiced stroke. Pressure built inside her, threatened to burst into flame.

She clenched her pussy muscles around him, as if that would hold off her climax. God, but he knew how to use his big, hard tool.

She was coming. Now. Waves of delicious sensation undulated in her pussy. They spread up and out, her whole body trembled with the strength of it.

Drake caught her soundless screams of satisfaction in his mouth, carried her through each wave of ecstasy, pushed her high, then higher. By the time he stiffened and shouted his own release, Erienne was a mindless, boneless heap.

*****

Night had come, cloaking the modest accommodations in black velvet, but a picture of the woman sprawled under the bedcovers next to him was etched indelibly on Drake's mind.

Strange. Usually he couldn't wait to escape his partner — or partners, he amended, thinking back to the scene with Deirdre and her cousin less than twenty-four hours ago — after he came.

He stroked the silky bristles of Erienne's hair while she snored softly, smiled at the realization that he was lusting after a woman so different from his usual playmates. The heady smell of sex filled his nostrils and had his cock leisurely lengthening and hardening again.

The first time he hadn't been able to wait for the niceties. He'd had to get his cock into her pussy, fuck her hard and fast. And from the way she'd come apart in his arms, she'd wanted it that way too.

The edge off his lust now, he wanted to taste every inch of her firm, compact body, make her come with his hands and mouth. And he wanted to watch her on her knees, working his cock with her full, sensual lips. Her tongue.

Hell, he wanted to fill her every orifice. And it had been years since any woman had made him yearn for more than reassurance about his own sexual prowess and, he reminded himself, the physical release of coming.

"I'm gonna work some magic on you, baby," he whispered against her nape before burrowing under the covers.

Gently so as not to wake her, he lifted her butt cheeks, draped her legs over his shoulders and settled in to feast.

He kneaded her bottom with one hand as he lapped her outer lips. God, but they were smooth. Silky as a baby's bottom. He loved it. Her musk filled his nostrils, made him acutely aware she was all woman. Grown-up, delectable woman.

When he turned his attention inward, he found her clit swollen and tight as if to beg his attention. He stabbed it with the point of his tongue once, twice, once again. Then he took it between his teeth and drew it inside his mouth. It hardened more as he suckled.

When he slipped a finger of his free hand inside her pussy, moisture gushed out. She was so damn responsive. Even while she slept, her hips lifted to his mouth and she made soft little sounds that drove him crazy.

Incredibly those sweet sleepy sounds got him hotter than any foreplay he'd ever had. Amazing, because he guessed he'd experienced just about every sexual act a man and a woman could perform on each other. And more, he thought with no little self-disgust when he recalled last night's threesome.

On the other hand, what he was doing now seemed right. His cheeks wedged between Erienne's firm, satiny thighs, his face buried between her legs, he stroked and suckled and drank his fill of her honey. His balls tightened and his cock throbbed, but he tried to ignore their demands, focusing instead on waking her to a gentle climax.

She slept on, her restless motions and arousing little whimpers the only signs that on some level she was enjoying Drake's efforts. Except for her dripping pussy.

He slipped a second finger inside her, then a third, while he continued stimulating her clit with his tongue and massaging her ass cheeks.

Her only response was to sigh and spread her legs a little wider.

But when he slipped the tip of his little finger into her anus, she came instantly awake.

"No!" Her tone conveyed disgust—even a little fear, he thought.

So she wasn't as sexually experienced as she pretended with her fuck-me clothes and musky perfume that would cause a hard-on on a corpse. "Yes," he murmured against her clit as he worked his finger slowly beyond her anal sphincter. "I'm not going to hurt you. You'll like this. I promise."

Most women did after they got past the initial shock. But Drake wasn't certain Erienne would. She felt incredibly tight there. Making no effort to invade her further, he wiggled his finger ever so slightly.

"Oh, yes." She sounded surprised, as if she hadn't realized pleasure could be found there as well as in her pussy.

"There are many ways to sexual delight, baby." He wanted to explore them all with Erienne. He blew on her clit, felt it harden more when he covered it with his mouth and lapped up the musky moisture that gathered there.

She tasted so good. And he'd never had a woman who seemed so perfectly attuned to his sexual needs from the moment they touched.

Moments ago she'd been dreaming—dreaming about Drake doing delicious things to her.

What his tongue was doing to her was magical. But like the tricks Drake performed onstage, the emotions welling up inside her now were only illusions. She had to focus on reality—on the fact she was here to learn if the man now licking her pussy was selling secrets to the enemy.

Just then he bit gently at her clit and sent her thoughts scattering.

Sensation. His velvety tongue, his warm moist breath, the strange but arousing sensation of his finger barely inside her anus right now.

Memories. Drake taking her against the wall earlier, his big hard penis pounding into her like a jackhammer—as though he couldn't help himself or spend the time for the sort of foreplay she was enjoying so much now.

She was going to come. Gently this time. A slow, warm glow began in her clit, radiated out, then up—her inner thighs, her belly, her breasts. Prickling sensations at first, then tremors took over as the bubbles of satisfaction rose, then softly exploded one at the time.

Not even Rob had made her feel so sexually alive. As though nothing mattered except taking Drake's penis inside her all the way, easing the ache he'd created when he made her sensual dream come true.

Chapter Three

ಬ

The afterglow still warm on her cheeks, Erienne tossed back the covers and slid off the bed. "Come here," she said, reaching for Drake and urging him onto the nondescript upholstered chair by the window.

Stars twinkled in the midnight sky, surrounding a crescent moon. When he thrust his hips to the edge of the chair and splayed his muscular legs, neon lights cast shadows of iridescent reds and blues and greens on the glistening tip of his penis and the large, satiny smooth scrotum that had drawn close to his body with sexual excitement.

Erienne went down on her knees, licked away the drop of lubrication and tongued the slit before taking him in her mouth. Cupping his heavy testicles in both hands, she took more of his penis and swirled her tongue along the ridge that separated its head from its long, thick shaft.

He tasted good. Clean, a little salty, and male, with no hair to catch between her teeth and spoil her fun. His moans and the gentle pressure of his hands silently urging her to take him deeper let her know he liked the way she gave him head, too.

"God, Erienne. Stop. Now." Jerking her head off his cock, Drake took several ragged breaths. "I want to come in your pussy." He pulled her to the bed, grabbing one of the condom packages he'd tossed on the night stand and ripping it open with his teeth while he watched her sprawl on her back and spread her legs for him.

Her gaze on him while he put on protection, she fondled her nipples. "I want you to suck them while we fuck."

"My pleasure, baby."

He was hard as stone and getting harder by the second. Erienne was a man's dream—hot, horny, and not ashamed to let him know it. Kneeling between her legs, he guided himself home.

He could easily get used to her tight, wet pussy. Her puckered, hard little nipples. Her mouth that had to have been made especially for his tongue and cock. Drake usually ascribed to the theory that once a night was enough, but it seemed his body was planning to make an exception to that rule.

Her nipples formed hard little buttons for his tongue to tease. Her pussy caressed his cock.

His balls tightened painfully. His cock grew bigger, harder. It pressed hard against the slick, wet folds of her pussy.

Slow wasn't an option. Not now. Maybe not ever, with Erienne.

He thrust hard, deep. She met his every move, fast, faster, harder, deeper. Sweat rolled off his body, mingling with hers and making her skin taste salty. Her moans of pleasure spurred him on. Finally he couldn't hold on. He slammed into her once more, his cock already spurting before he buried it all the way.

God. It felt so good, he had to scream at the intensity of each exquisite wave that poured over him. He was still coming when she clasped his body to hers and let herself fall over the abyss to her own release.

* * * * *

Too much pleasure. Too much emotion.

Erienne stood by the bedroom window the next morning, reminding herself why she was here. She should have been more interested in searching his luggage for incriminating evidence than in checking out what, if any, interesting toys he might have stashed away.

She hadn't found either.

No toys and nothing that could conceivably be a place for him to stash away state secrets. The underwear, jeans, and shirt she picked up from the floor held nothing suspicious. And all his luggage contained was clothing—two pairs of black silk boxers like the ones he had on last night, two pairs of black socks, one blue and one white Egyptian cotton dress shirt, a severely cut black suit—and the sort of leather shaving kit men always carried on their trips. She'd grinned when she noticed it contained an unopened box of extra-large prelubricated Trojans.

She even searched the linings and hems of the clothes and used a magnet to check the cases themselves for hidden metal objects. The only things left for her to look through were the items he emptied from his pockets last night.

Quietly so as not to wake Drake, she moved closer to the bed and perused the small cache: four foil-wrapped condoms, a slender black leather wallet, a few dollars' worth of change, some crumpled bills and what looked like an antique snuffbox.

It was about an inch and a half square, and maybe a half-inch deep. Its tiny gold clasp and hinges had delicate filigree work, unusually distinct for having been crafted in such tiny scale. On top was an intricate inlaid pattern of lapis lazuli, onyx, and mother of pearl. In the center of the pattern was an amazingly realistic-looking blue eye.

"Good morning," he said, rolling over and smiling. "I have more in my shaving kit."

Apparently he thought she was checking out the supply of condoms. That was a good thing since she'd been about to open the little gold box.

"Quite a supply for two days, isn't it?"

"One never knows what might come up."

The double entendre was delivered blandly, without facial expression. She'd heard Drake did deadpan well. Now she believed it.

"We should go and check the equipment your manager shipped to the theater," Erienne said.

She had to get them out of this bedroom, get some perspective. Otherwise she'd end up spending this whole assignment making up for lost sex—and not completing her assignment.

Hopefully she wasn't having sex with a traitor.

But if she was, she had to find out.

She was enough of a patriot to want to know it if Drake Conover was a spy. And enough of a fan of illusion that she was dying to learn how he performed his magic tricks—especially his trademark act, "The Deadly Dartboard."

* * * * *

He'd never before had a lover who took such a keen interest in the tools of his trade.

But Drake found he liked showing Erienne how he used them to create his illusions. He also enjoyed having her close, where he could steal a kiss whenever the urge came on.

"Erienne, George Moran, who keeps the shows running smoothly. George, this is Erienne Duval."

"My pleasure, Ms. Duval. Is Drake showing you all his trade secrets?"

She laughed. "He could show me every day for years and I still wouldn't be able to understand how he pulls off all these tricks."

"Illusions, please. Not tricks." Drake put an arm around Erienne, drew her to his side. "How's the setup going?"

"Almost finished. The extras the hospital hired are pretty good workers." George paused when someone yelled his name. "Oops, looks as though I might have spoken too soon. Excuse me."

Erienne looked up at Drake. "What's wrong?"

"Nothing George can't fix. He knows more about the equipment than I do. He wants everything right for the show. Right now he's pissed off with me because I let Bob and Renee—they're the ones who usually set up my props—take a few days to relax before we head to Germany and Belgium."

"So that's why you're laying out these things yourself?"

"Yes. Don't want to lose the best stage manager in the business." Drake turned to the prop table and started taking the props he'd need tonight out of a large wooden box.

"What's in here?" she asked, holding up a smaller box.

He grinned. "Scarves."

"What do you use them for?"

"Tying volunteers from the audience to 'The Deadly Dartboard.'" He gestured toward the shiny metallic dartboard situated at the rear of center stage. "I invented this one myself. Want to try it out?"

"I'm not sure. Something in your press kit mentioned that you throw deadly weapons at your volunteers. I'd have to see how it works before I'd volunteer. What's so special about the board?"

Drake opened another box and drew out a handful of lethal looking daggers. "When Jim flips a switch backstage, the board will start rotating on its axis. When it does, I begin tossing these daggers, slowly enough for the audience to build up a good head of terror, wondering when I'm going to miss and kill my human guinea pig. The trick is in coming as close as possible without hitting her."

"I think I'll wait until tomorrow. I want to see you do that to someone else besides me." Erienne's worried gaze shifted from the board to the slim, medieval-looking iron daggers in his hand.

"Come on. Let me show you how it works." Dragging her with him, he strode to the board—then hesitated. He never before had trusted anyone except his crew with the secret behind why his assistants always survived what appeared to be a sentence for sudden death.

But Erienne wasn't in the business of magic, and she'd given him no reason not to trust her. "Look at the outline of the woman," he told her.

She did, but she looked confused. "I see it. Is there something special I should be noticing?"

"One, the silhouette is several inches bigger around than any volunteer I'd choose. Two, it's made of a different material than the rest of the board. Finally, the silhouette doesn't have slots in it. The rest of the board does." Drake pointed out the closely spaced slots to Erienne.

"That's all?"

"No. Behind the board there's a very powerful sweeper magnet that moves slowly, horizontally, all the time the board is rotating. And these daggers are highly magnetic."

"Being magnetic keeps them from stabbing your volunteer?"

"No. But the sweeper magnet attracts the iron dagger—to all the areas on the board except the outline. It's made of a material called Fontax."

"Fontax?"

"Yes. It's a Taxal alloy, made of vacuum-treated chromium, cobalt, and titanium. It's used mostly to make surgical and biological instruments when it's vital that they be a hundred percent anti-magnetic. "

Her puzzled look turned into a smile. "I see. The sweeper magnet pulls the dagger toward it while the Fontax repels it from the section where you've got a volunteer tied up. And the daggers are pulled into those slots because they're attracted to the sweeper."

"It's a lot more complicated than that, but you've got the general idea. Magic's a matter of creating illusions, whether it's by sleight-of-hand or with help from high-tech devices like this board."

"It must be awfully heavy. Do you take it to all your shows?" Erienne stepped around to the back of the board and took a look.

"It is heavy—and tricky to pack. It has its own area of the tractor-trailer rig that trails me around the country. I don't ship it out of the country. Air freight would be prohibitively expensive, the way it has to be packed. Maybe someday I'll have another one made and keep it in some central European location to use on my foreign tours."

"Why haven't you?"

Drake reached out, ran his fingers through her pelt of short dark hair. "European audiences are more into sleight-of-hand illusions than ones like this that involve mechanical contrivances. I haven't needed it to attract big crowds over there."

Her pale blue eyes darkened with passion when he touched her. Or was it just wishful thinking to believe that she wanted him here and now? He pulled her into his arms, sure that in this public place she'd pull away.

She didn't. Instead she tilted back her head for his kiss.

What was it about Erienne that got him instantly hard? Drake wished he knew. Maybe, he thought as he held her, it was that she was a real, highly sensual woman—not the caricatures of sex symbols he'd been sleeping with the past few years.

A real woman he wanted to sample again right here, right now.

"Let's make love," she whispered.

"Here? Now?"

"In your dressing room. I want you to tie me up with those scarves."

So she was into a little light bondage. The prospect turned Drake on, too.

His cock pressed painfully against the zipper of his jeans. It obviously didn't give a damn if the theater manager and half his crew—even the hospital community relations manager who'd stopped by an hour earlier—might walk in on them.

Drake didn't care a whole lot either, though he'd have thought Erienne would have. "Come on," he said, grabbing a handful of his colorful, strong silk scarves and one of the strings of anal beads he sometimes used as props for one of his encore tricks.

Pity they were the only sex toys he had close at hand.

"There's no lock," he commented after closing them inside the star's dressing room backstage that held only a well-lit makeup table, a single bed, and a full-length mirror that covered up most of the dingy wall next to the door. "Someone may walk in on us," he said, wondering if knowing they risked an audience would heighten her sexual pleasure.

Her eyes sparkled. "I don't care."

"Neither do I. Take off your clothes and lie down."

Drake took her breath away. Tall, dark, sexy. And he intimidated her a little, though Erienne would never admit that to a soul. She didn't give an inch to men in the ordinary world.

Slipping her blouse off her shoulders, she focused on his lean cheeks showing the barest hint of razor stubble, his glistening sable hair, and those striking green eyes that seemed to read into her soul. The idea of giving over control to him terrified her, but it also got her incredibly aroused.

Sudden heat had flowed through her body moments earlier when they kissed. Now moisture pooled between her legs. Every cell of her body came alive at his simplest touch. Whatever else Drake Conover might be, he was one potent male specimen—and she had to have him again. *Now.*

She didn't care if some voyeur took home video movies. She didn't even care at the moment if her temporary boss should walk in and find them screwing.

She slid her skirt and panties off with one quick sweep of a hand, got rid of her bra, and lay down, eagerly anticipating whatever sex play might be his pleasure this afternoon. "I'm all yours," she murmured, spreading her arms and legs toward the four corners of the narrow bed.

"You'll not be sorry." Bending, he secured her arms first, then her legs, with the cool silk scarves. Then he tossed the fake-fur coverlet he'd swept off the bed over her belly, draping it so her breasts and pussy were exposed to his hot emerald gaze.

When she strained against her bonds, the coverlet shifted, its fur-like fibers caressing and arousing her as if it were a living thing.

Drake might be a traitor, might even now be conspiring to sell out his country again to the highest bidder. Nonetheless he reminded Erienne of a dark angel.

Part of her brain insisted he couldn't have done what her boss suspected. Not and cause the wild reaction in her that went past the physical—she liked him as well as lusted after him.

The more rational part knew even a master magician who drew down millions every year legitimately could be seduced by promises of even greater wealth to betray his country.

But at the moment all she could think of was how he'd look stripped of the trappings of civilization and standing over her naked and fully aroused.

A devastating smile on his sculpted lips, he sat beside her and tweaked her puckered nipples. The harsh lighting made him look darker, bigger, more intimidating than he'd been last night.

Erienne squirmed at the growing heat low in her belly, the tickling sensation of the fur as it slid between her legs. She imagined the silky feel of the hair on his hard-muscled chest against her nipples and groaned.

She'd die if he didn't fill her with his long, thick hard penis soon. "Please," she murmured, wanting anything that would soothe the burning need he evoked with no more than his all-encompassing presence.

He smiled, showing gleaming white teeth she hadn't noticed before. Then he reached out and ruffled her hair before lifting the furry coverlet and tossing it to the floor.

Stating his intentions would have been redundant. The way he wet his lips with his tongue when he raked her helpless body with a gleam in his eyes, made them crystal clear.

Still she wanted to see him. Straining to raise her head, she could see only his washboard abs and the ruby head of his penis that obscured his navel. Her mouth watered—she'd have that inside her soon.

He seemed in no hurry, though. Spying a feather some performer apparently had left on the dresser following another gig, he picked it up and sat cross-legged between her widespread legs. When he used the tip of the feather to trace a line from her lips to her quivering pussy, it sent chills slithering down her spine.

Drake's well-developed muscles rippled with every motion. God, but his shoulders were wide. A small crescent-shaped scar marred the otherwise satiny skin that stretched over his chest.

Erienne itched to touch him, to explore the masculine perfection of his gorgeous body. "Please," she whimpered, straining against her bonds.

"Patience, baby," he muttered, retracing the feather's path with his callused finger. "You're soft. Pale and precious." He produced a strand of very large, brightly colored beads and trailed them over her body. The beads were cool and smooth, but they sent hot currents through her every time they bounced against her body.

His gaze scorched her with emerald fire. "Do you want me to untie you now?"

"Yes." Moisture gushed from her body, as if to disagree. There was something terribly arousing about being helpless, out of control. "No."

"But I want to touch you." Writhing, she tried to pull free of her bonds.

"Be still, Erienne." The harsh tone shocked her, and her breathing grew ragged.

Did she want freedom or enslavement? She wasn't sure.

Drake's heat scorched her. On his knees now, he covered the silk that bound her wrists with his big, callused hands. While he hovered just inches above her naked body, she strained desperately to reach him—but he pulled away.

"No, baby. You wanted this. Now you're mine to do with as I will. I'm the master of magic tricks. You can't escape."

His breath came fast, warm and sweet against her cheek as he toyed with the knot at one wrist. He was so close, she felt his heart beat—yet she was powerless to feel his passion.

"Please. I've changed my mind. I want to touch you. Taste you." She wanted to explore every inch of his gorgeous body, rub her fingers over golden skin that felt like satin where he brushed against her.

Had she lost her mind? She must have, to have let her body forget she was seducing him for God and country, not for her own carnal pleasure.

Too bad, she told her conscience. The pleasure would be her bonus for a job well done.

It was as if their affair had been destined by the stars. As though she'd been made for him and him for her.

It had to be. Otherwise she wouldn't get as hot as a mare in heat every time she looked at him. And he wouldn't be randy as a stallion.

Trailing the beads over her mons and up her body, he let them rest in the hollow between her breasts. They seared her tender skin, but his moist breath burned nearly as hot before he covered her mouth and plunged his tongue deep inside.

Against her belly she felt his rock-hard penis, huge and rigid yet pulsing with life. She needed it—needed him—to fill the quivering void inside her.

A void she hadn't realized was there until she met the master magician.

The closely shaved stubble of his beard rasped her skin when he paused to nip and tongue her nipples. His tongue laved every inch of her mons before moving lower and lapping at her clitoris. When he raised his head, she saw the heat of his passion in eyes so dark they seemed almost black in the dim glow from the candles.

His gaze locked with hers, he took the beads, popped them one by one past her anal sphincter until only a few of them lay gently in her wet, swollen slit.

"Relax. The beads will bring you pleasure." He tugged them gently, sent a wave of sexual excitement that got her wetter, more needy.

"They feel...different. I don't know..." She'd never felt like this before, so helpless yet so exquisitely cared for.

"I want to look at you," she said, raising her head as far as she could.

"Here. Is this what you want?" Tucking a folded pillow under her head, Drake rose on his knees and slid forward until the glistening rosy tip of his penis nearly touched her lips. "Taste me."

Erienne ran her tongue over the tip of his cock, then slid down on him until she felt him throbbing against her throat. She wanted him inside her, taking her completely the way he did last night—and this morning. She wanted to convulse around him, take her pleasure while she made him give up his control.

He lifted her head, cradled it while she lapped off a salty drop of pre-come. "I love to feel your hair."

She loved the look of him. His penis was long and thick and fully aroused, and it curved gently toward his navel. His clean-shaven scrotum made her want to taste his balls, too. Savoring the taste and smell that was uniquely his, she clasped her lips around the swollen head of his penis and sucked him in.

Feeling him throb inside her mouth made the empty sensation in her belly more intense. Still she didn't want to let him go.

Suddenly Drake shuddered and jerked away. "Someday I'll let you take care of me that way. But not now."

He rubbed himself along her wet, slick slit. So hard, so hot, so ready.

Erienne couldn't move, couldn't wrap her arms and legs about his buff male body and draw him home.

He slid on a condom, then slowly penetrated her. His delicious fullness stretched her, filled her, made her feel tight and precious. Almost like the virgin she hadn't been for — she had to think back — nearly ten years now.

"You are mine." He placed soft, wet kisses on her lips, the action a sharp contrast with the hard, fast encounters they'd had last night. As if he appreciated that she was virtually helpless bound as she was, he withdrew slowly and slid back home, over and over. Deeper with each deliberate stroke. As if he had all the time in the world to pleasure himself in her pussy when every minute the chance of someone walking in on them increased.

Every few strokes he popped out a bead, and each of the quick sensations nudged her toward the edge. And he suckled first one nipple and then the other, drawing the areolas deep inside his mouth and bathing them with his tongue.

Drake might be her enemy but he was treating her like a precious gift — something only Rob had done before.

She'd never felt so complete. As if she'd found a soulmate as well as a bedmate. His smell, the way his muscles bulged when he braced his weight on his arms, the throbbing of his swollen penis in her pussy—the sensations merged in her head and drove her wild.

A hot, urgent feeling began deep in her belly and radiated outward. Her inner muscles clamped down when he withdrew, relaxed when he plunged harder and deeper with each measured thrust.

She needed to draw him closer. She yearned to wrap her arms and legs around him and never let him go. Liquid fire bubbled through her veins, centered where her skin touched skin. A kaleidoscope of sensations assaulted her, sent her flying.

When she screamed her pleasure, Drake's mouth clamped down on hers. His tongue plunged down her throat, its cadence in time with the rhythm of his hips.

Suddenly shards of pleasure imploded in every cell in her body. Before normalcy returned, his shuddering orgasm triggered another, gentler climax.

Chapter Four

༄

For the first time since he'd fallen for Cindy so long ago, Drake Conover was in love. Or maybe lust, but not the generic sort of sexual hunger that overtook him from time to time.

And for the first time since his mother walked out, he truly trusted a woman.

He didn't want to lose her. Didn't want to imagine how empty his bed would feel without her in it, how his cock would ache when thousands of miles separated them.

The snuffbox his old mentor had given him after one of his first performances lay in his pocket with a handful of condoms and some loose change. Drake fished it out during intermission the following evening, opened it. He tried to recall the devotion he'd had to his craft back then, when his illusions had consisted of performing card tricks and fishing a stuffed bunny out of an old silk hat.

Now his magic depended more on chemistry and physics than on his ability to fool an audience by sleight-of-hand. And his fans included the rich and famous from all over the world. By this time tomorrow he'd be back in Europe preparing for a six-week tour.

Damn it. For the moment he wished his next gig was in Hoboken, not Hamburg. If it were, he'd fly in, do the shows, and come back here to spend his nights in Erienne's arms. She'd have time for him, he knew, because she mentioned while they ate lunch today that her job with the hospital would end with his performance.

Of course he could ask her to go to Europe with him. In iffy economic times like these, there was bound to be another seat open on tomorrow's Concorde flight. They could stroll on the Seine, see the Eiffel Tower—dine on the *Champs d'Elysees* and make love in that *pensione* of pleasure where he'd spent several nights with several faceless lovers.

Drake's cock twitched.

Powerful thing, the mind, that it could conjure up pictures of him and Erienne making their way through each sensual adventure, taking sexual adventure beyond the ordinary…

Yes, he would ask her to join him. Two days at the *pensione*, then on to Hamburg to do his show. As he had for this performance, he would meet his crew at the theater. They need not intrude on his pleasure time.

Where was she? When he finished the first act, she'd been waiting in the wings. Now she must have gone off to confer with her boss. Drake strode from his dressing room, intent on finding her before he had to go back onstage.

There she was, looking through a box of gear he'd decided not to use tonight.

"Like the equipment, do you?" Coming up behind her, he caught her around the waist and nipped at her exposed earlobe.

She brushed her backside against his crotch. "I certainly do."

"Watch it. You might get more than you bargained for." He turned her around, held her by the shoulders at arm's length.

Her eyes twinkled, and her full lips curved in a playful smile. "Promises, promises."

"Come to Europe with me."

Her smile faded, and she averted her gaze. "You're not serious, are you?"

"Dead serious, baby."

"Then I guess my answer's yes. When do we leave?" She smiled, but he noticed the twinkle had disappeared from her sky-blue eyes.

Maybe she was a nervous flyer. Since nine-one-one lots of people were. "Tomorrow. We'll take the Concorde to Paris. Cheer up. I won't let anything bad happen."

"I know. It's time now for you to go back onstage."

"Okay. It's a good audience." He kissed her quick and hard before striding onto the stage.

He'd have time later to wonder why Erienne had taken him up on his offer when doing so clearly disturbed her in some way.

* * * * *

"Conover's no spy. I've done everything but a body cavity search, and he's got nothing to hand over to anybody." She'd done that, too, last night, but it had been for fun, not for her job—and she wasn't about to admit it to her boss.

"He hasn't been out of my sight since I met him at the airport. Except to use the bathroom on occasion. No, not a public bathroom. The ones in his hotel room and dressing room. Yes, I'm sure," she hissed into the pay phone outside the theater. "And yes, he's invited me to go with him overseas. Hardly the act of a spy, do you think?"

Her supervisor scoffed at that, said having her with him would provide the perfect cover. Nothing Erienne said dissuaded him from sending her with Drake. It seemed some microfilm had gone missing at the Pentagon last night.

Microfilm that would cause the government no little embarrassment if it got into the wrong hands.

Microfilm, Erienne realized, could easily fit into that snuffbox Drake never let out of his reach.

The one she hadn't peered inside.

Yet. And she didn't have the chance to look before she boarded an Air France Concorde at JFK with Drake the following morning.

*****

"Come on, let's join the mile-high club."

Drake spoke softly, but his deep voice carried. What if some of the other passengers overheard?

Erienne glanced around the plush forward cabin. Maybe no one did. In any case no one was staring at them. "Here?" she whispered.

Bending over and nipping her earlobe, Drake said, "In the lavatory. Wait a minute, then join me." He unfastened his seat belt and made his way down the aisle.

Should she? Her nipples tingled and got hard beneath her stretchy knit dress. Her pussy got hot and wet at the idea of having sex with Drake high above the Atlantic.

It was saying an emphatic yes. Unlike her brain, it obviously had no qualms about having magical sex whenever and wherever, with the magician who very likely had betrayed her country.

Without conscious direction, she unfastened her seat belt. Funny, she'd always heard it was men who did their thinking with their cocks. Maybe horny women's pussies took over for their brains. It seemed hers had.

Still trying to resist temptation but not having much success, Erienne stood. She tried hard to make herself sit back down, but it was as though Drake were that powerful sweeper magnet and she was a box of nails. She had to follow him.

She knocked once on the lavatory door and met his triumphant gaze when he opened it and pulled her inside.

"I knew you'd come." Sliding his hands under her skirt, he found her panties and tugged them down.

"Now step out of them." In the tight space between the door and the toilet, he held her, squeezed her nipples through her sweater. "Turn around."

She poked him in the ribs, eliciting a yelp of protest.

"In a hurry, are you?"

"Yeah. My cock's about to burst my zipper. Let it out." He dragged her hand back, molded it over his hardened flesh.

She fumbled, then caught the zipper tab and dragged it down while he ripped open the foil packet she'd noticed in the stainless steel vanity sink. "Ready?"

His erection nudged her ass when he stepped back far enough to sheath himself. Then he bunched her skirt up around her waist.

In the tiny enclosure the musky smell of sex surrounded them, made Erienne restless. There'd be no foreplay. No games. Just him ramming into her until they both exploded.

"Fuck me, Drake." She rubbed her ass hard against his crotch, and when he leaned over her and positioned himself, she bent over the toilet and braced herself with both arms.

"My pleasure." He nipped the back of her neck and nudged her legs farther apart. He was inside her now, hot and hard, his hands at her waist, holding her still for his powerful thrusts.

His penis stroked her G-spot. The angle of his penetration stretched her almost painfully.

When she whimpered, wanting more, he reached between her legs and stroked her swollen clit.

"Oh, God," he growled, withdrawing his hand and gripping her ass, hard.

"More." She wanted all of him. And she wanted him now.

His big hands grasped her hips. He thrust hard and deep.

"Drake." Her breathing was too ragged to get out more than just his name.

He paused mid-stroke, nipped at the nape of her neck. "Yeah, baby."

"I want all of you. Now."

He pulled her back and thrust forward. "Like this?"

"Yes." She clenched her muscles as hard as she could around his huge, hard penis.

"Do that much more and it'll be all over."

She loved the way he made love. He pulled out a little and slammed back, changing the angle just enough to make contact with her G-spot again.

"Oh, yes. God, yes."

"Found that button, didn't I?"

He pumped her hard, fed her wild contractions.

And she came again when he bit the back of her neck and buried himself inside her one last time.

He was shaking as much as she when he finally pulled out of her and discarded the condom.

Erienne didn't even care whether their fellow passengers realized they'd been fucking in the lavatory. Every cell in her body was celebrating at her initiation into the mile-high club — even though, she thought with a secretive smile, they'd done it more like six miles high, less than an hour before they'd arrive in France.

* * * * *

Paris had been Drake's favorite city since he came here with his mentor years ago. But seeing the familiar sights through Erienne's eyes added a new, exciting dimension to the bustling streets and familiar landmarks. The city burst with life, from the Eiffel Tower to the Seine—and to Madame Marie-Louise's *Pensione* of Pleasure on the Left Bank, where they'd checked in for the night.

The thought of acting out some of Madame's sexual vignettes with Erienne had his cock twitching in his pants.

This wasn't a good thing while he was sitting, in view of a thousand other tourists, along the rail at a sidewalk café.

It didn't help that Erienne was savoring every luscious mouthful of a chocolate éclair and not bothering with a fork. Her tongue darted out, licked a spot of creamy custard off her upper lip.

His cock got harder still.

She'd lick his come off that way, too. And if he didn't get a hold on his libido, he'd be wiping some off his pants.

"What's this show Madame said we should come and watch?" she asked, licking the last morsel of the creamy stuff off her full lower lip.

He wondered that, himself. "She stages something new each night of the week. Sexual vignettes acted out by her…" He wondered how best to describe the high-class prostitutes and gigolos who worked at the *Pensione*, "…employees."

"Oh. Do we get to join in?"

"No, baby, but we can orchestrate our own show if you like." Damn it, he couldn't get sex off his mind when he was with her.

They could have joined in the fun—if Drake hadn't cringed at the thought of any other man touching Erienne, even if as he suspected, most of Madame's buff gigolos were more into other men than women. Besides, Erienne was more than enough woman for him—he guessed his days of enjoying *ménages á trois* were over.

He looked forward to watching the show—or rather watching Erienne's reaction to the visual stimulation. He bet it would get her hot, as responsive and sexually adventurous as she was. Maybe she'd even see something in the show that she'd want to try.

"Come on, let's get back to our room. I want to change before the show."

* * * * *

Erienne had an idea. She'd get into that snuffbox tonight, and if it contained the stolen microfilm, she'd at least have one last erotic memory to keep her warm.

While Drake shaved and showered, she hurried downstairs to Madame's boutique. A black-and-red lace bustier that left her nipples exposed, black stockings, and a supple leather whip went onto the counter immediately. It took a bit longer for her to decide on the five-inch platform stiletto heels Madame insisted would complete her outfit.

No g-string. She wanted her pussy open for whatever Drake might have in mind. And she had her own handcuffs, ones she might soon be clamping on Drake's wrists for real.

No way could she walk around in public with her tits and ass hanging out for everyone to see. She needed some kind of cover-up. There. A long, stretchy sleeveless dress had a low, low neck and a slit in the side nearly to the waist. Drake wouldn't have any trouble figuring out how to get inside.

"Just this, please," she said, hoping Madame understood English.

"But of course. You did notice we have the iron cross and chains on the wall in your room, did you not, mademoiselle?"

No, Erienne hadn't noticed that particular feature—she'd been too busy taking in the mirrored ceiling and the basket of sex toys on the nightstand—but she smiled and said yes anyway. If she didn't hurry, Drake would be out of the shower and he'd find out she'd been gone.

"They are by the entry door. Do try them. Do you need handcuffs?"

"No, thank you." Erienne handed over her company credit card and waited while Madame prepared her bill.

Drake was still in the bath singing an off-key rendition of some French song when she got back to the room. From the time he'd taken already, she deduced he was shaving his sex, too, not just his face.

That was good. He'd gotten a little scratchy in the two and a half days they'd been together. When she thought of him all satiny smooth again down there, she creamed her panties.

She creamed them again when she looked at herself in one of the mirrored walls after putting on the bustier and rouging her nipples as well as her cheeks.

She'd just slipped on the sexy cover-up when Drake stepped out of the bathroom, gloriously nude.

"You shaved your chest, too," she said, reaching out to stroke the smooth, incredibly soft skin around his small, flat nipples.

He nipped the sensitive spot above her collarbone, then nibbled the upper curve of her breasts that the stretchy cover-up revealed. "Skin to skin. Nothing between us. That's how it's going to be, baby." Then he stepped into loose black linen trousers and zipped them over his glistening erection.

That was all he wore except his deck shoes when they went back downstairs and settled into box seats to watch the show. Erienne couldn't help thinking that if she reached over and unzipped those pants, she could play with his beautiful penis to her heart's content. Or straddle him and take an incredibly sensual ride, right out here where Madame's other customers could tell exactly what they were doing if they looked up from the main floor.

The curtain rose. Two buff, totally hairless men looked as though they'd been oiled from head to toe. They were chained to poles that ran from floor to ceiling through rings that protruded from their nipples and penises. Thick iron collars circled their massive necks.

A woman entered wearing a black catsuit with cutouts for her nipples and pussy. The skintight garment showcased her generous curves. She held a vicious-looking whip that she cracked menacingly before laying it into one man's swollen penis, shouting something in French that Erienne couldn't understand.

"What did she say?"

Drake leaned over, slipped his hand inside the slit in her dress, and whispered in her ear. "That she'd forbidden him to get a hard-on. That she's going to put him in a chastity belt as punishment."

Wide-eyed, Erienne watched the woman force the man's swollen sex into some sort of metal contrivance and locked the g-string-like chain to the back of the attached belt that circled his waist. He screamed in apparent agony when she left him and turned to his twin.

"Look, she's loosening the other man's chains. And she's clamped a leash onto his collar."

Drake grinned. "I'd rather look at you." Sliding her skirt aside, he exposed her pussy and tweaked her clit. "I'll bet that if I pull the top of this dress down I'll find your nipples bare."

Suddenly Erienne didn't care about the disturbing scene that was emerging on the stage.

"You'd be right," she told him, pulling down the stretchy fabric herself and exposing her rouged, puckered nipples to his heated gaze.

The second man, now on his knees between the dominatrix's legs, began to lick her pussy. His twin writhed against his bonds.

"He wants to get at his mistress, much as I want to get to you," Drake whispered, cupping her bare sex and putting delicious pressure on her clitoris.

Her pussy gushed when she looked at the way his erection tented his lightweight pants. "It would be easier for me to get to you," she said, suddenly hungry in spite of having eaten two of the éclairs she'd teased him with earlier. "I want to taste you, and feel whether you're as velvety smooth down there as you look."

Turning sideways in his seat, Drake unzipped his pants. "You can nibble later to your heart's content. Ride my cock now. That way we can both watch what's going on down on the stage."

Erienne didn't care if the actors and everybody in the audience looked up and saw them having sex. The prospect even excited her. She freed his penis, climbed on, and began a slow, rocking motion.

She clenched her inner muscles around him when he took one rouged nipple in his mouth and worried it between his teeth.

"Look," he said, lifting his head and nodding toward the stage. "Now she's doing the guy in the chastity belt. Want to do that to me?"

The woman had a huge strap-on dildo lodged in her victim's ass. Apparently she enjoyed hearing him scream.

"No. I don't." Erienne could never hurt Drake, and she liked being a woman. She'd never had the desire to take on a male role, even in play.

"Good." His breath felt warm against her neck, and her nipples beaded when he rubbed his smooth, clean-shaven chest against them. He swelled more inside her, stretched her almost unbearably. "I'm into pleasure, not pain."

His penetration was deep, complete. His scrotum pressed against her rear passage, reminding her of the scene being played out below. She wished they could stay this way forever, that she didn't have to go back upstairs with him and, very possibly, expose him as a traitor.

What if he wasn't? Could she convince him the search she planned to make while he was cuffed against the wall was no more than kinky sex play?

Erienne had to try. If, as she hoped, she found no evidence Drake was spying, she'd give everything she owned to continue their affair, see where it might lead.

When he flexed his hips and drove into her again, she couldn't think at all.

Her pussy clenched around his hard, hot penis. Tremors shot through her body.

Chapter Five

He could barely walk after the show ended, his cock was so hard. Erienne must have come a dozen times, but he'd held onto his control, savored being inside her while they watched the three sexual vignettes Madame had staged for her guests' titillation and amusement.

He had no choice. He'd forgotten to pop a condom in his pocket. No surprise, because he'd never needed one before during Madame's shows. He'd preferred to share his climax with a partner, and not until he drove her mad with pleasure. But Erienne had pretty much made his once-a-night climax rule obsolete.

From the way Erienne's hot little pussy had clenched around his cock, Drake guessed the last one, a funny sexual encounter between two male clowns and a female bareback rider, was her favorite—and that she liked the S&M act that had featured Madame's famous twin gigolos least. He had to admit, the *pensione's* proprietor had outdone herself with that one—maybe she had some important guests who were bigtime into getting aroused by pain.

He couldn't wait to get her in the bed and ease the ache in his groin. And she seemed eager to accommodate him, taking two steps to his one, keeping up as he practically dragged her up the stairs.

Once in the room, he dropped his pants and reached for her, but she stepped away.

"Not so fast. This time I want to be in charge."

Giving over control was something Drake never did. He didn't trust people enough for that.

But he realized he trusted Erienne that much. Trusted that she'd never harm him in any way.

He shrugged. Maybe she'd gotten more into that first act than he'd thought. But he found it excited him to play along. He held his arms away from his body and set his feet apart, making his cock and balls readily accessible. "I'm all yours, baby. Do your worst."

The handcuffs she clamped on his wrists looked awfully lethal for toys, but he gritted his teeth and let her chain his arms to the X-shaped cross that was bolted to the wall. Panic began to set in when she nudged his legs farther apart and clamped on leg irons to the rings on its lower arms.

Calm down. This is Erienne. And this is just a game.

She tongued his nipples, then slithered down his bound body and nibbled briefly on his cock. "I think I'll go get some toys," she said, gathering his discarded trousers and emptying his pockets before laying them over a chair.

Drake was desperate to come. Fucking her while they watched the show, denying himself release, had taken its toll. Now what little control he hadn't lost to his libido, he'd lost to her.

Deliberately, as if she had not a care for his pain, Erienne peeled off the black dress that left little to memory or imagination and stood by the bed perusing the basket of fresh sex toys Madame always restocked for each new guest.

Damn. In stiletto heels, black stockings, and that red corset thing that left her tits and ass bare, she made the most erotic picture he'd ever seen. In the black lights, her scarlet lips and heavy eye makeup provided an exotic contrast with hair the color of polished mahogany, hair cut as short as a little boy's.

Her pussy was no boy's, though. It, and the rest of her, was a hundred percent female. And hotter than hell.

He wished to God she'd find whatever she was looking for and come give him some relief. But she seemed in no hurry. No hurry at all.

In fact, she wasn't rifling through the basket at all—she'd opened and was looking inside his lucky snuffbox.

But she didn't look at it for long. Smiling at him all the time, she pulled out a small butt plug from the basket, lubricated it, and inserted it in her anus.

Drake's cock swelled more as she crossed the room toward him, her hips swinging, a soft leather cat o'nine tails in one hand and the basket in the other. "I won't need this, will I?" she asked playfully, swinging the whip a foot or so in front of his nose.

"No, Mistress." He *really* wasn't into pain.

Smiling, she tossed it aside, dug into the basket, and grasped his cock. "I think you do need this if this is going to last for long."

Soft leather tickled his freshly shaved scrotum when she pulled his balls downward. That same leather bit into his painfully engorged cock when she pulled it tight around its base and buckled the ring in place. He welcomed the coolness of her hands on him, because his sex was on fire.

"I'll be right back," she said, showing off her gorgeous ass as she turned around to get something else out of the toy basket. "Don't you move."

"What makes you think I could if I wanted to?"

She laughed. "Aren't you a master at escape?"

He wished. "That was Harry Houdini."

"That was Harry Houdini, Mistress." Her words were stern, but her eyes twinkled with merriment.

"Mistress."

"I don't have a collar, so this will have to do," she said when she came back and secured his belly to the center of the cross with a silk scarf. Then she stuck a ball gag in his mouth before he could protest.

In a flash, she was on her knees, sucking his cock. Her hands were on him, too, spreading his ass cheeks and trying to insert something cold and wet.

This was her gig, her game. He made himself relax so she could work the lubricated plug past his anal sphincter, grunted at the sudden discomfort that soon disappeared and had his cock swelling more painfully against the constricting ring from the pressure the plug put on his prostate.

She sucked his cock and rolled his balls back and forth in her hands. Blood pounded through his body, made him lightheaded. He had to come, but he couldn't. Not with that cock ring biting into his flesh.

His muscles tightened. He strained against his bonds.

Please. Let me loose and let me come.

But she didn't. She let him go but only long enough to turn around and go down on all fours, her ass aligned with his cock. "Fuck me now," she ordered, and he managed to bend his knees enough to seat himself in her dripping pussy.

Now he couldn't come for real. She hadn't thought to sheathe him. But he was in agony. And he couldn't get out more than a muffled sound around the ball gag. Every time she shoved her pussy up onto him, he came closer to the edge. And when she rammed herself into him all the way to his balls, screamed and milked him with her own orgasmic contractions, he shot his load inside her.

The cock ring was no match for his raging lust. Not when she clamped down on his cock as though she'd never let him go.

After she removed the ball gag and released the last of his bonds, he took her in his arms. "You'll have to marry me now," he said.

* * * * *

Erienne didn't think Drake had been joking last night when he offered marriage in the wake of her virgin performance as a dominatrix. Or when he held her in his arms all night, as though he'd never let her go.

Of course she wasn't pregnant—all female undercover operatives took quarterly Depo-Provera shots to prevent unwanted consequences from rape—or the voluntary sexual encounters their jobs might call for. She'd had her last shot a week ago, before going to Pittsburgh to seduce her way into Drake's bed.

But she hadn't told him that, though it undoubtedly would have eased his conscience.

This thing with Drake had gone far beyond duty. Beyond lust. She'd even gone several days now without grieving for Rob.

And now that she'd examined his lucky snuffbox and found nothing inside it but its brushed gold interior, Erienne was certain Drake wasn't the spy her bosses were so anxious to catch.

She had to contact her boss.

She'd left Drake sleeping and gone to the café where she teased him yesterday by making a sensual feast out of those custard-filled éclairs.

Considering the six-hour time difference, she couldn't really blame her boss for reaming her over the middle-of-the-night call—but she had to tell him he was wrong, that Drake Conover was no traitor.

If it wasn't Drake—and Erienne was certain it wasn't—then it had to be one of the members of his crew selling out to the enemy.

Surprisingly, the boss agreed. "Someone called yesterday into a line in Hamburg that German intelligence has tapped. The drop is set for day after tomorrow, before the first show."

The intercepted local call, made while Drake was chained to the cross in their room pretending to be her slave, proved someone besides him was contacting the terrorists.

She came away from the phone, chastised, with the boss's new directive ringing in her ears. "Find the microfilm. If it gets into the terrorists' hands it could mean disaster for us all."

From the first, anyone should have figured one of Drake's retainers could have made the exchanges. Erienne shook her head, unable to understand why her boss had been so certain it was Drake that he ordered her to cover him twenty-four seven.

Not that she minded the assignment, she thought, recalling how delicious he tasted. How he kept her wet and tingling with his lovemaking.

By the time she set down the payphone, she had a new assignment—to ferret out the traitor among Drake's hangers-on. What better way to do it than to accept his guilt-assuaging proposal and insist he include her in the inner circle of men and women who saw to the details of his shows?

She bit into a croissant, then sipped strong espresso flavored with amaretto. The cool, brisk morning breeze ruffled her hair, brought a mild odor from the fish market down the street to her nostrils.

Damn it, she didn't want to use Drake.

But she didn't see any way around it, not with less than forty-eight hours left to prevent another piece of vital information from getting into enemy hands.

What Erienne did want was to merge their lives, for real. And that wasn't going to happen when Drake found out she'd seduced him for God and country—never mind that it had been the most pleasurable job the Company ever assigned her.

Because she'd betrayed his trust. Was betraying it more even now, while she waited for the to-go espresso and croissants she'd ordered to take back to the *pensione*.

* * * * *

"Did you mean what you said last night?" Erienne asked while Drake sat on the edge of the bed and finished off the buttered croissant she'd brought him.

"Yeah. I did."

She gave his thigh a playful squeeze. "Then let's do it."

"Get married? Now?"

"Not now. When we get back home."

As late as yesterday, the idea of shackling himself to one woman would have been abhorrent, but now Drake found himself eager to move on to the next act in his game of life.

His cock was eager, too. With Erienne around, it was damn near insatiable.

But six weeks wasn't all that long to wait—not when she'd be with him anyhow while he did the shows he had booked in Hamburg and Brussels.

She brushed a croissant crumb off his chest, before moving down to encircle his cock with her hand. "Will that be okay?"

Hell, when she had him like this, he'd agree to damn near anything—except letting her go. "Yeah. You want to make the wedding a big deal?"

She shook her head, a bit sadly, he thought. "I don't have any family to speak of, and not a whole lot of friends. I guess I've been on the move too much..."

Suddenly it struck Drake that he didn't know anything about his future bride other than that she kept him in a constant state of arousal. And that she knew nothing about him but what she might have read in the tabloids—none of which recommended him as a candidate for marital fidelity.

"I've got no close family either. The crew I work with is my family, so to speak. You'll meet them all tomorrow when we get to Hamburg." In time he'd tell her why he'd taken nearly thirty years to find a woman he could trust after his mother's betrayal, how he'd grieved when his dad died in a mine accident the year he graduated from high school. And how a kindly old magician had taken him in, taught him all he'd known about the art of illusion and nurtured him along until he, too, died two years ago.

But not now. Now he wanted her in the sunken tub he'd filled with scented water while she went to the café. "Come on. Let's take our espresso and try out Madame's marble hot tub."

Chapter Six

Drake climbed into the swirling, scented water while Erienne stripped off her jeans and sweater. Steam floated around him, giving him an otherworldly look.

But he was real. Very real indeed.

As soon as she stepped out of her panties, he sat up, grabbed her, and set her down across his lap. "Hand me the soap, baby."

His big hands warmed her while he lathered her from neck to toes. By the time he finished, he'd sensitized every place he'd touched, made her crazy with wanting him.

"I need you inside me, Drake." She turned, straddled him, and began applying lather to the tantalizing, golden skin that covered his arms and torso.

She gave particular attention to his sex. Damn it, it was his turn to go a little crazy.

But he didn't take her teasing for long.

His biceps bulging, he lifted her, impaled her. His huge unsheathed penis hit her G-spot before sinking deeper, pressing hard against her cervix. Her climax built in her pussy and flowed slowly outward, sending little shocks to every cell in her body.

While he fucked her pussy with his penis, he used his tongue to make love to her mouth. His hands were busy making magic on her aching breasts. Slowly, then faster, he advanced and retreated.

The fragrance—something sweet yet unbelievably sensual—swirled around them on the steam that rose into the air. Warm, silky-feeling water bubbled noisily around them, lapped her skin. On his tongue she tasted sweet espresso with a hint of amaretto.

It was as though every possible sensation assaulted her, heightened the feel of Drake around her, in her. Played accompaniment to the sight of him, dark and dangerous, his face tight with passion. The tastes and smells and sounds surrounding them worked together to make her climax brighter, more intense than any she'd had before.

Erienne shuddered as her inner muscles clenched around him, and moments later shared his triumphant shout when he shot hot semen uselessly into her womb.

Grinning when he'd caught his breath a few minutes later, Drake splashed water on her neck, then gave her breast a playful squeeze. "Want to do it again?"

She laughed. "Sure. But you'd better save some energy for later. Weren't we going to do the tourist thing today?"

"Yeah." With fluid grace, he stood, stepped out of the hot tub and held a bath sheet out to her. When they had dried off, he lay across the bed, watched her search through her single suitcase. "Get dressed. I want to go buy you a ring."

* * * * *

The ring he'd given her earlier today, a deep blue sapphire with diamond baguettes, was beautiful. The sex they had before and after they went to buy it blew Erienne's mind.

The climax they'd shared an hour ago was deeper, sweeter, and lasted longer than any she'd had with him before, because tender emotions had tempered the fire.

Hers as well as his.

Erienne slipped out of bed and stared out the narrow window at the street below. Fog obscured the view, making the quaint round streetlights look eerily like fallen moons upside down in a smoky gray sky.

She had to tell Drake she was with the Company. That getting close to him, seducing him had been her job as well as her pleasure. And she had to tell him one of his trusted crew members had to be a spy who regularly sold out his country to its enemies.

But she couldn't wake him now. Not when he was sleeping so peacefully.

She didn't want to tell him at all. Didn't want to lose him now that she'd fallen in love.

Maybe if she caught the traitor first...

Drake said they'd be meeting six of his crew in Hamburg tomorrow. Damn it, she should have paid more attention when he introduced people to her before his Pittsburgh show.

Of course not all of them had come to work the benefit—the hospital had hired two local men to help set up Drake's props, and Drake did some of the more complicated setups himself.

She should have spent less time lusting after him and more doing her damn job.

Straining her memory, she came up with two names: Jim Dugan, who had seemed to be in charge of the special effects during the show. And Drake's stage manager, George Moran.

Erienne hoped it wasn't George. From the way they interacted, she'd gotten the impression that he and Drake were long-time friends, not just employee and employer.

She couldn't recall the other man's name—the one who'd been smirking at them when they'd come out of Drake's dressing room breathless and probably flushed from the explosive orgasm they'd shared.

Dave something-or-other, she thought. But she could be wrong.

Drake said all three crew members she'd met, and three others, would meet them in Hamburg. Drake's agent, Myra Stern, and the married couple who kept props organized—the ones he'd given time off who hadn't been in Pittsburgh. The man, Drake said, also worked the lighting and helped Jim with more complicated special effects.

That meant she had four possible traitors. Her boss had said the caller last night had been a man. Of course there could be more than one traitor—considering the amount of money that apparently changed hands, that was a distinct possibility.

By the time she and Drake got to Hamburg in the morning, she'd have only twelve hours to ID the spy and prevent him from passing along whatever secrets were on that piece of microfilm.

She twisted her beautiful ring around on her finger, staring at the sparkling stones. Then she thought of Rob and all the other decent men and women who'd died because of the terrorists and their seemingly random acts of violence. Other lives might be saved if she caught this traitor before he could put more ammunition into the monsters' hands.

She had to confide in Drake, ask for his help. And hope he'd forgive her and believe her when she swore her love for him was real.

* * * * *

When Drake awakened the next morning, he was alone in the big brass bed. Blinking, he looked around. Where was Erienne? Following the sound of running water, he headed for the bathroom.

The outline of her compact body behind the translucent shower curtain put his cock on instant alert. His heart swelled with new, unfamiliar emotions.

He'd never thought he'd love a woman the way he loved Erienne. Or that he'd give one his absolute trust.

But she'd swept away all his old insecurities, made him believe he was her world, her soulmate.

He stepped inside the curtain into her arms. Her voracious kiss seemed almost desperate, as if they'd been apart for months instead of the few minutes she'd been up while he slept. He returned it, intensified it, drew her closer.

When she slid down his body his balls tightened, as though anticipating her touch. His cock stood straight against his belly. His pulse raced. A gentle spray of warm water pelted both of them. Glistening droplets cascaded down her body, plastering her hair to her neat, round skull when she went on her knees and circled the knob of his cock with her tongue.

All he could do was cradle her head in his hands while she stroked his balls and loved his cock with her mouth. And enjoy the rhythmic motion of the fingers she curled around the base.

Drake took immense delight in the erotic picture of submission that she made there on the shower floor.

She was his. Only his. Not just now, but for the rest of their lives.

He wished she'd take his full length down her throat, suck him until he came. But when he realized he was pushing her head down on him, he stilled his hands. Didn't want to force her.

He loved her too much.

But he didn't need to. As if she sensed his need, she lifted her head, looked up and met his gaze.

"I want to taste your come," she told him.

Then she took him in her luscious mouth again until his cock met the back of her throat. When she swallowed and took another inch, she squeezed gently on his balls, as though she couldn't wait for them to empty into her hot, tight throat.

He couldn't wait, either.

His muscles clenched. He pressed his fingers into her skull, held her steady, thrust his hips into her mouth as if it were her pussy.

When she swallowed again and clenched her lips around the base of his cock, he started to come. Once, twice, three times he felt his cock spurt down her throat, felt her swallow and coax out more.

After that he quit counting. Gave himself over to the wildest orgasm of his life.

His strength gone, he finally slumped against the shower wall and watched, enchanted, while she licked the come off his now flaccid cock and balls.

* * * * *

She should have talked to him before they'd left the *pensione*. Or on the short flight from Paris to Hamburg.

But she'd been a coward then.

She was no less afraid now. And here at the theater where Drake would perform tonight, she'd had no opportunity to get him alone. Not to mention that observing the four men who made up his backstage crew hadn't given her a hint as to which one was most likely to have the stolen microfilm.

Her observation was hampered by Myra Stern, Drake's agent, who had arrived in Hamburg an hour before them and now seemed intent on badgering Erienne for details about the wedding that probably would never happen once she told Drake the truth.

But Erienne couldn't dwell on her personal problems now.

Bob and Renee Forester seemed joined at the hip. They congratulated Drake, welcomed Erienne, and immediately went back to their job of setting up the small props Drake would need during the show. Erienne doubted Bob would make any move, much less take on spying as a lucrative sideline, if it meant he'd have to do something without Renee's participation.

For the moment she took the apparently devoted couple out of the running.

And Dave Lloyd, the prop man who'd leered at them when she and Drake came out of his dressing room in Pittsburgh, was nowhere to be found. Erienne's antennae went up when she heard stage manager George Moran tell Drake he hadn't seen Dave since early this morning at their hotel. Jim Dugan, George said with a shake of his head, was pissed off about having to do his own work and Dave's, too.

For a moment Erienne grasped the news of Dave's absence like a lifeline. Maybe she could finger him and Drake would never need to know. Then she came to her senses. Her boss had told her the drop was scheduled to take place tonight, during the show's intermission, not during the day.

Most likely Dave was out screwing some German whore. If her first impression was on the mark, he did most of his thinking with body parts other than his brain.

She still had four suspects and less than four hours to narrow them down to one. Which meant she had to talk to Drake. "Can I talk to you alone for a few minutes?" she asked when he paused in his conversation with George. "It's important."

Drake shot her that devastating smile of his. "Of course. I'm never too busy for the woman I love."

The dressing room where he led her was nicer than the one in Pittsburgh, not that atmosphere mattered now. She took a seat on a straight chair next to the bed. "I'm not a rich lady from Pittsburgh who gets off volunteering to rub elbows with the stars," she said after he had seated himself at the makeup table and met her gaze.

He looked relieved. "I never thought you were. And I think I'm rich enough for both of us. If you love me the way you say you do."

"I do love you." If only it were that simple. "But I'm a CIA agent. I was assigned to get to know you and to get your help to find a traitor in your crew."

"What?"

"Someone who travels with you—a man, my supervisor said—is delivering classified information each time you do a European tour to agents of a Middle Eastern terrorist organization."

Drake stood, his fists clenched so hard the knuckles turned white. He paced, then stopped and met Erienne's gaze. "You thought it was me, didn't you?"

"My boss did, at first. Until the German intelligence people intercepted a call night before last, when we were in Paris. A man set up a drop for tonight during intermission." She paused, the hurt in his eyes tearing at her soul. "After meeting you, I knew you couldn't be the one."

"Because I'm good at making you come?" His voice dripped with sarcasm.

"No. Because you're a good man, period. People who sell out their country for money don't put themselves out to help people less fortunate than themselves—at least not to the extent you do."

"I suppose I should say thank you, but at the moment I'm not the least bit grateful."

His rage was palpable. If she hadn't known deep inside that he'd never hurt her physically Erienne would have feared for her life.

"Drake, nothing that's gone on between us except why I managed to meet you in the first place has been a lie."

"You'd have fucked with me just for the fun of it, when we were virtual strangers?" He laughed, as though the very idea was incomprehensible.

I would have fucked with you even if I hadn't wanted you the minute I laid eyes on you, because it would have been the quickest way for me to get close enough to do my job.

But Drake didn't need to know that. "I did make love with you for fun. My job was to get friendly with you, not sleep with you. Sleeping with you was—is—my pleasure."

"Why do I have trouble believing that?"

"It's true. I love you."

"Cut the pretense. I can't believe I trusted you. Loved you when you were no more than a prostitute selling your delectable little body for—for what? Love of country? Reminds me of a joke that went around my high school. Wrap a flag around the ugliest whore in school and fuck her for God and country. Ha, ha, ha."

"Drake, please." Tears welled up in her eyes, but she held them in. He didn't need to see he could reduce her to blubbering tears. "Believe what you will. But you have to help me now."

The look he cast her way was dubious. As though he'd like to toss her out on her ass and national security be damned. Erienne held her breath while he paced the length of the room.

If he refused to help her...no, he couldn't. "If we don't get him, the people he's dealing with may kill us all."

Finally he sat back down, rubbed a hand across his brow. "All right. We can sort out our personal issues later. If what you say is true, we have less than four hours to stop this so-called traitor. Do you have any idea who he is?"

"No. Have any of your people been tossing around unusual amounts of money lately?"

Drake shook his head. "Not that I know of. But a spy wouldn't necessarily flaunt his ill-gotten gains, would he? Wouldn't he be more likely to squirrel it away somewhere so as not to draw suspicion?"

"Probably. I was hoping the guy got careless. How about strange behavior?"

"Acting odd or secretive, you mean? Dave, I guess. He's never missed a setup before. But I can't believe—"

"I don't think he's the one. If he were, he wouldn't want to call attention to himself by cutting out now, and then again tonight."

Drake shrugged. "Nobody else has done anything weird that I know of. But then I don't socialize a lot with the crew.

Want me to call George in? He'd be more likely than me to have noticed anything unusual going on."

"No. I'd rather not take a chance."

"You suspect George?" His tone implied disbelief.

Erienne didn't want to, because she sensed the man was more than a casual friend of Drake's. She'd already hurt him, without rubbing salt into the open wound. But she had no choice. "He's male, he's been with your crew on every European trip since the exchanges began, and he doesn't have any alibi that I'm aware of."

"I've known George since we were kids together in western Pennsylvania. I can't believe he'd..."

As though he'd been hit, he braced his elbows on his thighs and lay his head on his outstretched hands. But when Erienne went to him, tried to rub the tension out of his neck and shoulders, he cringed.

"Not now, baby."

Not ever, if she read him right.

After spending the most painful moments she'd endured since Rob's death, Erienne had zeroed in on the two likely culprits: Jim, who always seemed in need of funds and had a juvenile record for theft—and George, Drake's childhood friend and confidant.

Motive? Anything she came up with as motivation for either man to sell out his country was a serious stretch. Obviously the crook was selling secrets to the terrorists for money. But Drake didn't know of any of his crew who might have serious financial difficulties. When she'd pressed him, though, he admitted that both George and Jim occasionally ranted about the government taking care of the rich and ignoring people like them and their families.

Both men had opportunity, because both had been with Drake during the tours when secrets had been delivered to the terrorist organization's buyers. And she supposed both had the means, since passing the information so far had involved nothing more complicated than meeting with someone and exchanging it for cash.

But a piece of the puzzle was still missing.

Erienne closed her eyes, visualized the flow of information. Someone with a high-level security clearance stole it from State or Defense in DC and passed it along to the courier. The courier then brought it to various places in Europe where Drake's show was booked and delivered it to the buyer's agent.

That was it! Which one of Drake's people had some sort of connection with the bastard in Washington who was stealing the secrets?

How could the courier be connected with the thief?

"Drake, do you know if anybody you work with has contacts in the State Department? Or the Department of Defense?"

"No." Then he looked at her, his expression grim. "Yeah, I do. George's brother-in-law works for the State Department. I think he's a translator."

"Do you know him?"

"No. I just remembered George mentioning the connection right after nine-eleven. As far as I know George and his sister aren't close. She's several years older—she was out of the house before I met George, and that would have been twenty-seven or twenty-eight years ago." His shoulders slumped, as though he thought he'd betrayed his closest friend.

Maybe he had.

Erienne hated seeing the wounded look in Drake's eyes. First her admission that she'd used him to do her job, then his realization that his closest friend very likely was involved in espionage—the double blow had to have decimated him.

And he wouldn't accept comfort from her. When she tried again to hug him, he pulled away. When he spoke, his voice was tight.

"Call your boss, whoever he is, and have him put tails on whoever he needs to. I'll tell the crew I've hired extra security because I'm worried that someone may try to sabotage the show. That ought to explain away any questions they may have, seeing armed goons running around backstage."

"Do you want me to stay?" Blinking back tears, Erienne slid off her ring and held it out to him.

He shook his head. "You'd better. Seems to me this is no time to blow your cover. You went to enough trouble to set it up." He gestured toward her left hand. "Better put that back on, too. At least for now."

Chapter Seven

That night Drake went through the motions of performing—the smile, the sleight-of-hand tricks, the dramatic flip of the scarlet-lined black cape that always seemed to enchant the females in his audience.

But his tricks were just that—harmless illusions. Erienne had outdone him, tricked him with the most cruel illusion of all. The illusion of love.

A burly CIA man stood next to her in the wings, a lethal-looking handgun at the ready in an easy-to-reach shoulder holster. He assumed Erienne had one, too, stashed somewhere under the black satin evening tuxedo she'd put on for the performance. Two more operatives lurked backstage, someplace where they presumably could keep an eye on Erienne's two prime suspects—his closest friend and the quiet, unassuming guy who'd handled the setup of his more complicated tricks for nearly five years.

For the first time since he began performing seventeen years ago, Drake's heart wasn't in the show. The audience's cheers didn't spur him on to earn even more effusive praise.

He just wanted this farce to be over.

When the curtain came down, signaling intermission, he looked for Erienne. But she was gone.

* * * * *

In the shadow of a crumbling brick building several blocks from the theater, George Moran hunkered down against the chilly wind.

From twenty feet away, Erienne saw him trembling. Whether from cold or fear, she didn't know. She and Mick, one of the Company men her boss had sent as backup, ducked into the shadows when he stopped and glanced their way.

George looked back, then to the left and right.

Then as if by magic, he disappeared into the blackness of the night.

"Come on. We can't lose him." Erienne moved out, leaving Mick to follow.

Nothing. No one. George had seemingly disappeared without a trace.

Erienne backtracked to where they'd last spotted George and ran her hand along the crumbling wall. "Here," she whispered. "I feel an opening of some kind. He must have pushed this open and gone inside."

Mick put his shoulder to the spot she indicated and leaned into it. It opened only a few inches. "He can't have gotten through here."

"Listen." Someone was inside. Voices, low and furtive, floated on the wind. Erienne strained to hear more, but the words were muffled.

"Move back." Mick stepped back, then slammed into the opening with enough force to widen it. Something it dislodged clattered to the ground.

Erienne wiggled her way inside, holding her Glock in both hands, ready to fire. A flash of light momentarily blinded her, followed by the loud report of gunfire.

She fired at it as she fell, her chest burning until everything went black and she faded into a painless void.

* * * * *

Her ring lay beside his makeup case, next to a note that somehow managed to retain her familiar scent.

Drake stood there for a long time. He wouldn't read it. Wouldn't put himself through seeing her betrayal in black and white. Wouldn't think of her out there doing her job, arresting the traitor she'd been seeking since before they met.

As vividly as if it had happened yesterday, he pictured himself standing with his father at the door of their modest cabin, trying to figure in his seven-year-old mind why his pretty mom was leaving them for the old man in the big shiny car. Recalling how tears had streamed down his dad's rugged cheeks, Drake vowed to keep a tight rein on his own battered emotions.

"Thirty seconds, Drake," Jim called out as he banged on the dressing room door.

The show must go on.

He could do it. Damn Erienne and damn his good friend George.

After all, wasn't Drake Conover the master of illusion?

Crumpling the note in his fist, he stuffed it and the ring into his pants pocket.

For the next hour he played the crowd. By rote, he did his magic tricks, made all the right moves, built up the audience's excitement for the night's final illusion.

When the final curtain came down, Drake wiped the sweat from his brow.

"Hey Drake. I told this goon you hired that you had to do curtain calls, but he won't pay me any mind." Renee sounded royally pissed off, and she was doing her damnedest to hold the goon back.

The agent named Mick shoved her aside. "Conover. Thought you might want to know, your fiancée took a bullet when we arrested your friend."

Images of Erienne flashed through Drake's mind. Her sassy smile, the taste of him on her full, expressive lips. The way she kept him hornier than he'd been since he left his teens behind.

The way she'd cried and insisted she loved him even after admitting her deceit.

"Where?"

"The hospital. She took a hit in the chest. "

"George?" *If that bastard hurt Erienne and got away –*

"He's in custody. His contact is dead. Erienne got him as she was going down."

Jim touched Drake on the shoulder. "Time for a curtain call. Listen to that audience."

"She asked for you," Mick growled.

"Screw the audience. I've got to go to Erienne." He turned to Mick. "Take me to her."

* * * * *

He got to the hospital too late. The bullet had struck her aorta. She was critical. The specialist consultant had taken her straight to surgery, Mick told him after talking with the emergency service registrar in fast, fluent German that was beyond Drake's ability to understand.

Hell, he couldn't have understood if they'd been talking plain English. He'd be lucky if he could manage to remember his own name through the shock. The pain of knowing he might never see Erienne again. Never have the chance to tell her he understood.

Like a zombie, Drake followed Mick down a narrow hallway.

"They said we can wait here," the CIA operative said when he opened the door to a small room with some words written in German on the frosted glass door. "Want some coffee?"

Drake sat on one of the hard wooden benches. "No."

"Are you okay? You look like you're about to pass out."

"It's the stage makeup. Audiences expect magicians to look pale. Like Dracula, I guess." Of course, knowing Erienne was fighting for her life had undoubtedly drained the blood from his face, contributing to his pallor. Drake's pulse raced, and he had trouble breathing.

Mick looked him in the eye, his expression fierce. "You hurt her badly, you know. Worse than Rob hurt her when he got himself murdered over in Karachi."

"Rob?"

"She didn't tell you?"

Drake searched his memory. "No."

"Rob was her fiancé. He was with the Company, too. They were partners, and they were supposed to have gotten married the week after he died."

Drake shook his head. "She never said a word…"

Erienne hadn't told him much of anything about herself except that she loved having his cock in her mouth and her pussy—and that she loved him.

The thought that she might die, that he might never revisit the past four glorious days with Erienne, brought tears to his eyes.

He dug into his pocket, closed his fist around her ring. Not more than a day and a half ago he'd slipped it on her finger, thinking she completed his world.

She did, even if she had arranged to meet him under false pretenses.

God help him, if she made it, he was going to get it back on her finger. Get her back into his life and never let her go.

She had to pull through. For him. She was the soulmate he'd never expected to find.

Paper crackled in his pocket, reminded him she'd left a note along with the ring. He drew it out, smoothed the wrinkles he'd made when anger and hurt had made him crunch it in his fist.

These might be the last words she'd ever say to him, and only lack of time had kept him from shredding and burning it. But he couldn't make himself read them now.

Folding the note neatly, he returned it to his pocket.

Please God, let her live. If only so she could tell him to fuck himself when he begged her for forgiveness.

The ticking of the clock on the wall grew more ominous by the minute. Mick's breathing grew ragged, as if he too felt the tension that had Drake on edge.

When a nursing sister offered coffee, he drank it down, hardly registering the scalding heat that seared his throat. "Goddamn it, what's taking them so long?"

Mick shrugged. "I don't know."

"Why the hell didn't you protect her? Where the hell were you while she was taking a bullet? Goddamn it, man, she's a woman."

"A woman who's as able as I am to take care of herself. She'd have stayed at the theater if she'd thought you wanted her there."

"I did want her with me. I just didn't know it." Drake turned away, focusing on the view of an ink-black sky framed in the peeling sill of the only window in the room.

By the time the surgeon came out, the sky showed signs of light. Five hours had passed. Unable to understand more than a few scattered words of the rapid German, Drake turned to Mick as soon as the surgeon paused.

"She's alive. Barely. Lost a lot of blood. The next twenty-four hours will be critical," Mick told him.

If she doesn't make it… No, he couldn't let her go.

Drake turned to the surgeon. "I want to stay with her," he said, calling up the simple German words from somewhere far back in his memory.

* * * * *

The ventilator hissed, its sound permeating the silence of the cubicle in the surgical intensive care unit. Erienne lay pale and deathly still, her only movement the expansion and contraction of her chest to the rhythm of the noisy machine. Incomprehensible red numbers flashed on the monitor above her head.

The surgeon had shrugged when he asked to stay with her, as if his presence wouldn't matter one way or the other. Erienne's special nurse, though, had taken pity on him. She'd offered words of comfort in halting English and brought him a washcloth and a basin of water to remove the stage makeup where his tears undoubtedly had etched macabre streaks.

"You frighten her if she wakes, seeing you like this," she'd said.

Her finger looked naked without the ring, so he slipped it from his pocket and put it back where it belonged. But her hand was limp, cold—not vibrant with life the way Erienne had been before...

A chill ran through him.

She was with him here, yet she wasn't.

He was so tired he let his eyelids droop. He'd rest just for a moment. Then he'd be strong again for Erienne.

Suddenly he stood in a field of flowers. Their rainbow colors were pale, surrealistic, but they grew stronger and more vivid as the scene slowly came into focus. There was Erienne in the distance, smiling as she floated closer to him, holding out her arms in invitation.

She wore something soft and filmy. Shifting pastel colors of the rainbow. The gown wasn't at all like the sexy, provocative garments he'd become accustomed to seeing her in. The burnished mahogany hair he loved to tunnel into with his fingers kissed her shoulders now. He itched to gather it in his fist, savor its silky texture against his skin.

He reached out to touch her, but she stayed just beyond his reach. Very slowly, keeping her gaze on him all the time, she slid the garment down and stood before him naked and unashamed, her legs spread slightly as if in invitation.

His cock rose, eager to sink into her glistening pussy. His mouth turned dry. As if by magic his own clothing disappeared, whisked away on a whirlwind along with her silken robe.

Suddenly a bouquet of flowers appeared in her hands — velvety roses. Roses of every imaginable color. Legend had it that red ones stood for passion, he recalled when an especially beautiful scarlet bud disappeared from her hand and materialized in his own.

"I love you," said a voice that seemed to come from the rose.

The bud unfurled, slipped from his hand. Its petals caressed his lips, slid down his torso before gently surrounding his cock.

Illusion. It was only illusion. But the full-blown red rose had him swelling and hardening with its sensual undulations.

He looked at Erienne, watched her bury her face among the fragrant blossoms.

As though she'd willed it, a white rosebud came his way, it petals unfurling as it seemed to whisper, "I am worthy of you."

The ivory petals filled his nostrils with their sweet, spicy fragrance, then floated downward. They cupped his scrotum, caressed his balls with a slow, seductive rhythm.

A yellow rose followed, its message plaintive. "Try to care."

There was no way he could deny that plea when it joined the red rose, caressing his cock, combining efforts to bring him to climax.

The roses floated from Erienne's hands until only one remained. It was pale pink, like her satiny mound that he longed to touch — to kiss. As it left her hands, it begged him to believe her. To believe she loved him.

He did. The rose petals unfurled, brushed his body the way Erienne's satiny skin caressed him. They curled around him almost like her hand, lending their strength to the other petals to bring him to an orgasm like none he'd had before.

For a long, long time he came while the petals clutched him in their velvety fist. All the while he looked at Erienne, loved her. Wanted her as he'd never wanted a woman before or since.

But she was slowly going out of focus. Fading away, out of his reach now and practically out of sight. On a gust of wind, a sprig of verbena came his way. "Pray for me," it said, its voice not its own but Erienne's.

When Drake awakened, he was clutching the branch of an almond tree. The scent of its delicate blossoms filled the room. Confused, he stared at it while snatches of a flower field of dreams emerged from the far corners of his mind.

"Is a symbol of hope, the almond blossom," the nurse said when she glanced across the bed at Drake. "You make it with your magic?"

"I wish I had." The monitors flashed their neon messages, incomprehensible to him. "How is she?"

"The same."

She still hovered somewhere out there between darkness and light. Somewhere beyond his ability to reach her. The ventilator's sucking sounds reminded him that if not for that lifeline, she'd be gone. He barely managed to hold back the anguished scream that rose in his throat.

"Perhaps if you touch her…"

He snatched up the crumb of hope in the nurse's halting suggestion as if it were a lifeline. "I'd not hurt her further?"

"Must not touch tubes. But gentle touch work magic."

Pity his magic didn't extend to the laying on of healing hands. But Drake would try anything. Do anything. He laid the almond branch in her still, cold hand, then bent and brushed his lips on her pale, dry cheek.

After moving to the foot of her bed, he burrowed his hands beneath the scratchy cotton blankets that covered her feet. Very gently he caressed her toes.

At least they were warm. Not icy cold like her fingers.

They were unresponsive now, but he imagined her stretching, curling her foot around his hand.

Massaging the pads of first one toe, then another, was getting him hard. Hell, everything about her kept his cock twitching like a stud horse with the scent of a mare in heat.

A stud who might just never get it up again if he lost her.

He slid his hands higher, ran his fingers over her high arches, past those slender ankles that looked so dynamite in the killer heels she liked to wear. Would he ever feel them hooked over his shoulders again, enjoy the pleasure-pain of her short pink fingernails biting into his flesh while he drank his fill of her honey?

Her calves, even now, felt firm and muscular beneath his searching fingers. But she didn't beg him for more when he stroked the highly erogenous zone behind her knees. He might as well have been stroking a department store mannequin for all the reaction his touch evoked.

Tears streamed from Drake's eyes, but he didn't care. Hope withered like the almond blossoms he'd placed in Erienne's still, cold hand.

He sensed her slipping away.

Chapter Eight

❧

Eternity called out to Erienne, lured her out of incredible pain into the blessed darkness of oblivion.

She was cold, so cold. Every agonized beat of her heart took more effort than she could bear.

A bright light shone at the end of that tunnel of blackness, powerful in its lure. She found herself tumbling, falling, seeking the peace that came with death.

But something held her back.

Hands on her feet. Her ankles. Her calves.

Let me go.

"Stay. I need you."

Drake. How cruel could fate be, to have brought him to her now, when the soul that belonged to him was about to leave her tortured body?

Warmth radiated from her knees. Just warmth. Not desire. She was beyond sexual arousal now.

But not beyond wanting Drake.

His voice came as a husky whisper in her ear. She couldn't bear to tune out this last earthly contact.

"Imagine my mouth on your pussy. My tongue teasing your sensitive little clit. Remember how you love having my cock stuffed inside you, feeling me shoot you full of my come?

"And having me roll one hard little nipple between my thumb and forefinger while I'm suckling the other one?

"You can't go now. I'm not ready to come with you. We've got years yet, more adventures to take together. Babies to make and

watch grow up. We haven't even begun to sample all the paths we can take to pleasure."

No, Drake. She cried out his name, but her voice wouldn't work. She hurt too much, was too far gone.

Her heartbeat slowed. Stopped.

She slipped further down the tunnel.

"Please, baby. Come back and I'll work my magic on you." But his voice was anguished, as if he knew illusions couldn't bring her back.

Suddenly he appeared, blocking the ray of light she sought. His magnificent body glistened, golden in the darkness. His big, beautiful cock rose hard and proud against his belly, its ruby head aglow on a burnished golden shaft that darkened as it merged into his bronzed velvet sac.

In one hand he held the paper roses he used in one of his acts. All red—except for one pale pink bud.

"Come, take my love and my passion. Please believe I love you." His deep voice broke in an anguished sob. *"Don't go. If you do, you may as well carve out my heart."*

How could she leave Drake to the sort of agony she herself had suffered when Rob died? She couldn't ignore her love's passionate entreaty.

Slowly, painfully, Erienne marshaled her strength. Willed her heart to beat again. Steeled herself to accept the pain she'd so desperately tried to escape.

She took one torturous step, then another, until she felt Drake's strong arms surround her, drag her back to the world—and him.

* * * * *

Three months later Erienne and Drake lay naked on an out-of-the-way private beach in Monaco, a reddened scar along her breastbone the only visible sign of the ordeal she'd endured.

Not so visible was her mounting sexual frustration.

In the month since he finished touring and collected her from the hospital in Hamburg, he'd treated her like a fragile flower. And she'd had enough of it—though she had to admit they'd learned the little things about each other that a couple really ought to know.

She'd laughed when he told her how that small crescent-shaped scar was a souvenir of his only excursion into crime. Pity she hadn't known the mischievous six-year-old who'd caught himself as well as his flannel shirt on a chain-link fence he'd tried to climb to get at a neighbor's apple orchard.

Now she wanted sex. Hot, uninhibited sex like they'd enjoyed before she confessed to Drake about her deception. Before that Arab terrorist put a bullet through her.

He'd told her she'd have to seduce him when she was ready, that he wouldn't subject her to his lust until she proved to him that she'd completely healed.

That worked for Erienne. She was ready and able to blow his mind.

And she had the ammunition she needed in her beach bag, purchased yesterday in an out-of-the-way shop at the village, from a wizened old woman who claimed her potions worked real magic.

Drake lay on his stomach, eyes closed. The picture of relaxation.

That picture was about to change.

Erienne sat up, opened the penis-shaped red glass vial the woman sold her, and poured some of its contents onto the smooth, darkly tanned skin of Drake's tight ass. Straddling him, she began to massage the oil into his muscular flesh.

The sounds that came from deep in his throat reminded her of a big cat's purring.

A pungent, exotic scent rose, surrounded them both in a sensual haze that Erienne could only describe as otherworldly. It smelled of roses and almonds, and something else—an elusive something that made her nipples bead and tingle, her pussy drip its juices onto Drake's velvety scrotum.

She reached into her bag, drew out a string of large translucent pearls and anointed them with more of the oil, warming them between her palms while rubbing oil into each bead.

His anus looked like a rosebud, pink and puckered even before she circled it with a heavily oiled finger. It unfurled for her when she pressed each bead inside, closing and reopening with each insertion.

The purring noises he was making morphed into hard breathing and low-pitched growls.

"You need to leave a few beads outside," he said, lifting his head and inhaling the scent that already had her desperate for release.

"I know." Some of the beads he'd inserted in her in that Pittsburgh dressing room had lain in her slit. "Spread your legs for me."

When he did, she rubbed more of the oil into his scrotum, rolling his testicles between her palms as she stroked the velvety sac. "You've kept it smooth," she said. "I like it."

He groaned again. "I know."

And she knew he liked her sex to be silky smooth for him. That's why she'd had her pussy waxed again three days ago, while Drake played faro at the casino in Monte Carlo. She could hardly wait for him to evaluate the cosmetician's thorough job.

"Want to do my cock?" he asked, his casual tone belying the tension evident in his muscular body.

"Later. Turn over. And keep your hands behind your head." He'd have his turn later, after she took her fill of him.

His small brown nipples hardened when she anointed them with her oil. Good. She wanted him so hot, he'd forget being gentle, forget her injury. She'd have him so aroused that his only concern would be satisfaction.

As aroused as she was now.

Her mouth watered. His penis, marble-hard and distended to its full impressive length, stood straight up, its head curving slightly toward his washboard abs.

His cock, he called it.

She'd never much liked the word when Rob or her other partners used it. But it sounded right now. Erotic.

Drake's cock, long and thick and gently curved, all of it standing ready to give her pleasure.

Erienne had never seen such a beautiful cock. Never wanted so much to touch a cock, lick a cock, take a cock inside her pussy. Her abdominal muscles contracted, and her mouth went dry.

She met his emerald gaze. "I want to suck your cock."

His response consisted of a tortured sounding groan.

Bending and running her tongue around his ruby cock head, she smiled up at him. "I want to suck you dry," she amended.

"Yesss."

Taking the base of his cock in one hand, she circled its ruby head with her tongue before closing her lips around it and sliding them down the satiny shaft. When she splayed her fingers and gently squeezed his balls, his cock twitched against her throat.

His cock felt like hot silk over steel to her tongue. It tasted like the sea and hot, aroused male. It had been so long—too long—since she'd given him head before they left the *pensione* and embarked onto their journey into hell.

"God, baby. Bite me."

She sucked harder, scraped her teeth lightly against his shaft while she took him deeper, swallowed, caressed his cock head with the convulsive motions in her throat.

She wanted his come. Now. Wanted to hear him shout with pleasure while he shot hot, salty semen down her throat.

Bracing herself on one elbow, she moved her hand off his cock and balls, swallowed more of his big cock. When she found the protruding beads, she gave them a tug.

Another. And another.

All the while she loved him. Loved his big, beautiful cock twitching wildly inside her mouth.

"Stop. For God's sake stop. I'm gonna come. My God, I'm coming. Don't—don't stop."

His hot sperm shot into her mouth, down her throat, triggering a climax that started in her dripping pussy and spread like wildfire throughout her body. His come overflowed around his throbbing cock inside her mouth and dribbled out onto his velvet-smooth scrotum. When he lay back, spent, she licked his cock clean.

Then she lay between his legs and sucked his balls into her mouth, one at the time, watching his cock spring back to life a few minutes later when she removed the rest of the anal beads.

Drake lay in the sun, spent, his heart as full as his cock was empty.

Erienne was back, whole and well. And she still loved him in spite of him reacting like a prick when he'd learned he hadn't been her primary mission when they were enjoying mind-blowing sex in Pittsburgh and at Madame Marie-Louise's *pensione*.

Life was good. And his wrung-out cock was coming to life again.

This time would be all for her.

He started with her mouth, savored the taste of his come on her generous lips. Since the old woman's "magical" oil from the glass penis still had him tingling everywhere she'd rubbed it on him, he returned the favor, anointing her round, firm breasts, then massaging oil into the scar that still made him shudder.

How close he'd come to losing her!

And how happy he'd been since she turned in her resignation from the Company.

He slid his oily hands over her concave belly, imagined her growing round there with their child. Not now, but not too far in the future, either.

But first he wanted them to explore every possible sexual pleasure. Together, as man and wife. He'd waited two months to consummate the marriage he'd insisted be celebrated the day he took her from that Hamburg hospital.

She obviously didn't want him to wait any longer to begin their sexual adventures.

Neither did he.

He dribbled the sensual oil over her plump, pink mound, watching as it made its way around the hard little bud of her clit, in and around her vagina, past her puckered rear opening where his hand now waited to massage it into the satiny flesh.

Someday he'd use the strap-on he bought yesterday after she mentioned how she thought she'd like to be fucked in the pussy and the ass at the same time. He'd indulge that fantasy, as long as it didn't mean letting another man's cock into his woman.

But not now. Today he'd return her favor, drink her honey until she screamed with pleasure, then sink his cock in her wet, tight pussy and make her come again. And again.

No toys. No beads or dildos. No bondage games and no watching sex acts on a stage or screen.

Just Drake and Erienne this time, beneath a springtime sun with no one to see them but the birds and an occasional passing boater with strong binoculars.

He lay between her outstretched legs, holding them down while he covered her pussy with his open mouth. While he sucked, he worried her clit between his teeth and tugged gently at the hard nubs of her nipples.

Her little groans spurred him on, made him desperate to please her. As soon as he felt the tremors of her first orgasm on his tongue, he slid up her body, buried his cock to the balls in her pulsating pussy when she raised her legs and locked them around his waist.

"Taste yourself," he ordered, taking her mouth and thrusting his tongue inside.

Mindful of her recent ordeal, he moved in her slowly, smoothly, deeply. Everywhere they touched, the exquisite friction sent waves of excitement through him.

Excitement heightened, he imagined, by whatever potion the old woman had put in her "magic" oil.

Erienne felt it too. The flush in her cheeks, the way she stroked his shoulders and upper back while she met his every deliberate stroke, the gentle contractions of her tight pussy around his cock—they said more than words that this was more than fucking.

More than a joining of their bodies.

They were merging their souls.

When he came this time, she led the way. Her sweet, hard contractions set off his own, and they slid together over the edge to mutual satisfaction.

"I love you," they said later as they lay in each other's arms.

It was their belated wedding night, celebrated in the sunlight of a spring afternoon in Monaco with no one as witness but the Fates who'd let Erienne come back from the darkness.

Drake couldn't have conjured up a better wife and lover if his magical powers had extended beyond illusion. He said a silent thank you to the Fates, for Erienne had helped him move beyond his world of illusion to a real world—a real future—with the woman of his dreams.

COLORS OF LOVE

Prologue

The obsidian and its clear quartz mate generated gentle energy that warmed Selena Cross's palm, but their heat didn't reach her lonely heart as she watched her former lover's classic Corvette round the bend and disappear.

If only someday she might find the kind of love again that Garrett shared with his beautiful wife, the magic that crackled between the two. The sort of arousing, exhilarating relationship she'd once had with her dead Master, the love she'd once hoped to rediscover with Garrett.

Before leaving, Garrett had dropped the stones into Selena's hand and thanked her for sharing the talismans that had led him and Elaine to their runaway daughter and brought them back into each other's arms. "Save them for someone else in need. Elaine and I will make our own magic now," he'd said, and then he'd bent and brushed his lips across Selena's cheek.

Just that momentary contact had made Selena hot and wet, recalling when not so long ago she'd lain in his arms, felt his big cock pulsating inside her while his heart had beaten a strong, steady cadence against her nipples. Nipples he'd coaxed to hard points with his teeth and tongue that now puckered against the restraints of her practical cotton bra.

She'd known from the start that to him she was a pale substitute for the woman who still held his heart, yet she'd wanted so much to rediscover love. He'd brought her body back to life after a long dormancy, but to him she'd only been a friend who'd given him much-needed comfort.

For a long time Selena had been content, remembering life with her Master, performing for others the sex magic they'd once performed with love…with caring. Now, though, she wanted more. She wanted to finally wish her Master's memory farewell, ignite a sensual flame in a new lover's eyes, the kind of flame that sizzled so obviously between Garrett and Elaine. But no, her magic didn't extend that far. She tried hard to banish the longing and the loneliness that held her in its grasp.

Closing her eyes, she clutched the stones and concentrated. She visualized a house on the beach, a coltish teenage girl jogging across a wide expanse of sand while her parents watched from the shelter of their patio. The woman was beautifully pregnant, and the man's big hands surrounded her burgeoning belly. Garrett and Elaine, united with their daughter, beamed with happiness as they awaited a new baby, apparently anticipating a life filled with love.

Selena choked back a sob. Seeing the reconciled couple together these past weeks, and now looking into their future, made her own life here on the Suwannee seem bleak, isolated. She constantly fought loneliness despite the guests who came and went, seeking solace and solitude, healing and respite from the pressures of an unforgiving world. At the river's edge, Selena sank onto a stone bench and rubbed the magic stones together between her palms.

Someday, the magic you bring to others will come again to you. That voice, faint but distinct, wafted across the river on a gentle breeze, bringing Selena hope where despair had so recently laid her low. *It's not time yet, though, for first you must let your Master rest in peace.*

That was true. Though she'd performed sex magic for many guests, even made what she told herself was love with Garrett Bryant, her dead Master still owned the better parts of her. Seven years had passed since He'd left her, but still she wore His jewels, went to sleep each night with His memory foremost in her mind. She had to banish Him from her heart, much as she banished the mischievous auras in her Wiccan rituals.

It would take time and effort to find the inner strength to let Him go.

Meanwhile, she'd serve her guests, bring them the magic she so wanted for herself. The stones warmed at her touch, the obsidian and the brilliant clear crystal quartz. Her talismans. They'd worked to bring Garrett his heart's desire. Perhaps when she'd cleansed her soul of memories, they'd work for her.

Colors of magic. Each day she'd come here by the Suwannee, close her eyes, and ask the Lord and Lady to banish her dead Master from her heart, to make room there for another love. One day if they granted her wish, she'd rub the colors of magic together and see His face; the face and colors of love.

Chapter One

୪

It wasn't as though she didn't like sex. Not at all. Selena Cross sighed as she looked out over the Suwannee River as it meandered sluggishly toward the Gulf. It was a peaceful scene, no speedboats out today, scaring birds and sending the gentle manatees into hiding. Not at all. She should have been planning the magic rituals she'd promised to lead next week, not standing here moping and staring at the river. After all, sex magic was a large part of the services she offered her guests, along with psychic predictions and more conventional Wiccan rituals.

But damn it, even witches needed release, and she never found it when orchestrating other people's sex magic.

This last group—the guests who'd checked out this morning—had left her emotionally drained and physically aroused yet unfulfilled. Four couples, every one of them determined to go as far as the next, with her orchestrating the orgy, had been almost more than she could handle. What Selena could use now was a partner with whom she could make some magic of her own. Preferably a Dom. She was tired, so tired of taking a Dom's role and leading the sex rituals she'd learned to savor as her Master's beloved slave.

Unfortunately, she was all alone and would be until later in the day when she anticipated the arrival of one Timothy Alexander. He would be a new guest, referred by her long-time client James Fortner. If her luck held out the way it been doing for the last few months, the only R&R Mr. Alexander would want would be a weekend spent sleeping alone in his room while she cast stones and wove magic spells to help him achieve relaxation and stress release. Either that or there just wouldn't be that connection—the indescribable something that occasionally burst into flames when a man and a woman met.

Only rarely did she and a guest connect with that instant chemical attraction that led to making explosive, mind-clearing sex magic. Even it did not give her the emotional fulfillment she craved. But no one had been able to do that, not since the loss of her Master, the man to whom she'd given her heart. The man she'd lost to death nearly eight years ago.

Selena sighed. For all that she preached that self-stimulation raised magical energy as well if not better than sex with a partner or group sex magic, doing it solo was getting pretty old. Her pussy throbbed, demanding release that didn't want to come. Idly she stroked the hard nubs of her nipples, flicking them gently with her fingertips and enjoying the mild arousal the action brought. A gentle breeze caught the fabric of her flowing skirt, causing it to slide along her inner thighs and tease the damp folds of her freshly shaved labia with soft fleeting contact. Cool, smooth, and impersonal, much like her own fingertips felt as they caressed her breasts and throat through the thin material.

What if someone was watching her from the opposite bank of the Suwannee? She imagined a lover, spying on her from a vantage point across the river, pictured his eyes darkening, glittering with carnal appreciation. His cock would be hardening by now, his breathing becoming ragged with lust. She grew damp, swollen, as needy physically as she was emotionally.

That fantasy died away, replaced by a vivid memory of her Master's face, the hot anticipation in His gaze while He watched her pleasure herself. Anticipation she'd never experience again, just as she'd never again know the pleasure of serving Him, finding ecstasy in pleasing Him. Tears stung her eyes, spilling over and drenching her cheeks with hot, salty pain. Her throat tightened, then burst loose with a primal cry.

Enough was enough. Selena swallowed the next scream that tried to wrench itself from her wounded heart. Eight lonely years was too long to have grieved. Too prolonged a period to have hovered in the darkness serving only others' needs. It was time—past time—to bid her beloved Master farewell, wrench His precious memory from her soul.

Time to commune with the Goddess, for herself rather than for the series of transient guests who came to seek her counsel. To pray for a new Master, not a temporary substitute or a client with his own needs to communicate to the Lord and Lady. Turning away from the river, where there was not a soul in sight, not even a lone boat making its way toward the Gulf, Selena stepped inside the special circle—the one she hadn't visited since her Master had been gone.

The closely planted hawthorn shrubs had grown, now stood almost as tall as she. They'd been three-foot babies when she and her Master had turned the warm spring earth and planted them so long ago. Their branches had spread upward, not out, as though they knew they mustn't encroach upon the circular clearing. As if they realized that the circle in the mossy ground, paved with smooth stones her grandfather had harvested from the riverbed long before her birth, was inviolable.

Though discovery was unlikely, the very possibility of it made Selena's pulse race when she stepped inside the circle. She reached into one voluminous pocket of her loose, sky-blue dress and retrieved the sacred objects designed to stimulate and drive the practitioner of sole sex magic rituals, arranging them precisely within a large pentagonal indentation her grandmother had carved years ago on a smooth, otherwise round river rock near the center of the circle. Anticipating release she feared would be more physical than emotional, she sat beside the rock on a carved stone bench that rested securely on the jutting penises of two smiling satyrs. One by one, she released the buttons down the front of her dress, anticipating her sensual commune with Nature.

Each satyr grinned up at her, as if they anticipated taking part in her solo act of desperation. As if they heard and understood her murmured invocation to the Goddess, smelled the musk of her arousal, and reveled in each inch of honey-gold skin that she uncovered. Selena smiled first at one and then the other before straddling the bench, slipping the dress off, folding it, and arranging the material so it would cushion the crossed arms of one satyr where she'd lay her head. For a moment she stood there, enjoying the motion of the breeze against her naked skin, the cooling effect it had on the wet, swollen folds between her widespread thighs.

Then she reached in the smaller pocket of her dress, found the salt she'd placed there, and sprinkled a handful of salt around the circle. She raised her face skyward, seeking the Sun God to complete the Moon Goddess…beseeching Them to send her a Master to fill her circle of life. Golden particles danced before her eyes, and she concentrated on them…on love, health, tranquility…as she visualized the negative auras of hate, disease, and anger leaving her body on a cloud of smoke, wafting away, leaving her ready to make her magic.

She couldn't banish her frustration and need, her hunger for love and fulfillment, though. She hoped the Sun God would understand. She closed her eyes, visualizing the crescent candle of the Moon Goddess and silently chanting an ancient prayer:

"Oh Mother Goddess, Creatress of Life
In this sacred Circle of Light
I do pledge myself to honour and
Serve Thee
And to abide by the Wiccan Rede
For as long as I shall live."

When she visualized the Sun God's candle, a tear slid down her cheek, chilling where it touched.

"O Great Horned God, Lord of the Woodlands
In this sacred Circle of Light
I do pledge myself to honour and

*Serve Thee
And to protect the secrets
Of the Ancient Ones
For as long as I shall live."*

Eyes closed, she held her open hands to the sky. Glowing light, two white beams of it, streaked down from the sky into her hands, and a familiar warm sensation spread through her body. A feeling of purity, a state devoid of negativity.

Opening her eyes, she greeted sunlight filtering through the towering oaks, dappling her body, reflecting off facets of stones in the ends of gold barbells that pierced her nipples. It warmed the moonstone that filled her navel and centered a brilliant starburst tattoo she'd gotten on the orders of the Master who'd taught her the magic she'd been practicing now for nearly ten years.

As always, she paid Him homage. Bending, she lifted the huge carved rose quartz phallus from the pentagon and took its smooth, bulging head between her lips. Her tongue ring vibrated when she licked it, as though it were a real man's cock. Rigid. As He had been, only He'd been alive, responsive to the gentle touch of her fingers on His testicles, the rasp of her teeth on His warm male flesh when she worshiped Him.

For when I can't be here for you. That's what He'd said when He'd given her this. Though it had been years since He'd lost His battle with the Grim Reaper, and though she'd made sex magic many times in the course of her business, Selena had never found another Master...another man who could give her more than orgasm, more than release like the one she now planned to provide for herself. A picture of her lost Master firmly in her mind, she slipped the dildo between her swollen labia and sank it to its crystal balls within her dripping cunt.

She ran the fingers of her other hand through her short, pale curls on her head, remembering how He'd loved stimulating her that way before becoming ill. How He'd enjoyed thrusting His callused fingers beneath the wig she'd bought after He took her hair in a healing ritual, baring her naked scalp as well as His own to the Sun God's light.

The guttural words of the healing incantation still rang in her ears. Not that His spell had worked any better than the surgery and debilitating rounds of chemotherapy He'd undergone. No modern medicine, no magic, no prayers, and no healing rituals had managed to slow the progress of the cancer that had eaten away at Him cell by cell until He'd finally died, leaving her nothing but an empty husk. And memories she'd visited every day and every night, memories she'd visit one more time as she asked Divine help to lay them to rest.

How she'd loved the feel of His fingers and tongue on the nape of her neck, her temples, the incredibly erogenous area over her occipital bone. Idly she found that spot, stroked it through the cap of soft curls. Her cream flowed, wetting her thighs.

Bending again, she picked up a large pink gel anal stimulator, still dripping with the lubricant she'd just applied on its shiny surface. She widened her stance, bent further, and looked into the glowing ruby eyes of the south-facing satyr as she worked the plug in, a little at a time. She shuddered at the cool invasion. Goddess, if it were only a man's hot cock filling her there at her Master's bidding, another's filling her cunt where her old Master's dildo now lay embedded. But not just any man. A Master to fill the empty spots in her body and her heart. The Master for whom she'd begged the Goddess each time she made magic but only now believed herself ready to let fill the void in her soul.

Slowly, her ass stretched to take more and more, until her sphincter muscle clamped down on the narrow stem of the device, hugging its round base tight against her nether hole. Goddess, but she felt full as her cunt and ass contracted, the sensitive tissue stretched to accommodate the toys.

Selena clenched her inner muscles, clasping the dildo as firmly as she encouraged new practitioners to clamp down on their partners' cocks, while she strapped on the butter-soft black leather harness that would hold both objects firmly in place while parting her labia and exposing her throbbing clit.

The Sun God was strong today, His morning rays warming her skin and making her welcome the coolness of the stone bench. She lay down, rested her head on the Earth satyr's padded arms and her legs over the shoulders of the satyr who represented Fire. She closed her eyes, said another silent prayer to the Goddess, and lost herself in the sensations of sex magic.

She imagined her Master there, straddling her, forcing her to take His hot, pulsating cock deep in her throat, to accept His spurting seed while He sucked her swollen clit. While His hands stroked her belly and His smooth, hard-muscled chest abraded the rock-hard points of her nipples.

Today Selena found it hard to visualize Him, to feel Him and see His compelling features in her mind as she brought herself to climax. It was past time for her to let Him go, to find a new Master to fill the empty spot in her heart. But she couldn't, not yet. He hadn't let go of her emotions, and she had a feeling He wouldn't, not until she found another Master to take His place.

Concentrating on sensation, she murmured the ancient prayers. Listened for response in every chirp of the birds overhead, each rustling noise of an animal moving through the forest. Opening her eyes, she sought the emptiness of the sky above her, seeing nothing but feeling the presence of Sylphs in the air, the moisture from the river with its Water sprites. She smelled the fertile element of Earth around her, reveled in the passion of the Sun God's heat. His fire. Cool stone caressed her back. The soft breeze, sylphs kissing her skin, stimulated all her sensual places. The rippling sound of water tumbling over rocks at the river's edge filled her mind.

In answer to her entreaties, Earth, Air, Fire, and Water joined forces to arouse her. Her cunt pulsated against the dildo, setting vibrations in the thin wall of tissue that separated her two stretched holes. Her clit twitched, wanting more stimulation than the sun's heat and the caress of the wind. Her nipples swelled against the gold that pierced them, as though reminding her of when her Master had pierced her and put them there.

No. Goddess, help me. Cleanse me of His memory. But the Goddess didn't seem to be listening. Strange. Selena never had problems surrendering her own self to the Goddess when leading clients in their group rituals.

"Your Master is your God, but you must gather your strength, find the way within yourself to let Him go. If you do not you'll never find peace, never achieve another love."

As though compelled by the Goddess, Selena began to stroke her own skin, warming it with her fingertips, paying special attention to her throat, her belly, the sensitive hollows behind her knees. She avoided touching the highly erogenous places that had appealed so much to Him, for doing that would have reminded her too graphically that He was gone, never to return.

Goddess, help me let Him go. Free me from the prison of my memories so He can go to His eternal reward. So I can find fulfillment here on Earth, reconnect with its energies.

Hesitating only a moment, she began to stroke her nipples, aroused at the way they beaded at her own touch. With wonder, she explored the wet, warm folds of her pussy. In her mind's eye she saw not her Master but a new lover...a lover whose beckoning smile welcomed her back to Earth and all its wonders.

Tension rose within her, at first gently, then building to a wild crescendo. Her clit and nipples felt as though they'd turned to crystal. Crystal that burned with fire one moment but froze the next, while her cunt and ass contracted feverishly against the rigid toys that filled and stretched them. As her orgasm came, she began to shake.

"Thank you, Goddess," she gasped.

When she opened her eyes moments later, the smiling satyrs stared down at her, their carved stone features almost human looking now—as though they, too, had found a measure of satisfaction in her climax. As though they, too, realized the Goddess had shown her the way to let go of the past, celebrate the Earth and her life on it.

Methodically, as her Master had taught her, Selena withdrew the instruments of her pleasure. First the harness which she folded neatly. Then the anal stimulator, and finally the Pyrex dildo, now warmed from the heat of her body. Those she set on the stone while she retrieved her dress and slipped it over the sensitized surface of her body. Rising, she tucked the harness in her pocket and scooped up the other toys. One in each hand, she held them as though they were holy icons as she glided to the water's edge.

Not the river, but a cleansing spring beside it that brought clear fresh water bubbling from deep below the Earth's surface. Her Master had said it provided the purest water, fit for cleansing the most tortured soul. She knelt at its edge and cleansed the toys, wondering as she glimpsed her reflection on the crystal surface of the water whether she would ever again see contentment there.

"It's time for me to let You go, You know. Past time. Time for me to find magic with someone new. To celebrate life the way You taught me to." Selena spoke the words she'd mouthed a hundred times. A thousand. Now as never before, though, she felt perhaps it was time, truly time to let His memory go and move on.

Sex magic was best when shared with a living breathing partner, not bittersweet memories, faceless Deities, and a handful of phallic symbols. For the first time since she'd come home eight years ago from the vanilla funeral His parents had orchestrated, Selena shed her dress and slid naked into the cool, bubbling spring where she'd thrown His collar.

And dived in after it, for she hadn't been ready to let Him go. Then, when she hadn't been able to find it, knew it was lost to her, she'd wanted this spring to take her, drag her in a whirling vortex beneath its surface. She wanted it to propel her to whatever eternity she might share with the Master she'd loved and lost. But the Goddess had known better.

She'd known that someday Selena would embrace life again as she was doing now. Effervescent bubbles caressed her skin, confirmed life and renewed the life forces within her. When she rose from the water she lifted her hands to the sun, let Nature evaporate the moisture with the sun's warmth, the wind's soft breeze.

Goddess, send me another Master. Another with whom to share the miracle of magic...of love.

A sense of peace and serenity flowed over Selena, as though the Goddess had heard, would consider her plea. Taking a cleansing breath, she gathered her clothes, then moved into the clearing by the river, letting the Sun God kiss the water from her body.

She should have gone back to the house, prepared for her new guest's arrival. That could wait. Shrugging into her dress, she took a seat on a bench, let her mind wander with the Undines that darted above the water near the river shore.

In time her plea would be answered. Another Master would come her way. The breeze cooled her, lulled her into a dreamy mood where she saw Him, as clearly as though He'd materialized before her eyes.

Strong. Rugged. Attuned with her in every way, devoted to mastering her to give her pleasure...as much pleasure as He'd take from her. A Master the gods of darkness wouldn't take away, who'd stay and celebrate life with her.

* * * * *

Zachary Lang glanced at the road map, then checked his rearview mirror. Good. It seemed that he'd finally lost the dark blue sedan that he'd noticed on his tail most of the way since leaving Tampa. Must have happened when he made that last turnoff from the main road.

Damn, he hated having to live like this, keeping an eye out for danger during every waking hour. Even on this quiet secondary road northwest of Gainesville, Zach lived with the constant knowledge that someone could spot him, sell him out to the mobsters who'd apparently set an army of hit men on his trail.

He was learning the hard way it wasn't healthy to tangle with the mob. Why the hell had he insisted on supervising construction of the new county building he'd designed? If he hadn't, he'd never have caught the general contractor skimping on materials and started this nightmare that wouldn't end until he'd given his testimony and sent the culprits off to prison. A nightmare that grew in scope as the state attorney's investigators peeled off layer after layer, exposing ties between organized crime and high-level politicos all the way from Tampa to Tallahassee and beyond.

Zach sighed. Trauma was too pale a word to describe the hell his life had become. He saw a certain irony in the fact that his exposure of the fraud to the authorities might have saved a lot of workers, while it could easily be the death of him.

If someone hadn't noticed the substandard components going into that project, the next big storm might have blown the building down on top of several hundred innocent workers. Knowing that made Zach feel good that he'd been the one to discover and report the fraud, even though he hadn't gotten a decent night's sleep in the two months since taking his suspicions to the state attorney.

Two months during which they'd shuffled him from one safe house to the other, each one now riddled with bullet holes. Safe house, hell. They were hardly any safer than his own high-rise apartment would have been, since it had taken virtually no time for the goons to find each new rat-hole as the Tampa police had tried to keep him one step ahead of death.

Obviously the mob had connections with at least a few dirty cops.

He'd finally refused yet another shuffle after a shootout had left two of his bodyguards dead. Slaughtered, their blood spattered over the floor of the so-called safe house. It didn't matter that he'd barely escaped with his own life. Zach couldn't help remembering sitting around playing cards with the two men, listening to Tony teasing Carlos about getting soft around the middle, Carlos replying that Tony might someday find a good wife and kid to keep him out of the gym instead of a string of hot-blooded Latina girlfriends.

Shit. It was Zach's fault they'd died. His fault Carlos's kids would grow up without a dad, that Tony wouldn't find that special woman who'd have made his life complete.

Zach had no close family. No one to mourn him deeply if the next volley of bullets snuffed his life. He'd made his decision. He wasn't endangering anybody else to save his skin. He'd get in his damn car and drive around for two or three days until the trial, let them try to hit a moving target. Somehow, his friend Jim had talked him out of running indiscriminately, persuaded him instead to come to this out-of-the-way place where he could rest and be reasonably safe.

Afraid of endangering more people, Zach had said no at first, until Jim had explained about this place. About the proprietress being a witch who protected the perimeter of her property with wardings. His first reaction had been, "You've got to be kidding," but Jim had assured him he wasn't. Although shocked to learn his friend was into Pagan beliefs and rituals, he'd let himself be persuaded that this low-tech early warning system might protect him where more scientific means had not.

For the moment, Zach felt almost safe. It was as if when he'd turned onto this narrow road that ran parallel to the Suwannee River, he'd stepped back into an earlier era. A peaceful, slow-paced era where things moved slowly and crime rarely raised its ugly head. Even the air up here smelled fresher. Jim had been right. Getting away from Tampa and his problems just might help keep him sane as well as alive.

Where was this pagan bed-and-breakfast, anyhow? Jim had said it was out-of-the-way, and he hadn't been kidding. Zach hadn't seen a thing except weathered utility poles, fallow fields dotted with wildflowers, and blackberry brambles for the last five miles. It had to be around here somewhere.

He almost missed the weathered sign practically hidden in a blackberry thicket. *Cross Bed and Breakfast.* The delicate script perched above an arrow that pointed toward the Suwannee. Braking sharply, Zach made the turn, kicking dust up on the gravel road and scaring a blue jay that apparently had been looking for a berry for its dinner.

As he approached the river, the vegetation became thicker, lusher. Long-leaf pines and century-old live oak trees shared space with gum trees now pale green with new spring growth. As he rounded a bend in the road, he spotted a clearing with a breathtaking old home, large and sprawling behind flowering shrubs. It was as beautiful an example of old Florida-style architecture as he'd ever seen.

Cross Bed and Breakfast. The sign looked almost the same as the one he'd seen along the road. Discreet, as though someone had lettered it in a flowing feminine hand. When he stopped the car and looked back the way he'd come, all he saw were trees. Not a sign of civilization, not even the blacktop ribbon of roadway that led back to the Interstate.

His lifelong friend Jim had this place pegged. No one would think to look for him out here in the middle of nowhere. Not at a little-known retreat whose patrons Jim had mentioned were mostly believers in sex magic, psychic healing, and the casting of magical stones. Zach hadn't been particularly impressed with the idea of taking up modern witchcraft, although Jim had assured him that his own lifestyle as a Dom wouldn't clash—after all, it, too, was an alternate path few followed, a path the witch who ran this place understood and embraced along with her spells and incantations. In any case, if he could get a few days' respite from the dire threats and flying bullets, he'd take it and be content.

Jim must have realized the old house would fascinate him. With a practiced eye, he took in every detail, from the raised foundation to a chimney made of natural stone. Typical Florida style design, like what he'd studied in a residential architecture class and planned to incorporate into his own home once he settled down. If he lived to settle down.

Zach figured this sprawling frame home probably been built seventy-five or eighty years ago. The place was pristine, its façade lovingly maintained yet seemingly unchanged by time. A tin roof glittered in the sunlight, its brilliance illuminating the ground and casting shadows onto a wrap-around porch behind beds of flowering bushes. The place exuded peace…quiet…a gracious sort of living long gone from Florida's bustling cities.

Suddenly a sense of contentment flowed over him. This was exactly where he needed to be, not only to dodge the mob's goons but also to restore the emotional balance he'd disturbed when his terrible discovery catapulted him out of his element into a shadowy criminal world. When Zach got out of the car, he glanced toward the river and noticed a woman staring out at the water from a bench near its edge.

Something compelled him to head down the path, to go to her.

Could the woman be as entrancing up close as she seemed from a distance? The jungle-like setting with its lush greenery, pastel-colored spring flowers, and the woman's flowing sky-blue dress reminded Zach of a Claude Monet painting. "The Waterlilies", if he recalled the name correctly.

She didn't deserve being put in danger. Didn't need her quiet life disturbed by him and the problems he'd created for himself. Zach turned, determined to leave before putting her more at risk, but something compelled him to look back at her.

What was she thinking? She looked at peace, yet incredibly sad. As he drew near, he caught a scent of something clean and sweet mingling with the brackish smell of the river. Honeysuckle?

"Welcome. You must be Mr. Alexander." Sweet, softly spoken words flowed from her lush pink lips, the sound welcoming and soothing.

But she had his name wrong. Then Zach remembered. Jim had made the reservations under one of the false names he'd been using. "Yes, I am. You must be Ms. Cross."

"Selena." Her motion as graceful as an Ionic column, she rose and held out her hand.

"Zach." Her palm felt warm in his, soft yet strong.

"Zach? You are Timothy Alexander, aren't you?"

Damn. He'd forgotten again. This ducking would-be killers was getting too complicated. "Yes. But I go by my middle name." How the hell had he let Jim persuade him to use false IDs and credit cards? Zach had no talent for subterfuge, as he'd already proven by getting half the *mafiosi* in Tampa on his trail.

"Your secrets will be safe here, Zach." Selena smiled, as though she sensed his lie but wouldn't come right out and accuse him. "Come on, let's go back to the house. I'll show you to your room."

* * * * *

The man was running from something. Something dark and frightening, and deadly.

A chill spread through Selena's bones, even though the late April day was typically warm and humid. The obsidian and quartz stones Garrett had returned to her a year ago today clicked together in her pocket while she prepared a simple supper. The tinkling noise rang out a warning. Of some unseen danger? A sense of peril lay heavy in the still evening air.

Timothy Alexander, or Zach, which she thought more likely to be his real name than a middle name, had a haunted look in his dark eyes. Furrows had been etched — by worry, she imagined — on a perfectly chiseled face otherwise unscathed by time and elements. With one breath, she wished he wasn't her only weekday guest, because she sensed danger — and a compelling attraction she wasn't sure she should explore. With the next, she thanked the fates that she didn't have to explain his unsettling presence to anyone else.

Selena sensed an aura of danger about him despite his cultured manner, gold Rolex watch, and casual clothes of a quality far beyond her means. A small scar bisected one dark, arched eyebrow, the only blight on his otherwise classic good looks.

Who was this man? Had he struggled to earn the trappings of wealth he wore so easily, or had he enjoyed such luxuries all his life? Was he as alone as he appeared, or had he left a family behind, wherever he came from? Who or what was he was running from?

Because Selena had no doubt that Zach was running. From whom or what, she couldn't say.

One of the first things she'd noticed about him was his long, slender fingers. Perhaps he was an artist, but most likely not. His hands bore small nicks and scars that suggested his work might be more physical than creative. And she got an impression of tensile strength, barely controlled, when she watched him move.

Trying to banish her worries about her mysterious guest, she filled a ceramic bowl with bananas, apples, and grapes, and set it on the round oak dining table.

When Zach appeared in the doorway, the stones warmed in her pocket, exuding a strong heat against her thigh. A troubling energy. As though they tried to tell her — warn her of something — their energy increased when he came closer. Did they sense danger, treachery? Or were they merely reflecting the sensual energy this man set off within her body?

Like a panther, sleek and graceful yet full of raw male power, he commanded her full attention when he crossed the room. She couldn't help noticing his powerful thighs, and the impressive bulge between them. She needed no reminder that this was a man— a dark, dangerous stranger who had her growing warm and wet.

She was no longer alone in her big old rambling home.

When he sat down, she forced her mind to the mundane task of feeding them and ladled a generous helping of savory beef and vegetable stew onto his plate.

He murmured his approval, then made short work of the meal while she went outside to gather some fresh mint leaves for their tea.

"Do you take care of this place all by yourself?" he asked as he set his napkin beside the bowl.

"No. During the winter season, I have three full-time workers. Now, though, most of my guests come for weekends, so I get along by myself during the week. My help comes in Friday through Sunday."

"This seems like an awfully isolated place for a beautiful young woman like you. Surely you miss having things to do, friends nearby to visit with."

If she had a dollar for every time a guest had said something like this, she'd be well on the way to wealth. "Not really. I like the seclusion. I've never known life in the city."

"No husband or lovers?" he asked, smiling.

She needed no psychic power to tell she attracted him sexually. Barely leashed desire was evident in the heat of his gaze.

"Not any more." For the first time, saying those words no longer caused a tearing pain in her heart. "When He was still alive, we lived here together. I can't imagine calling anywhere else home."

Zach shook his head, his expression a silent offering of sympathy. "I'm sorry. I hope my asking didn't bring back sad memories."

"It's all right." Selena smiled, realizing it finally *was* okay to remember.

"You know, Jim was right when he said I'd find this place fascinating. I take it the house was built sometime during the 1920's."

"Yes. How can you tell?"

"The construction materials. The banks of long, narrow windows that open outward from the bottom. The tin roof, although that's typical of Florida homes built as far back as the late 1800's and as late as the mid nineteen-thirties."

"You make a habit of studying old houses?" Selena asked.

"I had to learn a bit about them in architectural school. My specialty is designing commercial buildings, though. How long have you lived here?"

"All my life." This was Selena's home, her refuge from people who thought she was crazy because she cast the stones and sometimes "saw" things that hadn't happened yet. Some of the simple country folks who lived nearby probably would have stoned her if they'd been aware of the sex magic rituals she sometimes led with her guests. As it was, they whispered and pointed at "the witch woman" when she came to town, but they liked her guests stopping at their produce stands and craft shops, and so they generally treated her well.

"My great-grandfather built this house in 1924 as a refuge for Pagans who had to practice their beliefs in secret. After my parents died a few years ago, I turned it into a bed and breakfast of sorts, though the breakfast part's a misnomer since I serve three meals a day. Most of my guests come here to recuperate from some physical or emotional trauma. Or to rediscover the magic within themselves."

"Just what I need. Peace and quiet. Recovery." He paused, as if considering saying more, before looking away.

Selena imagined he'd tell her about it in his own time. "Could I get you anything else?" she asked when she picked up his plate. "Some coffee or tea?"

"I believe I'll pass tonight. Get some sleep." Sleep had been in short supply these past weeks, while Jim had shuffled him back and forth among half a dozen safe houses, hiding him out from hit men.

Selena's gentle face lit up when she smiled. "You look as though you could use some rest. Go on. I will call on the Goddess to bring you healthful rest. Perhaps tomorrow you'll feel like joining me in the circle. My guests often find the moonlight ritual soothing. Some even manage to set aside their worries."

"Worries?" It probably didn't take any psychic ability to interpret the haggard look on his face or the wary expression in his eyes. Hell, he saw desperation every time he looked in a mirror, and he was no clairvoyant. In his situation, who the fuck wouldn't worry? Worry was too mild a word. Who wouldn't be terrified that the next man who looked him in the eye might have been sent to kill him?

Zach wasn't ready to die just yet. Especially not now, when he felt this inexplicable pull toward Selena. He had things to do, places to go, dreams to realize. If by some miracle he got through this ordeal alive, he intended to live life to the fullest in ways he'd never done before. Since his mortality had been so pointedly demonstrated the first time a bullet had whizzed by his ear, scant inches off its target, he'd begun to realize just how many things he had yet to experience.

How many life events he'd missed out on so far in his thirty-seven years of life. Things he'd always thought there'd be time for later. Love. Family. A special connection with a special woman who understood his particular sexual needs. Selena? He glanced her way, let himself imagine for a moment he wasn't a marked man and she was the submissive of his wildest dreams. A sub who'd stand by him, through good and bad, even when doing so endangered her very life. A sub totally different from Andrea, his last sub playmate who'd walked out on him the minute the goons had started gunning for him. She'd been more interested in exploring fetishes typical of the BDSM lifestyle than in the underlying relationship.

Perhaps he'd explore the inexplicable, instant attraction he felt toward this modern-day witch woman whose deep blue eyes looked as though they could see into his soul. An attraction he sensed she felt, too. Until then, he had to remain aloof, walk alone down the treacherous road he'd chosen. Without answering Selena's question, he pushed his chair back from the table and stood. "I'll see you in the morning."

When she laid a small, soft hand on his forearm, electricity crackled between them. "Have peaceful dreams, then. I'll make your breakfast in the morning whenever you're ready."

Later as he lay in the canopied bed, watching shadowed moonlight create shifting patterns on sheer curtains that framed the floor-to-ceiling windows in his room, it seemed all he could think about was her. Her soft curls, her gentle smile. Her pink, inviting mouth just made to take his tongue…his cock. He imagined his hands kneading her firm, round ass cheeks, his lips dripping with her honey.

His hand went to his cock for the first time since this whole mess started. He'd been too tense, too preoccupied to think of that, but now he couldn't resist the urge to stroke himself, imagining it was her mouth serving him, her fingers, her heated cunt. Then he came, in steaming bursts that had lain pent-up inside him all these months and grown to unbearable proportions while in her company. Still his deprived body demanded more.

As he held onto his own pulsating flesh, Zach felt Selena's warmth, sensed the silent invitation he'd seen in her eyes. An invitation he dared not accept lest he drag her into the danger he lived with every day. He considered briefly that he could engage her for the sort of sexual ritual she performed as part of her profession. But that would smack of using her as a prostitute, since he knew so little about sex magic—about magic of any sort for that matter. From all he'd seen and felt about her so far, he knew the wanting went deeper than flesh. She'd burrow inside his psyche, and he couldn't afford to draw anybody into him that way. Not now.

His emotions overwhelmed him as he gripped his cock in one hand and tried to picture Andrea. All he saw in the darkness was a gentle, graceful witch, bending over his prone body and paying homage to his sex…moonlight dappling her pale, smooth skin, the short soft curls on her head.

When he felt another climax coming on, he reached again for the folded hand towel he'd brought to bed and caught the hot bursts of semen as they left his body, wrenched free by his own hand…or was it a witch's magic?

* * * * *

Selena lay in bed, but sleep wouldn't come. Instead, an aching, pervasive desire tormented her. She tossed and turned, her legs parting. The cool night air did little to appease the heat or slow the flow of juices that drenched her labia and moistened her inner thighs. She was in heat, desperate with wanting. Wanting not her dead Master, for she'd finally bid Him farewell, but the tall stranger with the dark, haunted eyes, who for some reason felt it necessary to conceal his true identity.

She was lusting after a man she didn't know. Wanting Zach.

Her eyes closed, she lay in bed, the picture of his handsome face etched indelibly in her mind. The warmth of his hard-muscled forearm, the only part of him she'd touched, stayed with her still, tantalizing her with sensual promise.

She imagined those long fingers stroking the erotic hills and valleys of her throat, her breasts, her belly, and felt herself responding. The walls of her vagina clenched, as though preparing to be claimed by the full, impressive cock she'd noticed beneath his khaki trousers. She shuddered at the sudden bombardment of sensation...the congestion and the heat building deep inside her and bubbling over, soaking her slit and the pulsating tip of his erection.

"I want to fuck you."

His deep, honeyed words rang in her ears, as real as though he'd been beside her, whispering them. She imagined his breath, hot on her breast, his lips clamping onto her pierced nipples one by one, his tongue flailing them, arousing them. Arousing her.

Goddess, but she was so hot, feeling each burst of his breath on her sensitized skin, taking in the rhythm of his every simple command. His heart beat in time with hers, hard, fast, urgent—a reflection of their mutual need. Her breath caught in her throat, preventing her reply, so she opened herself wider, draping her lower legs over his tight buttocks. His heat and hardness seared her when he seated himself deep within her channel. He throbbed with life...passion, awakening emotions in her which she'd let lie dormant far too long.

A generous lover, he stroked her slow and deep, deeper with every thrust until she felt his long, thick cock knocking at the door to her womb, his heavy testicles nestled within her hot, slick labia, resting against her anus. His silky chest hairs brushed her nipples when he took her mouth again, stroking her tongue with the same maddeningly deliberate cadence. In and out, stoking her flames.

Goddess, but this felt so real. Selena threw back the quilted coverlet, too hot now to need its artificial warmth. She opened her thighs wider, making more room to cradle Zach's narrow hips while tightening the hold of her calves against his muscular ass. The rough texture of his rock-hard thighs contrasted with the smooth surfaces of her own, and the satin tip of his hard, ready cock probed within her damp, swollen folds.

His breath smelled incredibly sweet when he took her mouth. Clean and fresh with some citrus scent, it made her tongue tingle when he forced her lips to part and thrust his tongue inside.

Sure, deft, supremely confident, he claimed her body inch by inch, imprinting it with the warmth of his hands, the heat of his mouth. The seductive, kneading pressure of his hands sent waves of anticipation through her when he cupped her breasts, bringing them together, abrading the small, sensitive mounds with his cheeks and chin. Her nipples tightened, grew longer as he sucked first one and then the other, nipping lightly with his teeth and bathing the sensitive flesh with his tongue.

The pressure built inside her, growing and expanding until it burst in a white-hot flare of pleasure, taking her to a world where nothing existed but this man and this moment.

Selena woke, suddenly cold, for Zach was no longer with her. A chilly night breeze connected with her sweat-soaked skin, making her shiver. Her teeth chattering, she wrapped the tangled sheet around her and sat upright in the middle of the bed. Maybe if she concentrated hard enough, he'd come to her again…this time in the flesh.

She had a sinking feeling he wouldn't, no matter how strong the connection between them, not until or unless he conquered whatever had him on the run. She sensed he was a man of honor who wouldn't draw a woman into danger. Perhaps even now he was reconsidering being here, exposing her to his life. But she also sensed he had few places left to go. If he stayed until morning, she'd invite him to enter her magic circle.

A problem shared was a problem half-solved.

Chapter Two

ၸာ

Zach looked more relaxed this morning. Perhaps, as he'd told Selena when they left the house for a walk after breakfast, a night away from the city had been just what he'd needed to regain his emotional balance.

She couldn't help noticing the deep creases at the corners of his mouth seemed less pronounced. His step seemed surer, too, his attitude more confident. They strolled through the woods, pausing every now and then to watch forest creatures scurry toward a pool in the bend of the river created by fallen limbs and debris. Funny creatures, they dipped their morning catch into the water, then ate it as daintily as any highbrow lady might.

When a good-sized bass suddenly jumped out of the water as if it intended to steal a bird's intended breakfast, Zach laughed. "He must be hungry."

As hungry for food as Selena was for Zach. "Uh-huh. This is why I love it here. The peace. The freedom. The knowledge that here we can be one with the Elements, and no one will disturb us."

A shadow crossed Zach's face, but his smile quickly returned. "Tell me about your magic."

"It's Pagan. Wicca, based on polar opposites, the Sun God and the Moon Goddess who control all magic. Earth, air, fire, and water, the elements which command us all to a greater or lesser extent, depending on many factors. As a priestess, I help believers achieve balance, contentment. My magic can be as simple as casting the stones, seeing a client's future. Or as complex as helping them discover sexual nirvana."

"All that?" Zach shook his head, as though trying to take in what she imagined must seem incredibly complicated to someone not steeped in Wiccan practice and ritual, as she'd been all her life.

"If they believe. If, like you, they aren't practitioners of Wicca, I can sometimes help them set aside their troubles, see the beauty inherent in Earth. In us all." Selena paused, found a seat on a fat oak log, and stared momentarily at the tall hawthorn hedge that concealed her private circle—the place no guest had ever been. Suddenly she wanted to take Zach there, coax out the magic she sensed lay deep within his stoic shell.

But it was too soon. "Come, sit beside me. Listen to the birds' song, the rush of the river toward the Gulf. The silence of the forest with all its secrets." When he joined her on the log, she took his hand, felt the tension flow from him. "Close your eyes, Zach, and let me banish whatever demons are troubling you."

His eyelids fluttered, then drifted shut, improbably long dark lashes forming a lacy contrast against his olive skin. He let out a sigh that said more than a hundred words of explanation about his skepticism. It emphasized a sense of hopelessness in him that she doubted he'd trust in her enough to put into words. "If only you could."

"Relax. Tell me about your life. What does a successful architect do once his workday is done?"

"I sailed. Fished. Watched the sun set over Tampa Bay. Visited the clubs…played."

He said it as though he never expected to go back. "Past tense?" she asked, keeping her tone easy, non-threatening, and rubbing her palm along his exposed forearm.

"Seems that way sometimes. What does a witch do for entertainment?" Opening his eyes, he looked down at where she touched him and laid his free hand over hers. "Make all kinds of magic?"

"Mmm." From the hot look he sent her way, she guessed what magic he meant. Sex magic. "If you'd let me, I'd cast the stones, look into your future," she told him, though her sex twitched with anticipation of something more. Much more.

"Maybe later. Right now I'm enjoying the peace and quiet. This is a great spot to relax." He stretched long legs out in front of him, and leaned against the slender trunk of a sweet gum tree.

"All my guests seem to like coming here. It shows the best of water and earth, flora and fauna. I thought about putting up a gazebo or something so folks could relax in comfort, but I don't want to disturb the pool or the view of the river."

Zach stood, backing up a bit and looking intently at the pool and the small clearing. Then he picked up a slender stick and began to trace something in the sand at his feet. Intently, he gazed up at his surroundings, then turned back to whatever it was he was drawing.

When he'd finished, he strode to her and took her hands. "Come over here and take a look. I believe I've solved your problem."

"A treehouse," she murmured, imagining how the pentagonal structure would look, anchored to two massive oaks and suspended atop three slender columns. A circular ladder snaked around one of the trees, providing access as well as a bit of whimsy. "Would the trees support the weight?"

Zach hunkered down close to the ground and pointed out the beams. "Steel crossbeams concealed beneath the gazebo floor will provide all the support that's needed. Nestling it in the limbs of the trees is just for window dressing. That way, your guests can look down on the pool, out at the river, or back into the forest. They can have their creature comforts without disturbing nature's bounty. You could leave the sides open above the rails, or screen it. What do you think?"

"You're a genius." In a few minutes, he'd solved a problem she'd grappled with for years. "How much would something like this cost to have built?"

"If you want, I could..." His words trailed off, and his expression sobered. "...I could draw this up for you on paper, then work up some rough projections of material costs." No way could he surface now and contact any of his associates. If he did, he'd be exposing Selena to the danger he'd come here to escape for a little while. "I—I haven't any contacts with builders up in this part of the state, but I can draw the specs so any competent contractor should be able to execute them. The only tricky part, engineering-wise, will be to make certain the beams are set deep enough and anchored firmly. Florida sand, particularly near moving water, is notoriously unstable."

"I'd be glad to pay you." When she knelt beside him, his skin prickled with sexual awareness.

Blood rushed to his cock, but he managed to stifle the groan that rose in his throat. "No pay needed. As you see, this took no more than five minutes. Besides, as I told you, my specialty is designing commercial buildings."

"From what I see, you're pretty good at designing gazebos. I'll take you up on your offer to draw this up. It's just what I've imagined having here but couldn't visualize the way you've done. Come on. The least I can do is pay you with a good meal."

He'd rather have laid her out on the fuzzy beach-colored blanket she spread over a flat spot in the clearing, but he had to admit the food looked good. Walking around her property had stimulated his appetite for food as well as for her. Zach sat cross-legged, watching Selena set out plates, cups, and plastic forks.

"Here. Can you open this?" Smiling, she handed him a bottle of wine. From the label, he recognized that it came from the Dakotah Winery, a local vineyard he'd passed by on his way here. Around its neck hung a corkscrew with a carved wooden handle in the shape of a grinning satyr.

He peeled away the outer wax covering, then started to work the corkscrew into the cork. "I drove by the winery where this came from. Don't think I've ever tasted any of their wines."

"I think you'll like it. It's made from native Florida grapes. This one's a blush."

Like the slightly pink cast to her cheeks. Zach worked out the cork, inhaling the fruity fragrance of the wine before pouring them each a glass and setting the bottle back in the split-reed picnic basket. "To you, and to this peaceful, restful place," he said, lifting his and enjoying the tangy, slightly sweet burst of flavor on his tongue.

"To you. And whatever problem brought you here for rest."

At this moment his troubles seemed far away, Selena all too near. The full skirt of her soft wraparound dress lay in enticing folds over her thighs and calves. The light fragrance she wore mingled with delicious scents of roast-beef and horseradish in the two crusty sandwiches she set out alongside fat purple grapes on brilliant yellow plastic plates that reminded him of the noonday sun.

Simple yet elegant. Like the lines of a favorite building, the picture of this day would stay with him, the variegated greens of the oak and pine leaves blending with sunlight and the warm moisture blowing in from the river on a gentle breeze. Selena sat quietly, as though a true submissive and not a pagan priestess, waiting for him to take the first bite before beginning to eat.

He plucked a grape from the cluster on his plate and held it to her lips. "Here. Take a bite."

She hesitated. "You first."

He hardened his voice, stared into those fathomless blue eyes. "Open for me," he ordered, keeping his tone gentle but compelling.

Holding her gaze, he rubbed the dark-purple sphere back and forth over lips more rose than red. Natural lips that needed no added color. "I said to take a bite," he ordered, noting a sudden realization in her eyes as he spoke to her more roughly.

Her eyelids fluttered, and her mouth opened to accept his offering. The crunch of teeth against tender skin, the burst of juice and the flick of her tongue against her lower lip to catch a droplet that escaped her mouth punctuated her slow, sensual capitulation to his order. Desire slammed into him, hard and swift, when he imagined those lips closing over his cock, taking him in, licking droplets of lubrication from his cockhead much like she savored the sweetness of the grape.

"Don't look at me unless I command it," he told her when she glanced up at him, her expression questioning.

Her gaze lowered, as though she was accustomed to taking orders—as though she welcomed his command. The thought of her, head bowed over his swollen phallus, taking pleasure in serving his needs, had him hard as stone, his testicles drawn up and aching. "Now feed one to me."

The grape, an unusually large and juicy one, glistened darkly between her dainty fingertips when she brought it to his lips. He took a bite, nipping her fingers as he did, noting the tremor that went through her at this first carnal touch. He imagined sucking grapes like these from her cunt, tasting the sweet-tangy mixture of the grapes and her succulent cream. Listening to her moan with ecstasy at his mastery.

He wouldn't have to restrain her. A word from him would have her hands raised over her head, her legs spread for his pleasure. From her manner, her look of pleased submission, he gathered it would take no special toys, no contrived threesomes, none of the trappings of a dungeon for her to find joy in submitting to his will.

But he didn't have the right. Not now, maybe never. To become her Master, then desert her when he did his duty and most likely lost his life, would be his shame. Reluctantly, he swallowed the grape she fed him, staying her hand when she reached for another. "We probably should eat the rest of our lunch before the flies get to it," he said, his tone deliberately casual.

Her soft smile warmed him, made him want to forget about lunch. Forget about everything but taking her down to the ground, sinking his fingers into her short, chestnut curls. Covering her slender body with his own and claiming her, as though it were his duty as well as his pleasure. Smiling across that blanket and restraining himself from touching her was one of the hardest things Zach recalled ever having had to do.

For the rest of the day, he stayed away from her as much as possible. But Selena's presence was everywhere he went. When he walked by the river, he heard her laughter. Her soft hum carried on the wind while she worked in her garden. He went indoors to read the paper in the parlor and smelled her fragrance lingering on the fabrics. A glimpse of her hip and shoulder, and the rustle of her clothing distracted him when she came into the kitchen and arranged cut flowers on the table. He took his dinner into his room, but when he was finishing the last of the savory stew and saw her walking down toward the river, toward her fragrant garden, he couldn't resist any longer.

After supper that evening, he weakened and followed her into the fragrant garden behind the house. Inexorably drawn, he stepped into a small rock-lined circle where she knelt as though in prayer. A crescent moon shone in the starry sky, augmenting the flickering flame of a pair of ceremonial candles.

Her gentle voice rose and fell, its soft tones mesmerizing as she cast two stones, one as black as night, the other crystal-clear, its facets reflecting the flickering light from the candles and the moon. Arms raised toward the heavens, she thanked the Moon Goddess and the Sun God for all its elements: earth, air, fire and water. And for the bountiful food that fed their bodies and their souls.

She turned, held out her hand. As her gaze met his, he felt something in her reach out and touch his mind, connect with him in a way so tactile it startled him with his intensity. "Tell me," she coaxed him. "Share your hopes and dreams and problems, and the Goddess will help me show you the way."

Zach would have resisted, but some force outside himself compelled him to unload his problems here, on this sweet witch, as though she might have some magic that would alter his dismal future. "The mob's after me," he said. "They're gunning for me because I'm set to testify next week in a case of criminal fraud down in Tampa."

"What have they done? How do you know they want to harm you?"

He didn't intend to tell her, but somehow it seemed as though it wasn't Selena he was telling but some Force far greater in that circle. Somehow that reassured him and let him go on, as if it weren't Selena's frail shoulders on which he was laying his troubles. Zach began to reveal his deepest secrets and his fears, concealing nothing, baring his soul. He found something in her faith that touched him, washed away his doubt, made him want to believe in her. In her magic.

When he fell to his knees, his head bent in supplication, she touched his cheek, her fingertips soft as a breath of spring. Worry marred her gentle features. "It will be all right," he said, not knowing if it would but unable to bear her worry. "The trial is in two days. After that time…"

I'm free. Not necessarily. Burgeoning belief warred with a lifetime of skepticism. The trial could drag out for weeks or months. And there could be repercussions. Still, he found himself believing this woman, believing he might survive. He'd concentrate on the most pleasant of possibilities. Freedom. With luck, he would be free.

He couldn't say it yet, couldn't jinx it that way, but suddenly the idea of being free to come back here, see her, gave him new purpose, a purpose oddly stronger even than his desire to survive, to live his life as he'd always lived it.

"I could look into your future," she said softly.

Logic told him she was crazy, yet he found himself believing this woman had special powers, that she might actually be able to see things hidden from most mortals' jaded gazes. "I believe you can."

Did he dare ask her to? Zach's breath caught in his throat, making speech impossible. Yes, he needed to dispel the doubt, to know what he would face next week.

"Tell me," he said, meeting her solemn gaze.

"All right. Select one of the stones. Don't think, just choose. Choose as you choose a lover, with the guidance of your heart and body, not your mind." Selena gestured toward the stones that ringed the circle where they stood.

How could he pick one from among so many? Zach's breath caught in his throat as he bent and picked one up, not consciously reasoning his selection. The stone exuded heat—not so much as to burn his palm, but more like a residual warmth from the sun that had set several hours earlier. A glow.

From her pocket, Selena extracted two more stones, one black and the other crystal clear like the ones already glistening in the center of the circle. Zach handed her the dark red cabochon garnet he had taken from the circle's edge. For a moment she held all three stones, a rapt expression on her face.

She then cast them into the center of the circle, lifted her face toward a sky of black velvet lit only by a few stars and a crescent moon. She began to chant, words he didn't understand on a conscious level, but which touched him somewhere far deeper than the surface of his brain.

Taking both of his hands, she sank to her knees within the circle, drawing him down with her. Their hands barely joined over the sparkling stones, she met his gaze with the eyes of a priestess, not the malleable woman he'd shared lunch with earlier. "Rid your mind of all thought. Dispatch your fears, your worries. Sit here with me, your mind and heart open.

With the help of the Moon Goddess, I will look deeply into your life...your future. "

They sat cross-legged, knees touching, the tips of their fingers barely making contact. "Breathe deeply," she told him, and when he did, it was as if their minds became as one, their life forces merging, generating a heat that was sexual and yet so much more. A joining of minds and hearts and bodies like nothing Zach had ever imagined, let alone experienced.

What a profound connection! Selena had performed this ritual before, reached into others' minds, but not like this. It was as though all the *chakras* opened, flooding her with his very being. His hopes, his fears...his future, mingled with hers as only the essences of true soulmates could.

The stones glittered in the moonlight, their colors muted, then bright as though the Moon Goddess beamed all Her light within the magic circle. Selena blinked, and the picture cleared.

What did she see? Success or failure, life or death? A future...or a void? She knew Zach wanted to know, for his pulse throbbed and a shudder tore through his body, despite the subtropical warmth of the night. Candles on the altar flickered, casting his handsome face in shadow, revealing the horror in his expression.

Horror she knew mirrored her own, now that she saw clearly. "Someone will try again to kill you, Zachary Lang," she told him, the words wrenched painfully from somewhere deep within her. Somewhere full of pain. Of horror at what she saw.

If Zach hadn't believed before that Selena possessed special powers, he'd have believed it when she spoke his real name.

Desperately Zach wished he could deny what she'd said, but he'd seen it, too, knew it was true. He rose and left the circle, unwilling to involve Selena further, fearing he would place her in danger along with him. Without a doubt, he knew now that Selena felt that instant attraction that had struck him the moment he'd seen her along the riverbank the day before. She couldn't not care for him, yet become so horrified at one glance into his troubled destiny.

Unable to walk away, he turned to her one last time. When she stepped forward, her face full of compassion, he held up his hand. "I'm not going to involve you in this Selena," he said, deliberately making his voice sound hard, resolute. "I want you. But I can't risk having you."

What irony. It seemed he might have found a soulmate only days before his enemies would try to cruelly wrench his soul from his body. A soulmate he dared not claim.

* * * * *

Late that night Selena tossed and turned. The usually relaxing pale blue walls and sheer curtains over French doors leading to the balcony seemed forbidding, the moon making eerie patterns much like a macabre dance. Her canopied bed, normally her nocturnal refuge, suddenly reminded her of prison bars. The top sheet tangled around her, catching her flailing limbs and immobilizing them. Failing to stop the troubling, tumbling visions that plagued her, the sweat-dampened bed linen held her as though it were a shroud. Visions not unlike those she'd seen with Zach in the magic circle, yet more vivid. More terrifying.

Though torn asunder by what she had seen, she dared not scream. Her heart pounded in her chest, and her blood ran cold. Zach lay in a pool of blood, deathly still, while two laughing gargoyles stood over him, the acrid smoke from their dull black pistols scalding her nostrils. The metallic smell of blood surrounded her, making her gasp for breath. Screams of a terrified bystander filled her ears, the sounds reverberating in her ears as if the scene were happening live, and not a hideous nightmare.

Fighting her way out of the covers' grip, she stumbled from the bed. The open dormer window lured her, with its panoramic view of the night sky. Golden light twinkling in a velvet night beckoned. She needed light, demanded release from the terrifying vision that still held her in its grip.

Ignoring the chintz-upholstered window seat, she sank to her knees and stared through the wavy old glass panes. Usually moonlight calmed her, but not tonight. Not while a vision of Zach's murder lay indelibly inked onto her mind. Her knees ached, and her temples throbbed.

Selena had experienced visions before. Visions that had later become reality. But she'd never before witnessed death. She'd never seen cold-blooded murder in her mind.

As he'd stripped his secrets away in the sacred circle, Zach had revealed himself to be the man she'd prayed for to the Goddess. The soulmate with whom she was destined to spend the rest of her life. The emotions he evoked in her were as real as Zach himself. But the danger Zach faced was real, too. Graphically real. The men who wanted him dead would be going on trial in Tampa next week.

Though she realized the ways of the Deities were beyond her understanding, she'd seen enough of the way the cycles of the world worked to know the Lord and Lady's purposes were always true. Still, Selena couldn't help asking the silvery Moon Goddess in the jet-black sky why She'd brought a soulmate for Selena to love for a few short days, only to snatch him cruelly from her arms.

She couldn't beg him to stay with her, to keep safe in her isolated world. Honor demanded he must testify or lose his soul. When he did, he could easily lose his life. The vision she had just seen foretold that he would die, in graphic, horrifying detail.

But maybe that vision had been flawed. After all, she hadn't been within the magic circle, either this one where she worked with guests or the sacred circle her grandparents had built near the river, the one she'd shared with no one but her Master. She hadn't called upon the Goddess or cast the stones. Her mind had been playing tricks on her. It had to have been only a cruel twist of her mind, brought on by her fear for Zach and what he had to do.

That was right. It had to be. Selena had never had a vision before, except within the magic circle. She'd go there, enlist the Goddess's wisdom. The fates willing, she'd learn that what she'd just seen was no more than an aberration. Quietly, so as not to wake him, she slipped from the house.

Alone and naked in the darkness, with the moon and stars lighting a velvet sky and Spanish moss-draped oak limbs swaying in a chilly breeze, she knelt in the circle. Very carefully she murmured entreaties to the Goddess, casting the stones again and again until she saw the Sun God beginning to light the eastern sky.

Each time she cast the stones, she saw tragedy. Death. Dark, disturbing emotions thankfully mingled with a few rays of light. Why could Zach's future not be as bright as the sun, as carefree as the meandering river?

She watched the sun creeping slowly toward its zenith, determined to use every magical power she might possess to battle the evil forces bent on destroying the man she loved. She would leave this refuge from a doubting world, go with Zach. Grasping the obsidian in her hand, she squeezed it as though she might obviate its dire predictions, choke its evil power by force of will. Then she rubbed it against the quartz crystal and the garnet before she laid all three stones in a row along the circle's edge.

Propelled by forces outside herself, Selena slipped back to her room, removed the jewelry that had belonged to her Master, and donned a gossamer robe the color of the sunset. Down the stairs, past two empty bedrooms, she crept as quietly as a thief to the door of the room that had belonged first to her great-grandparents, later to each new generation, until every member of the Cross family but Selena herself had died.

A gentle breeze ruffled sheer curtains that filtered the light from a rapidly rising sun. Selena stopped beside the oak four-poster bed where she'd been conceived and watched Zach toss restlessly in his sleep. She imagined he was nude beneath the soft, old sheet that twisted around his torso and wondered if the dark hair on his long, muscular legs would feel as soft against her skin as it looked.

Dropping her robe to the wide planked, highly polished floor, she crawled into bed behind him and began to stroke him through the top sheet.

Muttering in his sleep, he flung himself away from her, on his side. Selena slid her hands up and down his damp back, soothing him. He felt good beneath her fingers, all hard, lean angles and satin-smooth skin. When finally he lay passive under her seeking hands, she slipped beneath the sheet, daring more. His heart beat slowly under her fingers when she tangled them in his silky chest hair in her search for the small flat nipples that hardened immediately at her touch. He sighed, inching closer until his firm buttocks rested in the cradle of her hips.

Danger. She felt it in every beat of his heart, each sigh that accompanied her brazen exploration of his upper torso. She wanted to feel his weight bearing her into the mattress, his legs forcing hers apart to make room for him. She wanted to feel his penis throbbing inside her vagina, stretching and filling her and driving away her fear.

Still half asleep, Zach rolled over.

He opened his eyes to a vision—a vision of Selena that had never been far from the forefront of his mind since he first saw her watching the river flowing lazily toward the Gulf. It was as if his subconscious knew he was coming here all along, not for his safety but for his soulmate, for there was no denying what they'd felt in the circle when they'd sat together, their spirits merging. He reached out and touched her pale, full breast, expecting another disappointment but finding warm, real woman instead. Her nipple hardened, and her cheeks took on a rosy glow.

"I want you, Zach," she told him, her tone so quiet he thought he only imagined what she said.

She caressed him with gentle hands, trailed fleeting kisses and love-bites along his chest and neck until she found his lips. The reality beat the dream all to hell. When she parted her soft lips over his, desire slammed into him.

He wanted her, too, more than he'd ever wanted another woman. Her touch, the sweet scent of her, the salty taste of dried tears on her flushed cheeks, even the escalating pace of her breathing banished thought and left him only with feelings.

More than he needed to survive, he needed to be close to another human being. Close to Selena. Fear of the ordeal that lay ahead became nothing but a fading memory.

White-hot desire threatened to turn him into a ravening beast. His cock throbbed. His balls ached. He couldn't remember ever having wanted a woman so much. Couldn't recall ever having needed so much to take one, claim her. Mark her as his own.

He dragged her hard against him, desperate to release the pent-up fever inside him, wanting nothing more than to crawl inside her soft, fragrant skin and feast on her bounty. To feel her submission, see to her pleasure.

Though every cell in his body screamed to take her hard and fast and now, he gentled his touch, tracing the gentle curve of her spine, cupping her ass cheeks, kneading them, insinuating a finger between them and ringing her rear entrance. Her sigh, and the slight shifting of her legs to give him room to penetrate her there, bespoke her willingness to let him lead, to follow him on whatever of passion's pathways he might choose.

He'd take her there, and feed her his cock. Fuck her every way that brought pleasure to a man and woman. But not now. Now he had to claim her, pump out his life into her womb where it might take root, create his own immortality and hers, mingled in a way he'd never wanted before. A way he'd never expected to want. Cursing the necessity for it, he pulled away and put on a condom.

"Lie on your back and spread your legs for me," he ordered hoarsely when he stroked her satiny folds and found them wet and welcoming. That she did, without hesitation, got him hotter and harder than he recalled ever having been. So hot he damn near lost it when he thrust home in one smooth motion and felt her tight pussy clench him like a fist.

He hadn't lost control that way for years, since leaving his teens behind. Fighting the urge to come, he stayed still inside her, savoring the way her cunt milked him, its rhythmic welcome strangely soothing—incredibly arousing. "Are you all right?" he asked when she shuddered beneath him.

"Yes." There was wonder in her voice, as though awestruck by the power of the emotions that accompanied their joining. He began to move. Slowly, to prolong the exquisite agony of wanting, then harder, faster as she lifted her hips to meet each thrust. The sting of her teeth on his shoulder, the way she wrapped her legs around his waist as though to draw him deeper and consume him, brought him quickly to the edge.

The pressure built inside him, and then he started to come, his semen leaving his body in scalding spurts. Every whimper she made against his neck, each milking contraction of her tight, wet cunt around his cock, the pleasure-pain that stung his shoulders each time she dug her nails into his flesh— all triggered more fiery bursts of semen until she finally wrung him dry. A triumphant shout left his throat, mingling with her little whimpers and cries.

Afterward she cradled him in her arms, her warm, giving presence chasing away the shadows that threatened this perfect moment. Two days. He'd embrace them, embrace her, banish the coming ordeal from his mind…

And pray he'd survive to come back to her, pursue a life of peace and pleasure where he no longer needed to watch his back. Where he'd finally be free to offer her a future.

She had the makings of a submissive nature, but was that a momentary thing, or would she embrace the life he wanted with a mate? Feeling her in his arms, he knew it didn't matter. If they were destined together, in a Master-slave union or a plain vanilla future, he wanted her. Just her.

The next two days would be their utopia. He'd allow nothing to mar it but the certainty that it would end.

* * * * *

"How many other guests are you expecting this weekend?" Zach asked Selena later that morning when he found her setting down the phone.

"None now. The two couples who were driving down from Atlanta rescheduled their visit—one of the wives has just had an emergency appendectomy."

She looked adorable in shorts and a simple top, her cap of curls glistening wet from the shower she must have taken while he took his. Zach bent and nibbled her ear, then said, "How about keeping this weekend private, just for us?"

"I'd like that."

"Good. So what do we do?"

For a moment she was quiet, as though considering. "Zach. Would you be willing…interested…in what I do here? The more intimate rituals?"

"Sex magic?" He raised a brow, gave her a half smile. "I'd be glad to make some with you." At her serious expression, he lifted a shoulder. "Selena, I don't know much about it, but I'm willing to listen. I'm a sexual Dominant, which is an alternate path of its own. Just as I know nothing about communing with your Goddess, I'm sure you know little if anything about the lifestyle I've lived for nearly fifteen years."

When she looked up at him, he saw tears sparkling in her eyes. "You're so very wrong. Wait. I need to show you something, but first…" She bounded out of the room, leaving him to wonder…anticipate. In moments she returned, a sky-blue hooded cloak flowing softly around her graceful body. Tugging at his hand, she pulled him toward patio doors that faced the riverbank.

* * * * *

"Once I had a Master, as the Moon Goddess has her Sun God. Together we made sex magic in our special private circle where only I have been these eight long years. I'd take you there now, share with you what I've only shared with Him."

"What tore you apart?"

"Death." A shadow crossed Selena's expressive face, but only for a moment before she turned to Zach and smiled. "Before you arrived, I came here and made magic on my own. Sex magic. I purified my body and my soul, and called upon the Sun God and the Moon Goddess to free my memory and let me love again. To send me a new Master, a new soulmate, a new partner with whom to make the most powerful sex magic of all."

Before he could stop her, she led him behind her into a circle rimmed with hawthorn bushes in full bloom, painstakingly paved with native stone, its inner area lush with bright-green spring grass. A circle centered with a carved stone bench whose indentations could only be a woman's graceful curves set in relief. The huge cocks of two satyrs held up either end. One satyr's arms were crossed in front of him, at the perfect height for a sub to rest her head, while the other had arms outstretched to hold the woman's knees draped over his bent elbows. He couldn't help noticing the boulder next to the bench, or the pentagonal niche carved into it.

"I cannot be your Master. Not now." Not while, for all he knew, this day might be his last on Earth. Still, his hands went to his belt as he imagined lashing her to the incredibly erotic fucking chair...claiming her and giving her the pleasure she so obviously expected.

"But I can be your slave." Slipping her hands into her pockets, Selena pulled out several leather strips, a soft flogger, and assorted tools of their lifestyle, placing them with unusual care within the indentation carved into that large round stone. "For today, for as long as you're here, we can make beautiful magic together. Magic I promise you'll remember when you've gone back to your ordinary life."

He looked at her steadily, took a step closer. Suddenly, where she'd been taking the initiative, pulling him into the circle, now he was in charge. He had no doubt she could tell, in the way his gaze met hers, in his body language. "No," he said softly. "If I am your Master, I am your Master forever, Selena. Not just for today. But I cannot take that step now, because my forever may end very soon, and that isn't fair to you."

She shrugged out of her robe and knelt at his feet, taking his hand between her much smaller ones. "Time is different to the God and Goddess. If my forever with my new Master is only a day, then that is the time given to us. I'd take that time, however short it may be. I accept you, Master. I beg You to take and accept me."

"Surely you understand. You saw it yourself, in the magic circle. Once I go back to testify, I'm as good as dead."

"Then live for now. Celebrate life, however fleeting it may be. Take me. Please."

How could he refuse her what she obviously wanted so much? How could he deny her what he wanted more than anything to give? He couldn't. Too struck emotionally by the depth of her desire to speak, he nodded.

Selena stood before him, sprinkling what looked like salt granules around the circle. A sunburst tattoo on her belly, visible clearly now where before it had been obscured by darkness, surrounded a smooth translucent moonstone in her navel. Fascinating. He'd never thought of tattoos as erotic, but hers was. Almost as arousing as the golden sunburst nipple shields with their paired slender chains that dangled between her beautiful, full breasts.

"If it pleases my Master, come to me and make magic. Sex magic."

Zach's mouth went dry. His balls drew up close to his body, and blood surged into his cock. His gaze settled at the juncture of Selena's thighs whose satiny surfaces beckoned his fingertips, his tongue. Without his conscious direction, his hands went to his shirt buttons and opened them one by one. The sun seared his naked chest, encouraged him to bare himself completely in the sylvan glade, to Selena's gaze and those of her gods and goddesses.

"I can't resist a goddess's call." Only a dead man could, and Zach was still very much alive. "Your safe word will be—" He looked around, saw the white flowers of the hawthorns that rimmed the circle. "—snowfall."

"I need no safe word, Master. But we must look into each other's eyes to make magic." When she held out both hands to him, he felt her heated gaze on every cell of his body, although she looked directly into his eyes. "I have the feeling you're a natural—that you'll take to this with only the barest hint of instruction."

Zach wasn't so sure. All he knew was that he wanted to get Selena on that fucking chair and claim her. Still...something made him squeeze her hands and curb that instinct for the moment. "You may tell me what I need to know."

"All right. You're facing East, toward Air. The mind. The metaphysical principles of life itself. Now I face West, toward Water, the element of psychic healing. Water represents the soul, the emotions, the principle of Love." She raised both hands, then straightened her right arm and pointed north. "In the north is Earth, foundation of the other three. Earth represents the physical body, the principles of Law."

"And in the South?" Zach asked, his gaze unwavering as he looked into her clear blue eyes. "Is that where I'll find Fire?"

"South is where I'll find Fire in You. A Master's fire. Fire is the element of transformation, passion, change, success, and health. When we make magic, You'll find Your ground in me, for that's the way the Sun God ordered the bench be placed."

Zach pictured her, lashed to that chair, her cunt glistening slippery wet, a quivering stamen within the creamy petals of her labia, her eyes on him, her lips open but silent. Waiting. Anticipating what he'd do to assuage her longing, feed the passion in her until it burst into Fire's hottest flames. His cock was already burning. "I've had enough of a lesson for now. Take your place on the chair," he ordered, selecting the five supple leather strips from one corner of the pentagon and clutching them in one hand.

She straddled the bench and rested her head in the satyr's outstretched hands. Her white throat was bared, vulnerable. She tempted him to taste it as she murmured imprecations to an unseen god or goddess. Gently, for he didn't want to hurt her, he threaded the first leather strip through an iron ring embedded in the satyr's wrists and wrapped it twice around her neck, bending to lave her there with his tongue before securing the bond with a simple slip knot.

One strip bound her wrists together, and another secured them to the ring in the satyr's nose. One at a time, he lifted her long, slender legs over the other satyr's outstretched arms, positioning them so as to open her cunt for his pleasure before securing them and bending to lap at the copious cream gathering in the cradle of her thighs.

"Oh yes, Master." The hunger in her eyes fed his own need as much as the arousing smell of sex, the glistening proof of her arousal.

The sun's warmth invaded his body, like the sunburst etched above her womb. It filled him with the need to possess, to conquer, but most of all to surrender to her Sun God. Worship the Moon Goddess he saw in her. Make magic and assuage the need to connect with another human being, to escape the uncertainty of his future.

Five. That seemed to be a magic number in this ritual she'd begun. Zach looked at the objects in the pentagram and chose at random. The flogger had seen much use, he thought, rubbing its carved handle as he looked at the soft doeskin strips and a single braided strand of thicker leather. Supple. Like the woman who said she wanted to become his sex slave. Testing her sensitivity, he ran the knotted ends over her cheek, down her body, across her lush, exposed mound and over the glistening folds that surrounded her cunt, around the inviting entrance to her ass. When her clit grew instantly hard at the feathery touch of the lash, his own cock rose rigid and pulsating against his belly. Hungering. Demanding its home within her mouth, her cunt, her ass.

Her tongue darted out between full lips now dark-rose and wet from the abrasion of her own teeth. She watched him while he laid the flogger blindly onto the rock, closing his hand seconds later around a good-size butt plug. As though she knew his intent, welcomed it, she shifted the angle of her hips on the chair, giving him better access to her rear passage. Moistening it first with her cunt-cream, he worked it slowly up her ass until its base rested against her body, and the rim of the fucking bench, which held it firm when she slid back into her original position.

Her breathy whimpers when he tugged at the chain between her breasts, the way she moistened her lips again as though inviting him there, summoned him as surely as if she were one of the sirens of ancient lore. Straddling her, he fed her his cock, a little at first, then more as he pressed deeper. Her convulsive swallowing motions milked him, made him desperate...

But no. From the East came tiny winged creatures floating on a cooling breeze, invading his mind as he invaded his lover's body. "What the…" He drew back, startled.

"They're elementals. Sylphs and Undines. Sylphs represent life. Communication. Undines personify love." Her tone was breathless, her look needy until he stepped forward, fed her his cock again.

The rippling of water nearby—he didn't think it was the river, but more likely a bubbling spring—calmed him, slowed his raging hunger and allowed him to look into her eyes as she sucked his cock. Now he was beginning to understand the magic. He was Fire to her Earth, nourished by Air and Water. Slowly he withdrew when he felt his climax building in his balls, shuddering when she dipped her tongue into the slit at the tip of his cock, still cradling her face between his trembling hands.

"Take the athame," she said, her voice urgent. "The knife."

"You want me to cut your bonds?" Experienced subs didn't beg to be set free, but maybe—

"N-no. Send the Sylphs and the Undines away. The time for communication and emotion is past. It's time to feed Earth. The physical body. Time to feed it with Your Fire."

Zach reached for the elaborately carved knife.

"Point the tip to the East to banish Air's Sylphs, then to the West to send the Undines on their way." When he lifted the knife, she shook her head as much as the lash allowed, her expression suffused with desire, showing him he'd distracted her sufficiently that she'd forgotten part of the instruction. "First thank each of them for their blessing and protection before you tell them goodbye."

The tiny winged creatures that were Air darted about them until Zach muttered thanks and farewell. Then, when he pointed the athame to the East, they flew away.

Tiny seahorses now danced before his eyes, apparently emboldened with the disappearance of the Sylphs with their pounding wings. "They represent the soul…and Love of the spirit more than the body. Thank you, Undines, for the emotions you bring to us," Selena murmured, her breath wet and warm on his throbbing cock.

"Thank you, and farewell," he said, pointing the ceremonial knife westward.

"Now we are alone, Earth and Fire. May You find a Master's pleasure in me. May You fill me with Yourself, sear me with Your fire, find a Master's peace within my body."

Moved by her words, Zach became even more intensely aroused. His cock rose against his belly, rock-hard and insistent. He reared back, positioned himself, and felt their juices mingling, her slick honey with the lubrication that oozed from his slit. Caught up in the magic he was only beginning to understand, Zach hovered over Selena, his eyes locked with hers for long moments. He positioned himself. Their juices mingled, her slick honey with the pre-come that oozed from his slit. He looked down at her, his woman, and he made sure her gaze was locked with his as he sank his cock inch by inch into her ripe cunt. She felt fertile. Warm and nurturing, as Earth should be.

A great sigh ripped itself from his throat at the depth of emotion inherent in this simple act of fucking. Emotion he'd never felt half as strongly before.

She was incredibly tight. Not only her cunt. Stretched by his cock and the butt plug, she throbbed around him as he moved inside her. Deep. She sucked him so deep he felt her womb. She squeezed his flesh as he withdrew, as though she didn't want to let him go. Heat flowed between them, Earth and Fire; the moonstone in her navel scorched his belly when he stretched out atop her, and the golden shields around her nipples warmed his fingers when he paused to stroke the tight, hardened nubs that jutted out from them while on his journey to fill her mouth with his own. Then he took his tongue and sucked it deep, as if it were another cock. Her taut little nipples bored into his chest. With every stroke of his cock into her cunt, she milked him as though to seize his fire and take it into herself. His balls tightened as she writhed beneath him, every cell in her body apparently focused on giving her Master pleasure. Just as he held back now to prolong hers. Protect her from the raging inferno within him that screamed to be set free.

Balancing himself on one elbow, he reached between them and stroked her clit. Once, twice, three times—before she erupted into a quivering mass beneath him, a willing receptacle for his seed. He was coming…but the Sun God help him, now wasn't the time.

It was the hardest thing he'd ever done, pulling out and spewing his Fire over the sunburst on Selena's belly. He kept up the manipulation of her clit, watching her writhe in the full measure of her orgasm to the very end.

Moments later, he bent to kiss the tears from her eyes. "Don't cry, my love."

"You denied me Your seed."

It tightened the fist around his heart and his groin, the plaintive need in her voice, the want in her eyes. Why had he been given such a gift when he might lose it in less than twenty-four hours? "I won't risk giving you a child to bring up without a father. I can't allow you to assume that burden alone."

"But I'd take the risk. I'd—"

"Hush," he said firmly, framing her face, letting her see the command in his eyes, stilling her with his mastery. "If I get through this testimony with my skin intact, I'll apply myself to the task of creating another little witch or warlock for us to love."

She stared up at him, those blue eyes like the eyes of the Goddess herself, but her voice when she spoke trembled as a mortal woman's would, every syllable in her voice speaking her love. "I will hold you to that, Master."

Chapter Three
ഇ

"Wrap your legs around my waist and tell me about yourself," Zach commanded.

He and Selena soaked in the cool, refreshing waters of the spring. The seductive way He played with the chains that connected her now-chilled nipple shields, and the feel of His huge, hard cock seeking entrance to her cunt, kept her from being cold despite the seventy-two-degree springwater that bubbled up all around them.

"Eight years ago I threw my old Master's collar into this spring. I wanted to sink down with it, to never come up again." She passed the palms of her hand over the water, gazing down at the depths until Zach put His hand under her chin, guided her face back to His. She laid her hands on His broad shoulders, felt the wet muscle and life beneath her touch. "I never thought I'd make magic with a soulmate again. Until I saw you walk toward me."

Zach was her soulmate, as certainly as her old Master had been. She'd felt it when He'd demanded her surrender and she'd wanted nothing more than to comply. To be His willing vessel, as the Moon was the willing familiar of the Sun. She threw her head back, sucked in a pleased gasp as He dug His fingers into her short hair, held her still as He seated His cock to the hilt inside her willing pussy.

"Tell me more," He ordered in a low voice.

"I..." She bit her lip, managed a smile. "...I was born on the Suwannee, have lived here all my life. I follow my grandfather's footsteps with my rituals, my old Master's teachings as to how sex slavery should be. Sex magic is a natural expression of a Master's dominance, a slave's submission.

"Did You not feel it?" she murmured, holding onto Him. "The merging of Earth with Fire when our climaxes came? Did You not feel closer to the Forces that order our lives?" Just the memory of His fire consuming her, merging them, had her cunt spasming now around the hot column of Zach's cock. "Did you not feel our spirits merge?"

Her muscles clenched around Him as He pressed His teeth gently to her throat. She was suffused with joy at the truth of it, the impact of her own words sinking in.

Zach raised His head, and she could tell His worries were coming back to His mind, for she saw the shift in His expression, that attempt to disguise His concern for what was to be…or not, behind a casual mask. "I felt the most mindblowing orgasm I've ever had, that's for certain." He tugged playfully on her nipple shields, making her nipples harden and swell against the barbells that held the shields in place. "I'm afraid I'm only a man, with a man's one-track mind. I wasn't thinking of merging forces when I started coming. Wasn't thinking at all. I liked it, though. Could get used to doing my fucking with the gods and goddesses orchestrating the action." He bent His head and nibbled on her earlobe. "I can't explain it, but I felt our spirits merge long before we performed sex magic. I sensed it happening when I first saw you along the riverbank."

He raised His head, drove His hips more firmly against her, earning another gasp from her lips as He made her feel His hard need. "My idea of dominance is obedience. I'd have you bow to my will without needing to restrain you. Pleasure me as I pleasure you. I'd mark you mine, if I had the right."

"You have the right," she said softly, her expression as open to Him as her body. "But I understand why you won't…now. I will be here, Zach. Master. And I can help you. If you believe, we can make good things happen."

* * * * *

Selena couldn't possibly know how much Zach wanted to believe that, how strongly he wanted to embrace her belief in magic, in the balance of the Elements. No one could possibly know how much he wanted to survive, to learn the mysteries of Nature with his loving slave.

He squeezed her hand as they walked through the woods early the following morning, with her pointing out each tree, each flower, every animal that crossed their path. It seemed in Nature there was perfect balance—balance that evil humors had skewed in him. "Because of you, I want to believe. More than anything I've ever desired, I want to go on living. For you. For us."

She spied a pinecone in their path, stopped to pick it up and sniff its pungent aroma. "Like the birds, the pine tree represents Air. Wind flows through its slender needles, bends it to and fro according to its fickle will. Look overhead. A blue jay's nesting in the first limb of the tree."

Inspiration, persuasion, perception...Zach mentally enumerated the values Selena had said belonged to Air. "Friendship," he said, leaning down to brush his lips across her cheek. "That's the most important thing I've found with you, a facet of a relationship I've never before discovered in my submissives."

"You've brought me love. Friendship, too. But mostly love and the Influence of a Master to make me whole. Look. Years ago, my grandfather planted that gardenia beside the little pond. Gardenias symbolize Water."

The sweet perfume of waxy white flowers lay heavy in the still air, tickled Zach's nose. It mingled with the pungent aroma of Earth renewing itself, fed with Air and Water and the Fire of the Sun God. Here the Elements found perfect balance in Nature, a balance undisturbed by his and Selena's benevolent intrusion.

Suddenly a sense of peace flowed over him. What would be, would be. Every cell in his body thrummed with life...with love...with desire to master his woman once again. He stripped off his clothes, toeing off his deck shoes before stepping out of his shorts and boxers.

"Undress. Be one with me, one with Nature. Brace yourself against that willow tree," he ordered as soon as she was naked. "Tell me how the smooth bark feels against your naked ass, then select the branch you'd like me to use to warm your pretty cunt for me."

The eagerness with which she complied fed his own desire, even before she spoke. "The bark feels cool. Like satin. Rigid, like the whip You used to warm me yesterday." Her eyes sparkled playfully, but her words flowed over him like nectar from the gods as she broke off a limber branch from the tree, murmuring her apology—and her thanks to the tree for its sacrifice. "The tree gives its arm to You, Master. Use it as You will."

Flexible, soft with its furry blossoms, the willow branch lay in Zach's hand, as though waiting...waiting to caress Selena's silken mound, her ripe breasts. The sunburst another Master had imprinted on her belly.

Gently, he traced around the hardened nubs of her nipples with the tip of the branch, then laid a few light strokes of the limber branch over her tattooed belly. He traced around the hardened nubs of her nipples with the tip of the branch. Watching the anticipation in her face and the restless movement of her body against the tree communicating her eagerness, he drew out both their pleasure by teasing her with the tip until she was panting. Then he flicked his wrist, slapped her tattooed belly with the whip-like branch. Several strokes, enough to send shudders through her body, ripple the sun tattoo.

Another Master had marked her. If the gods permitted him to live, he'd stake his claim from the inside, fill her with his seed. Zach bent, tracing around the glowing moonstone in her navel with his tongue, then moving lower to taste the glistening folds that hid her clit, her cunt.

Her little whimpers aroused him almost as much as the taste and smell of her honey that would soon ease his way to heaven. Voracious, he sucked her rigid little clit between his teeth and flailed it with his tongue. Oh, yes. He'd mark her here, adorn her where no other Master had. He imagined a slim gold band suspended from this incredibly sensitive nub, a band known and seen only by him—and the gods and goddesses she revered. A slim gold band with no beginning and no end, put there by him to enhance her response to his teeth and tongue and hands.

When she let out a shrill, ecstatic scream, he stood, positioned his cock at the hot, swollen entrance to her cunt, and plunged inside, lifting her off the ground, pinioning her between his pistoning body and the tree that had given of itself to feed their pleasure.

He took her mouth as he took her cunt, roughly, possessively, with no quarter given and none asked for. She sucked his tongue, mated it with her own. Her breath blew hot and heavy against his cheek, as his did on her. He fucked her harder, deeper, not letting up until her vaginal walls convulsed around his cock, coaxing out his precious seed. His essence. His lust and his love, all for his precious witch-woman slave.

It was hours later, as the sun set in the western sky and his time to leave drew nearer, that Zach's newly found hope began to waver.

* * * * *

That night they stood in the magic circle facing each other, not touching, connected only by gazes fixed upon each other's eyes. Selena sensed Zach's fading resolve, prayed to the Moon Goddess that she could help Him restore it for His coming ordeal. "Take me, Master. Take my psychic powers and make them Your own," she murmured, holding out her hands in supplication.

When He hesitated, telling her He didn't trust in the power of the Deities to empower her to do His bidding, she turned to the altar, using smoldering lavender scented incense to light two exquisitely crafted candles: one a blue lotus, the other a creamy gardenia just bursting into fragrant bloom. "Aphrodite, goddess of all things mystical, take my puny offerings, imbue me with your wisdom and with the power to transfer it to my Master. Join with Hermes to bring Him heightened awareness that he may survive those who wish Him dead." Selena paused, swallowing the lump of fear that threatened to choke her words.

Closing her eyes tightly, she began to meditate, waiting for the Goddess's power to enter her body. Her senses opened, enhancing her awareness of the world her great-grandparents had created here, the world she herself had enhanced with her own touches and magic. Every tree and flower, every bush, all of Nature's creatures together formed her home, her sanctuary. The circle of protection that had kept her safe...until now.

The protections she had on her home were a gentle illusion magic that simply distracted the thoughts of someone with malicious intent so that they forgot why they intended harm toward her or her home. But someone with a focused evil, a bent toward true violence...the wards would not stop them. They would warn her, though. The intrusion was a black ink stain invading her consciousness, a coldness that gripped her vitals and brought her surging to her feet.

"Someone is here," she said.

A fierce howl pierced the silence. A bobcat? Selena felt Zach's pulse racing, heard His sharp inhalation. Her own heart pounded in her chest, a hard, fast cadence that seemed to match muffled sounds of footsteps from far away, coming closer. Growing louder. The short hairs on the back of her neck prickled.

"Go into the house, Selena." Though soft, Zach's tone made it clear He'd issued an order, not a request.

An order she dared not obey. "I can stop them. Shield you. Don't ask me to desert you now. Please, Master."

She had to stop the intruder. Had to save her Master. Calling on every Deity with whom she could communicate, Selena closed her eyes, gave free rein to her other senses...her intellect...her faith. As though her touch might shield Him from harm, she clutched His hand.

Flames flickered beneath her eyelids, red-orange tongues that scorched her soul. An enemy lurked, one with Fire's passion to do evil, Fire's energy and power to achieve his goal. Zach had chosen the garnet, harbinger of His passion...but she knew now it also could be used as the symbol of a destructive power, His mortal enemy.

The wind strengthened, rustling the leaves of the massive oaks, coaxing limber branches of the willow trees into a macabre dance. The candles flickered, and for a moment she panicked. Could Zach's enemies be stronger than she or worse, could it be the Lord and Lady's intent that Zach be taken from her?

"Go in the house, I said." Zach grasped her forearm.

Though it tore at her heart to defy Him, she pulled away. "You need me here. I will stay."

As if some Higher Power had grabbed Him, He stepped back, His gaze steady on her, muscles taut for the impending action. "No time to fight you now. Take care, my love."

Fight Fire with Earth. Compelled by the goddess Demeter, Selena lifted a shield and pentacle from the altar, experienced a strength and patience — and new resolve to do what it took to save her Master, even if that meant disobeying Him.

She closed her eyes, allowed her intuition to lead her. Turning toward the aura of the intruders, she opened them again. Two men burst from the woods, their intent as obvious from the hard focus of their eyes on Zach as the automatics they carried at ready in their hands. Heedless of Nature, they trampled the fragrant herbs that had sprung up between the pavers that ringed the circle. Raising the oaken shield and clasping the pentacle close to her heart, she called upon Dionysus to help her destroy those who'd invaded her sanctuary. To give her the strength and courage to protect her Master, that He might survive to punish her for her willful disobedience of His command.

Zach rose, as though to protect her with His own body. Shots rang out, one shattering the altar and sending ceremonial candles tumbling to the ground, another slamming into the dirt at Selena's feet. A third volley shattered the brief, eerie silence.

They were doomed. None of her entreaties to the Deities had stopped the attackers. Desperate, Selena heaved the shield toward them. A bullet ripped through it, spinning it like dust in a tornado, propelling it…straight at the head of the bigger, meaner looking intruder. He went down like a boulder tumbling down a slope, his gun clattering to the stone-paved circle where he'd stood.

Zach leaped forward when the one man went down, launched Himself toward the other. He drove His shoulder hard into the man's generous belly. Though the man staggered under the onslaught, he soon regained his footing. Like an enraged bull, he plowed into Zach. Zach shoved him back against an oak tree. For a moment he gave way, and Zach almost got his gun. Almost. Not even Zach's pounding his gun arm into the tree worked to dislodge the pistol from his meaty hand.

Selena scrambled for the weapon of the man she'd felled with her shield. *Goddess help me. Give me strength to save my Master. Go on. Pick that up and use it.* Her movement wooden, she curled her fingers around that snub-nosed, lethal looking piece of blue steel. Zach grunted as the second man broke free from His iron grip.

The gun felt heavy in her hand. She couldn't do this. She must. Demeter took possession of her, and she raised the gun. She must stop this, whatever way she could, before a good man died. Zach. Her Master. Steadying the cold steel barrel with her other hand, she willed herself to stop shaking, do what she had to do.

Zach's remaining assailant had knocked Him to the ground. "All right, asshole, you're fuckin' hard to kill but it's gonna happen now. I'm gonna splatter your brains all over your lady friend's weird little temple, and then I'm gonna kill her, too. Maybe have some fun with—" Suddenly the man slumped over, fell across Zach's chest. His gun dropped from his suddenly helpless hand a split-second before hers hit the ground.

"What the hell?" Zach's breathing came hard, as though the goon had knocked the wind from His lungs. Without success, He tried to shove off the guy's dead weight. "Look over there," He croaked.

In the distance her mind registered that the grandfather clock inside had just rung twelve times. Midnight, the hour of Earth. Selena followed Zach's gaze until she saw what had put that shocked tone in His voice. Near, but well outside the sacred circle, a huge brownish-red bull pawed at the ground, his eyes gleaming red, his breath steaming in the cool night air.

The Lord and Lady had served Selena well. When she calmed herself sufficiently to shove the last man's unconscious bulk off Zach, she saw it: two large, deep indentations in his back that no doubt matched the bull's front hooves. Zach scrambled to His feet, still breathless, and eyed His two assailants, both laid out as if by magic. Bending, He picked up both guns and laid them on the altar.

"Are you all right?"

Unsure at first until she looked down at herself and saw no evidence otherwise, Selena nodded. "I'm fine. How about You?"

"I'll live. Obey me now, as you should have done before. Go in the house and call the police. Where can I find rope to tie them up?" He asked, gesturing toward the two unconscious men.

"Over there. In the shed behind the house. I'll bring it to You after I call Sheriff Soames."

"All right. Hurry, though. I've got a feeling it will be easier to tie them up before they come to."

When Selena looked over where the bull had stood, he was gone. Vanished, as if he'd never been there at all. Thunder rolled from someplace far away, as though Thor had seen and approved the magic she'd made tonight.

Quickly, she made her way into the house, called the sheriff's office, and grabbed clothes for herself and Zach. On the way back, she stopped and got several packages of the rope she used to tie up her tomato plants.

* * * * *

"I'll have to punish you, you know," Zach said while they waited for the sheriff to arrive. They sat on the bench where he could see the attackers, but he kept Selena turned toward him so she could focus on her beloved river, not on the violence that had invaded her sanctuary. The violence he had brought to her. Just seeing the scene play itself again in his head, he was filled with fury. At himself and at the men on the ground, for endangering her. "You could have been killed."

"As you will, Master. I did what my heart demanded. I'm sorry if I displeased You."

"Ms. Cross?" A gruff male voice came through the trees, along with the tramp of two pairs of feet. Zach tensed, but Selena touched his hand.

"It's Sheriff Soames," she said. "And one of his deputies." From the way her shoulders tensed, even more than they had been already, Zach suspected their invasion into her home was not much more welcome than that of the ones tied up on the ground. When he saw the deputy's mocking and derisive expression, he understood. He wrapped an arm around Selena, doing what he could to support her from this new attack, an attack he had to squelch the desire to resolve with his fist plowing into the deputy's face. It had just been too difficult a day for more bullshit.

"Over here," Zach said, wrapping an arm around Selena as if that act might shield her from this new invasion of her sacred circle.

They charged in, stopping in their tracks when they almost stumbled over the two thugs. "Don't tell me these guys were tryin' to horn in on your magic show," the younger guy said, barely managing to contain a snicker.

Zach's palms itched. He wanted to wipe that smug look off the deputy's face. No need to make a bad scene worse, though. He squeezed Selena's waist, hoping to convey his support—his regret for causing her all this trouble.

"I guess these are the fellas you called us about," the older man—Zach guessed he was the Gilchrist County sheriff from his air of authority—said, motioning toward the attackers. "Looks like you did a pretty thorough job of makin' sure they'd still be here when we arrived."

"We didn't have any handcuffs, Sheriff Soames." Selena smiled up at the lawman. "We did have a lot of rope."

Soames glanced down at the men, laughed. "Gags, too, I see."

"Well, they were making a lot of noise once they came to. You could have heard them clear across the river. What they were saying wasn't any too polite." Selena leaned a little closer to Zach.

Had they done too good a job, hog-tying and gagging their prisoners? The last thing Zach wanted was to bring the local law down on Selena and her bed and breakfast. "My fault, Sheriff. Having guys shooting at me makes me nervous. I wanted to make sure they didn't get away."

"No problem." The deputy knelt and cuffed each of the men, then drew out a pocketknife. "Want me to cut these ropes, or do you want to untie 'em?"

"Cut them loose." It wasn't as though he planned to use that rope on Selena. Besides, she'd brought out an impressive supply of the soft braided nylon while he'd held a gun on the unconscious mobsters. "It's just nine millimeter braided cord." The thought that her old Master might have been into *Shibari* annoyed Zach, until he imagined someday honing his rusty skill at that ancient art of rope bondage on her, for her pleasure.

The sheriff cleared his throat, then looked questioningly at Selena. "Ms. Selena?"

"Yes. Go ahead and cut it."

"Not gonna be much use for tying up tomato vines once Jack here gets through hackin' it off these guys," he commented.

He wouldn't correct the lawman, even though he doubted anybody would use the expensive braided nylon to tie up plants. Well, maybe Selena did. Zach had wondered—but then he was a complete novice about the care and feeding of tomato plants, and he knew Selena was into the BDSM lifestyle. He looked down at her while the lawmen cut the criminals from their ropes.

"I'd leave those gags in place if I were you, Sheriff," she said when they went to loosen them.

"Gotta find out what they were doin' here."

The gods only knew there were rotten apples in Tampa's police department barrel, and Zach's first impulse was to hide his identity, hope the sheriff would just lock up their attackers. He couldn't do that, though. From her reluctance to call the local lawmen, and from the deputy's snide comments about her "magic show", he gathered the clientele she drew into the sleepy rural county along the Suwannee didn't exactly endear her to what was undoubtedly a conservative Christian community.

As if she read his scowl correctly, she squeezed his hand. "They're not all like this around here. Most of my neighbors are tolerant. Even friendly," she said so quietly that only he could hear.

But they all left her alone, no doubt. Isolated. She'd been isolated too long. He wanted to bring an end to that, damn it. Damn it, damn it, he wanted it all to be over, so he could stand with her. Protect her from smirking glances as much as from any physical danger.

Now he must do what he could to protect her from cruel gossip. He stepped forward, gesturing toward the scowling goons. "They came here after me. I'm Zachary Lang. If you want to know why, call and talk to Jim Fortner at the state attorney's office in Tampa."

"These guys don't look like any cops I've ever seen," the deputy said, turning away from the altar. He didn't even try to mask his lingering expression of fascinated horror. "You runnin' from the law?"

The sheriff shot his deputy a disgusted look. "Don't be an idiot. It's obvious Mr. Lang is in some kind of trouble, but it's the kind involving police protection. Stop your gawking and get these men loaded into the car."

"I'm a witness in a trial coming up next week," Zach explained. "This isn't the first time someone's tried to kill me. Jim's a personal friend. He suggested I come here and try to relax, hoping I'd be safely tucked away."

The sheriff emptied the bullets from one of the thug's guns before tossing it all into an evidence bag. "How'd you two manage to take 'em down before they blew you to bits?" he asked.

"Desperation, I guess. Selena helped." Somehow Zach knew they wouldn't want to hear about the shield or the pawing, snorting—and disappearing—bull. "Is there any likelihood these guys will break out of your jail?"

"Nah. Haven't had a breakout in years. Jail's not like these new ones where they spend millions for the prisoners' comfort but not enough on thick walls and good strong bars. You won't have to worry about them again—" He gestured toward his prisoners, "—'til at least Tuesday. Longer than that if they can't make bail."

"Tuesday?" Zach asked, confused.

"Won't be any bail hearing on Monday. Judge won't be back in town. He's off somewhere, fishin' in a bass tournament. Anybody we lock up stays locked up 'til he gets back. Damn, Judge Morrow's trips play hell on my food budget. Wish they'd let us give 'em bread and water but no, the law says prisoners got their rights."

Zach almost pitied the guys the deputy was half-leading, half-dragging toward the dusty green-and-white SUV emblazoned with a Gilchrist County Sheriff's Department logo. Almost. The bastards hadn't hesitated to try to kill him. Selena, too. "I'll be out of here in the morning, Sheriff. I doubt they'll stay around long once you let them loose."

"Oh, they'll be stayin' around awhile. Judge Morrow don't take kindly to folks tryin' to kill his constituents." Taking his pocketknife, he pried another bullet from Selena's altar and slipped it into a plastic baggie. "Especially our resident witch. He'll set their bond so high, they'll more'n likely be my guests until their trials. Selena, figure out what damage they did, and the judge will make sure they make it good."

She smiled for the first time since the smart-mouthed deputy made the scathing remarks about her magic. "Thanks, Sheriff. I will. Do you need us to do anything more tonight?"

"We're about done, thanks." Sheriff Soames shook his head. "I still can't figure how you two managed to disarm those two bruisers. 'Specially with them both totin' heat. Not just any heat, either. Them was some mighty high-powered pistols they tried to use on you."

"Somebody up there was looking out for us. There's no other explanation," Selena said.

The sheriff glanced up at the starry sky. "I guess so. The Lord, He works in mysterious ways. Lang, how can we get in touch with you when we need to take your deposition?"

Zach gave out his address and phone numbers, not bothering to mention the likelihood that he wouldn't be so lucky next time and wouldn't be around to testify at this or any other trial. "If that's all, Sheriff, I'm sure Selena would like to get at least a little rest tonight."

"Guess you need rest, too, if you're taking off first thing in the morning." Soames adjusted his hat, then hiked up his khaki pants and started to walk away.

If that wasn't a clear invitation to get out of town, Zach had never heard one. "Don't worry, Sheriff. I'll be long gone by morning. I have no desire to put Selena or anybody else at risk."

"That's good thinking. We'll be in touch." With that, Soames sauntered toward the SUV where his deputy had already secured the prisoners.

Zach turned to Selena, saw her trembling. "Zach, we have to—"

"Ssshh...enough." He pulled her into his arms a little more roughly than he intended, but he wanted her to feel his fury, his love for her, his fear that she might have been taken from him because of her damn stubbornness. The stubborn disobedience that had saved his life. He wanted to bring her pleasure once more before he left her side, taking the danger he had brought away with him.

"I'm going to tell you what we have to do." He tipped up her chin, looked hard into her eyes. "We're going to go inside, and I'm going to give you your punishment. Do you understand, Selena?"

Her eyes were clouded with worry, but his words, his touch, the press of his body had her responding in another way. He felt the shudder of desire ripple through her trembling fear, and knew he could and would distract her. Their last night would be about love. He could give her, and himself, that gift.

"Zach, Master, let's cast the stones. What you know can save you."

Goddess, he wanted to believe her, wanted to hope he might have a future after all. He yearned to look forward to years, not hours, of pleasing Selena now that he'd found her. "Pick up the stones, then. You can cast them inside. I won't risk having you shot at by more hired guns."

The gentle curve of her spine when she bent to gather the scattered stones and the ripe firm swell of her buttocks beneath her long, loose dress aroused him as much as her instant acquiescence to his order. His fingers itched to warm that enticing ass, then knead it, soothe away the redness created by his loving discipline.

"Come now." This might be the last time he'd have to love her...the only chance to assert the dominance they both needed. Every one of the deities must have been looking down on them tonight, for if they hadn't been protecting them, he and Selena surely would have died. Reminded of his order, her putting her life at risk by disobeying him, and his promise, he added softly, "It's past time for you to receive your punishment. Come, let's make sex magic together."

Chapter Four

ஐ

Zach looked strong, forbidding, the muscles in His upper arms and shoulders rippling as He handled the flogger He'd chosen from several she'd fetched at His command. Even in the moonlight filtering through the closed sheer curtains, His barely leashed male power took Selena's breath away.

"Lie on your stomach across the bed," He ordered, not turning from the window to face her.

A moment later, without warning, for He'd moved so quietly, she felt the stinging tendrils of leather making contact with her tender flesh, bringing heat she hadn't felt for ages—a stinging heat that spiraled through her buttocks. Sensations curled through her body, bringing pleasure more intense with every lash. Pleasure merged with pain that morphed into anticipation as it traveled to her ass, her cunt, even her nipples, pressed as they were into the soft down comforter, creating heat and moisture and longing.

"Oh, yesss, Master. More." Her ass tingled, and her arousal grew. She'd counted ten strokes by the time He laid the flogger down and laid His callused fingers where He'd punished her. Restless, she opened her legs, offering Him the wet satiny folds of her pussy should He want to discipline her there, too. His hot breath seared the sensitive skin of her buttocks when He bent and nipped her gently with His teeth, insinuating two long fingers along her slit, delving into her wet cunt, tweaking her clit.

The slick slide of His tongue across her burning ass cheeks soothed the pain He'd inflicted. Aroused her as she hadn't been aroused in so, so long. Selena closed her eyes, pictured Him reaching across the bed, restraining her, invading her cunt with the blown-glass dildo He'd ordered her to fill with iced water while He plowed her tingling ass with His huge, rigid cock.

Would He use the ball gag she'd laid beside the dildo? She hoped so. For the magic to be at its most powerful, He needed to fill her every orifice, claim her completely so He might come away with magic of His own. Magic that would protect Him.

He moved, but His aura surrounded her. Eyes closed, she listened, visualizing from the faint sounds what He did to prepare for her. The rustle of tearing foil, a creak of bedsprings once, twice, three times, the jingle of a buckle told her He'd lifted the gag.

"Open for me," He ordered, taking her mouth and ringing it with His tongue, mingling His saliva with hers, wetting her. "Pretend you're sucking my cock." As she did His bidding, He withdrew His tongue, slipping in the ball gag and buckling it snugly at the back of her head.

His deft movements when He caught the restraints and buckled them around her wrists and ankles spoke of considerable experience, as did the easy way He placed the blindfold, depriving her of sight. She squelched the jealousy that rose at the thought of Him, her Master, pleasuring other women, concentrated instead on the joy of surrender—the magical energy bubbling up in her. On opening herself fully to Him, body and spirit, giving Him whatever psychic powers might help save Him from His enemies.

But Goddess, He was the one creating the magic now, with the soft abrasion of His tongue along her slit, the icy invasion of her cunt with the dildo. Her nipples tingled, stimulated by His nearness even though He hadn't touched them. Her cunt contracted, needing heat. Needing Him.

A finger ringed her ass, made her rear back, wanting…needing completion. "I love how you're wet for me," He said, spreading her honey around her rear entrance, sliding His fingers forward to caress her swollen tissue, to pinch her tingling clit. "Raise up."

When she did, He slid a pillow beneath her hips. "Such a pretty ass. So tight. Relax for me and let me in."

"Mmmm." The sound came from deep in her throat, muffled by the gag. Her cunt contracted hard against the icy dildo when He applied gentle pressure to send it deeper. His breath dampened, cooled her flaming buttocks when He kissed her there. Then He rose, His movement evident in the shifting of the mattress beneath her. The head of His cock suddenly pressed insistently at her ass, demanding entrance. Entrance she eagerly awaited.

Her Master slid the icy dildo almost out of her cunt, then drove it home as He breached her ass, seating His sheathed cockhead just beyond her anal sphincter. "Open for me. Goddess, your ass is so tight, so hot."

He branded her with fire and ice. Sensations at both ends of the spectrum. In the darkness behind her blindfold she saw the red-orange of His fire, the answering wing-beating of tiny undines. Sylphs fluttered.

I am Earth, seared by Fire, chilled by Water, nourished by Air. Demeter, in Your wisdom, make my Master's mind go blank, that I may share my paltry talents with Him. Help me keep Him safe.

Demeter must have heard, for Selena felt Zach's power surge, in the strength of His thrusts, the rising scent of His male musk, now mingled with the basil and sandalwood fragrances of the incense she'd lit to represent their elements. It was as though His essence pervaded everywhere as He filled her. She swirled her tongue around the smooth ball gag, tasting Him there.

Her cunt clenched the dildo, no longer cold but imbued with His fire. Again and again, He invaded her ass, driving away the pain with exquisite pleasure. Pleasure that sped through nerve endings, spread throughout her body as she emptied it of thought, of fear, of magic. Emptied all she was into her Master who filled and completed her now as she prayed He'd do forever.

"By all your Deities, I claim you. I take your offerings and vow to cherish and succor them." His voice sounded as though it came from far away, as if it were another talking as He lay over her back, His skin merging with hers as they began to shudder in unison. Master and slave, made one in mutual fulfillment.

Zach shook, not so much from the power of the climax that just claimed him as from the realization that he'd taken something precious. Something he must guard well. Selena had given him not only her body but her soul. Her magic powers.

And he'd done what he'd never thought he'd do—given a slave his heart. Gently, slowly, taking care not to bruise her with the restraints, he removed them, soothing away the slightly pinkened marks where the straps had touched her tender skin. When he removed the gag, he replaced it with his lips and tongue, giving all he was, promising whatever future the Deities might grant them.

Many hours later, fiery bright, the sun rose on the eastern horizon, reminding Zach he had to go. Quietly, so as not to wake Selena from her exhausted sleep, he slipped out of bed and took his clothes with him to the bathroom. No way would he expose his woman to the risks he faced.

* * * * *

He'd left her with nothing but a promise to return. Without Him saying, she'd known He'd go. She'd known, no matter how she begged, He wouldn't take her with Him, fearful of placing her in danger.

A good man. A good Master.

Selena understood Zach's need to fulfill His obligation, His desire to protect her from harm. Content to wait for His return, she tended her garden, digging in the rich earth, basking in the sun as it rose from the east toward its zenith. She had no choice but to trust the Deities they'd invoked last night—and the intuitive powers He'd taken from her to keep Him safe.

She worked the soil, dark and rich and warm from the sun, pulling weeds from beneath the large gardenia bush. The smells of earth and flowers, and the slightly fishy smell of the river on the wind combined, Nature's own perfume on a sunny, warm day. A good day, she thought, pushing down a sudden premonition that all might not be well.

Suddenly dark clouds obscured the sun. An omen? Dropping to her knees at the edge of the sacred circle, Selena closed her eyes, made obeisance to the Lord and Lady. She dug in her pocket, found the stones: the garnet He'd picked, and the obsidian and clear quartz ones that had been her special talismans for years, since they'd help reunite a beloved guest with his wife and daughter.

Thunder boomed. Lightning crackled over the Suwannee. She clutched the stones, murmured a desperate plea for the sun to return. For her Master to stay safe. *Cast the stones. Face whatever danger lurks. Don't be a fool, your ignorance will do Him no good.*

Her jaw clenched painfully with fear, she pried her fingers loose, tossed the stones into the circle. Clamping down her eyelids until tears flowed from the corners of her eyes, she focused all her psychic powers on the circle...the stones...

No. A primal scream exploded in her chest, at first no more than a low rumble, almost a growl, felt more than heard. Then it burst forth, a high-pitched keening that drove a nesting blue jay skyward, its wings beating a cadence like running feet.

Goddess above. There, more clearly now, she saw the same building she'd seen before in a vision, one she knew she'd never visited. Cold, gray concrete stairs, flanked by statues...gargoyles. No, not gargoyles, but statues commemorating fallen soldiers, long-dead images immortalized in sculptor's stone. The scene was ominously still. Foretelling of evil, or tragedy. Chimes in a nearby church belfry began to toll the hour. One. Two. Three. Melodic, high-pitched sounds assaulted her senses. Four. Five. Eleven times it tolled the hour, and as the last mournful tone rent the air Zach stepped through the revolving door onto the wide, shallow stair, His expression triumphant.

Then His body slammed forward. He crumpled to the ground. Blood. So much blood spilled onto the concrete, down the stairs. The wails of passersby, of the Deities, blended with her own screams as she clawed the earth, distraught, wanting to cease breathing, join her Master in eternity, escape the tearing grief, the years of loneliness that stretched before her in her mind. Again. Goddess, she couldn't bear it again, no matter what she had told Zach in the sacred circle. She wanted Him now, now and forever.

A feral cat, gray striped with yellowish-orange eyes, stepped into the circle, clawed the air, then sat back on his haunches, eyes aglow. Fire. Her Master's element. "What say you, Cat?"

It is only eight-thirty now, Earth-lady.

Seven words. Just seven words, a rise and stretch of his supple back, and he disappeared as quickly as he'd come.

But Selena knew what she must do. Gathering up the magic stones, she sprinted for the house.

Chapter Five

"Well, Zach, in a few hours this will all be over."

Zach glanced over at Jim as they stepped inside the courtroom. His friend was in his element, apparently oblivious to the smell of unwashed bodies in the hallways, musty carpets in need of replacement. Even the pungent odor of carnauba wax emanating from the worn wooden seating didn't seem to faze him.

"Does it always smell like this?" he asked, wondering how anyone could spend day-in, day-out in this building devoid of fresh air, sunshine.

"The smell of justice? Yes, though it's stronger than usual on Mondays because the cleaning crew polishes the benches on Sunday when no one's here. Come on, I know you'd like to propose tearing this relic down and putting up one of your contemporary masterpieces."

Four days ago Zach would have said yes and meant it. Now, though, the only proposal he wanted to make was to a sweet witch named Selena. The only place he yearned for was the sprawling Florida home next to the Suwannee where they'd made love. He wanted to build that gazebo in the air, the one he'd sketched for her in sand—build it with his own hands, then bend her over the slender rail he envisioned and fuck her while they watched the Sylphs cavort above that still, shallow pool.

He wanted to learn her witchcraft, perform with her those acts of magic she'd barely introduced him to. Wanted it so much he'd let Jim persuade him to wear this stiflingly hot Kevlar vest under the dress shirt and suit jacket that would have been plenty warm enough already.

Selena had given him hope that once the testifying was over, he'd be safe...no further threat to the mobsters and crooked politicians who'd kept trying to silence him. Confident that the security checkpoints at the courthouse doors would keep out potential assassins, he took a seat in the first row behind the prosecutor's table as Jim made his way beyond the bar. After over two months of fear, of furtive ducking and dodging bullies and bullets, Zach experienced a weird, lulling sense of peace, even when he glanced at the three defendants and their high-priced lawyers and noted their smug, malevolent expressions.

Then the trial began.

* * * * *

Selena had never tossed on the first garments that reached her seeking hands or fired up her balky old pickup truck quite so fast. *Please the Lord and Lady, let me get to Him in time.*

Why hadn't she gone with Him, insisted when He'd said no? Why hadn't she disobeyed Him, followed the moment He'd driven away? Knuckles white from clenching the steering wheel, she floored the accelerator, listened for the usual sputtering protest from an engine long past its prime.

Instead of the usual ominous sounds, the engine gave off a throaty purr, as though it felt Selena's urgency, heard her desperate prayers. Maybe it did, after all. Selena braked sharply, turning onto the main highway, picking up speed. She dared not close her eyes, but then she didn't need to. The picture of Zach lying there, His lifeblood spilling onto the cold concrete, had etched itself onto her heart—her mind.

Thunder crashed again, followed by lightning that crackled in a jet-black sky. Rain came down in torrents, testing the wipers' single speed. Steam rose off the asphalt pavement, a surrealistic image when caught in headlights that did little to guide her on her way. Trees near the highway bent with the force of a fierce wind. It was as though the elements conspired against her. Against Zach.

She watched the speedometer edge backward. Sixty. Fifty. At forty-five she pushed back down on the accelerator. Couldn't delay. When she turned onto I-75, she dared glance at her watch. Nine forty-eight. An hour and twelve minutes to go seventy miles in blinding rain.

Selena choked back a sob, held onto the wheel harder when a double-trailer semi sped past her, buffeting the light pickup and spraying the windshield with muddy water from the road.

Then the sun peeked through the angry clouds. The rain slowed down, no longer coming down with blinding force. Every muscle in her body protested now that she could finally let go a little…breathe.

Thank you. Thank you all. Please, please, hold back the storm. Let me reach my Master in time.

At ten forty-five she pulled off the Interstate, desperate now to reach the courthouse in a city where she'd been but once or twice. A city whose downtown streets ran one way, the opposite way it seemed from where she needed to go. Horns honked. Angry drivers swore at each other, making obscene gestures to punctuate their opinions of their fellow man.

She'd never make it. The courthouse was a block away, but it might as well have been on Mars. Slamming on the brakes and abandoning the truck in the snarl of traffic, she made her way on foot. Let the drivers curse her. Let the police tow her truck away. She had to reach Zach. Now.

At the corner across from the courthouse, she gasped for breath when traffic made her pause. A clock on a restaurant read ten fifty-nine. A church bell began to toll the hour, slowly, mournfully. She couldn't wait. Ignoring the red light, she darted across the street between honking cars and ran down the sidewalk. When she looked up the short staircase between the memorials to the soldiers, she spied Zach stepping outside a revolving door.

"No. Go back inside!" Though she screamed it at the top of her lungs, He must not have heard. "Stop!" she yelled again. He kept coming. Toward the street. Toward her.

Three times the bell had rung now. She spied a glint of silver from a window of an office building across the street. A gun. The clock's minute hand lurched, then moved. Selena sprinted up the stairs. Had to get to Zach.

He stood as though someone had glued His feet to the stone staircase. A clean target for the gunman. *Bong. Bong.* Mournful sounds marking the hour, coming faster now it seemed. As the bell tolled for the eleventh time, a shot rang out.

Selena reached Zach, spun so her back was to Him. She flung her arms out wide, shielding Him with as much of her body as she could. He muttered an oath, His hands closing hard on her shoulders to jerk her back. The bullet ripped through her.

* * * * *

Zach paced the surgery waiting room, his own flesh wound forgotten. Not much for prayer until now, he searched his mind for every entreaty he'd ever heard, to every higher being he'd ever heard of. Selena couldn't die. Not now, when he'd just learned he might have a future to share with her.

The police had caught the sniper, and according to his prosecutor buddy Jim Fortner, the hired gun had spilled his guts. The culprits would pay, not only for graft and corruption, but for attempted murder. "Pray God it won't be for murder," he muttered when he saw a masked surgeon come out of the OR suite and head his way.

Jim stood up, laid a hand on Zach's shoulder. "Easy, my friend."

"Well, Doctor?" Zach said, struggling to hold his voice steady.

"She'll be fine, Mr. Lang. These stones in her breast pocket deflected the bullet and saved her from getting much more seriously hurt." The surgeon smiled as he handed Zach fractured pieces of the obsidian Selena always carried, along with the quartz crystal—and the garnet he'd chosen as his own talisman.

The stones glowed in Zach's hand as he listened to the doctor say Selena should be able to go home within a few days. He stared, mesmerized, as they took on a brightness he'd never seen before. The clear quartz crystal might have been a diamond, its facets caught the light so spectacularly. In its glow the garnet's deep red brightened almost to the color of rubies, and the jagged pieces of the obsidian took on a sheen reminiscent of highly polished onyx.

Colors of love. The stones had saved them both. He would give her back the magic stones, along with the largest diamond solitaire he could find for her to wear, a gem that would shine the brightest of them all. "Colors of love," he murmured, closing his fingers over them hard, his eyes falling shut to give a prayer of thanks to the many deities who'd brought those colors to his aid, in the form of his own sweet witch.

"Colors of love," he told Selena the next day when he gave her back the magic stones, along with a large diamond solitaire that shone brightest of them all. "You saved me, and they saved you."

Epilogue

My Master.

Selena watched, her juices flowing at the sight of Zach stripped to the waist, putting the finishing touches on the gazebo of her dreams. Frogs croaked, fish jumped, and birds chirped merrily in the clearing where she'd brought Him that day a year ago when He'd been running from the mob. Dragonflies flitted like Sylphs over the mirror-like pool beneath them, darting among the tall pines and stately oaks draped with Spanish moss to dip into the Suwannee, paying obeisance to Aphrodite.

A light warm breeze ruffled the leaves of the hawthorn shrubs they'd planted to ring a new circle, none less sacred than the other two. The faint mingled fragrances of four fat candles, waiting to give off their distinctive scents when lit, tickled her nostrils. Dark-green, with the scent of pine sap in the springtime; creamy white as pure as the gardenias on the bush beside the pool; a wheat-colored one, its fragrance clean and elemental like the Earth; and the basil-scented candle of reddish-amber. Even unlit, their auras heightened her awareness, her arousal, her need to surrender once more to her Master's command.

His gaze was on her now, like that of the Sun God on the Moon Goddess. He set down His hammer and axe and laid His hands on the waistband of His tight, faded jeans. "Disrobe for me," He said. "I've dreamed of taking you here, in this place, since I thought that day last year would be my last on earth."

Selena loosened the tie belt on her loose, long dress, letting it fall to the pine floor of the gazebo as Zach stepped out of His pants. He was magnificent, His hard body bronzed by the sun, honed by the manual labor He'd put into this gift for her — for them. Thank the Goddess, He remained unscathed by those who would have harmed Him.

Her Master, pledged to bring her pleasure through her submission. Her Husband, pledged to honor and cherish her all the days of their lives, just as she'd pledged herself to Him.

Their unborn son kicked strongly in her belly, as though he felt her excitement, felt his father's love. In a few more months, they would be three, not two. The family she'd never dreamed a year ago she'd ever have. She stood very still, the only adornment on her naked body His gold-link collar and His rings — the two on her finger, one in her clit, and another in her navel.

"Light the candles. Call on the gods and goddesses of each Element to bless us, make us safe." His callused fingers touching her gently as they cupped her belly from behind, He traced the sunburst tattoo now centered with the garnet He'd chosen as His own. As she paid homage first to Air, then Water, then Earth, and finally Fire, He steadied her, kept her grounded in His love.

The fragrances of Nature swirled around them, and she felt the blessing of the gods and Their consorts: Hermes and Aurora, Poseidon and Aphrodite, Dionysus and Demeter. The sounds and sights and tastes of Nature surrounded them, drove all thought from Selena's mind, leaving only feelings.

"Take the Lady into yourself. Make Her you, and you Her." For the first time her Master spoke the words of the sacred ritual, though she'd sensed them in His mind more strongly each time they made sex magic. Her swollen folds, already tender with her advancing pregnancy, tingled, and moisture came, slick and hot to ease His way.

She felt the Lord invade Him as He invaded her with heat more intense than any she'd ever known. Aphrodite called, and she bent over the ornately carved gazebo rail, confident her Master wouldn't let her fall.

"You know, I dreamed of this, dreamed of taking you this way when I doubted I'd ever take you again," He whispered, steadying her hips in His big hands and seating His cock deep in her warm, wet cunt. "Gods in the heavens, how I love you."

The pressure built inside her, threatened to erupt now, before He'd even begun to move. "May I come, Master?"

"Wait. Watch the Sylphs and Undines flitting around us. Listen to the bluebird's song. Thank the Lord and Lady for all Their blessings, and savor the sensations. Feel my cock, filling you, fulfilling you. Listen to the squirrels chattering in the trees.

"Celebrate life and living." He began to move, slowly, gently, as though afraid to hurt her or their child.

Unlike other times, she had no need to say the ritual words, for today Sol, the Sun God, bestowed His healing heat, His light. His Consort, silent now at the zenith of Sol's power, had invaded Selena's body, filling her heart with joy.

Her climax built slowly, spreading through her until it burst into flame. Her Master tensed behind her, His cock erupting, flooding her with life. With pleasure. "Come now, my precious slave," He gasped as He sank deep within her, cradling her in His arms.

Each hot spurt of His semen triggered yet another tiny orgasm in her, until, drained, they sank together to their knees. In love, in lust, in anticipation of a future blessed.

Selena looked up, saw the rainbow above them. "Look, Master," she said. "See the colors of love."

"Forever." His arms tightened around her, gave her a feeling of safety, of comfort. "Beyond forever, if the Deities keep smiling on us."

COLORS OF MAGIC
ଛ

Chapter One

Battered bounty hunter Garrett Bryant lay on the bed, watching a gentle breeze ruffle the white gauze canopy above his head. His cock still throbbed, as if reminding him how long it had been since it had felt a woman's warm, wet pussy.

A hand job was a poor substitute for getting fucked, but it would have to do. An hour earlier he'd almost given in and taken his temporary landlady up on her silent offer to join him in bed, before memories of his cool, beautiful ex-wife had intruded and reminded him that he'd be giving Selena far less than that caring, loving woman deserved.

Damn Elaine to hell. She'd thrown him out before he left on the job that landed him in the hospital, close to dead—and served him with divorce papers as soon as she'd figured out she wasn't going to become a widow anytime soon. Why the fuck couldn't he put her out of his mind, the way she'd obviously forgotten him?

The fluttering canopy above his head reminded him of a see-through black nightie she used to wear, so he closed his eyes against the mental picture of her firm, full breasts, the hard nubs of her nipples that elongated when he sucked them into his mouth. Though she wasn't there and never would be with him again, every sensual curve haunted his memories, invaded his dreams.

Shit! He'd banish Elaine from his mind if it was the last thing he ever did. Maybe then he could get back some of himself, enough to offer in good conscience to a woman with the courage to trust him not to get himself killed. A woman who wouldn't tear his soul apart.

Garrett forced his eyes to close, swept those painfully arousing memories out of his consciousness. Finally he slept.

But Elaine still taunted him, even in his dreams.

She wouldn't let him go. And for that she was going to pay. She had no right to stand over him like this, her full lips slightly open while her gaze focused on his pulsating, lonesome cock.

He sprang out of bed, grabbed her, and flung her onto the sheets where he'd tossed and turned and suffered the agony of unrelieved lust. Her laughter infuriated him, made him wild.

Grabbing the plunging neckline of her black silk nightie, he ripped it from her body, feasting his eyes for the first time in more than a year on her naked breasts, the slightly convex curve of her belly. He groaned at the sight of her cunt, still shaved the way he'd insisted she keep it so he could see the hard little nub of her clit and rub his tongue along her satiny folds. She was wet now, glistening and hot for him the way she'd been since their first time, years ago.

His cock reared straight up against his belly, obviously eager to end its long dry spell. But the knowing smile on her lips reminded him she'd walked away before.

She wouldn't walk away now.

Ripping the torn nightie into four parts, he used it to bind her wrists and ankles to the iron posts that held up the bed canopy. For a minute he just looked at her, let himself imagine they were still together and still in love. When she squirmed against her bonds and whimpered the way she used to when they made love, his heart leapt with…hope?

He knelt between her legs and rubbed his cockhead along her hot, wet slit. His balls tightened, and pre-cum mixed with her slick, warm juices.

"Go ahead, fuck me. You know that's what you want." Her voice poured over him like honey, taunting him as she arched her hips, offering him her prize.

Shit, if he fucked her now, it would be over in seconds. She'd come and he'd come, and she wouldn't get the message that he was boss, at least here and now.

"I don't think so, *wife*," he said, sliding his hands up her body to cup her tits and pinch the nipples into hard, rosy points. "Not until you take the edge off for me."

He followed his hands, straddling her torso while he moved higher and pushed her breasts together until they cradled his erection. Her nipples throbbed against his fingers, as though asking him for more.

Writhing against her bonds, she let out a little moan. "For God's sake, Garrett, I can't take much more."

"You don't have a lot of choices."

"Fuck me now."

He knew from the desperate tone of her voice how much she wanted his cock rammed into her cunt, but he wasn't ready to oblige her yet. "I'm going to eat you instead. And you're going to take my cock down your throat and like it." *Like you never did, not once, when we were together.*

Turning around to straddle her face, he fed her his cock before cupping her sweet ass in his hands and lifting her cunt to his hungry mouth. Her nipples poked at his belly, as if they missed the attention he'd been giving them, and slick hot juices dripped down from her satiny cunt, drenching his fingers.

Her soft moan reverberated around his cock when she sucked him deeper down her throat. If she kept that up he was going to drown her in cum, but no way would he let her stop. It felt too fucking good.

When he licked her satiny outer lips, she swirled her tongue over his cockhead, and when he sucked her hard little clit between his teeth and gnawed, she nipped him in retaliation. He spread her ass cheeks and sank two fingers into her weeping pussy, loving the way she deep-throated him while he finger-fucked her and sucked her clit deep inside his mouth.

She squirmed, as if needing more. Who else had she been fucking? he wondered, but it didn't matter now. His own control was nearly gone. With his other hand he spread her pussy juice around her asshole and worked his finger past her tight sphincter muscle.

She liked that. Always had. She'd even enjoyed a gentle ass-fucking from time to time, long ago before they'd become virtual strangers. He moved his finger deeper, wiggled it in time with her helpless hip-flexing. Her pussy gripped his fingers, milking him as more hot, wet juices streamed onto his hands and face.

She sucked harder on his cock, took him deeper yet. His balls tightened against her open lips, and his orgasm built from somewhere deep inside his torso and bubbled through him. He was coming in her mouth. No stopping him now.

For a minute he lay on her, drained, but when he turned to release her bonds there was no one there. No Elaine and no shredded black nightie.

Only his semen on his hand and on the crumpled bed linens, mocking him with the proof that he was nowhere near over his goddamned ex-wife.

And then, before he could go back to sleep he got the call. His daughter had run away from home.

* * * * *

His heart beat way too fast, and the pulses pounded in his neck and temples. Elaine's terrified voice rang in Garrett's ears as he stuffed his things into a duffel bag and limped outside as fast as his gimpy leg would allow.

Moss-draped oak trees, a meandering river, and the grand old house that had been his place of refuge for the past three months suddenly seemed ominous, forbidding. If he hadn't been hiding out here, Leah might not have taken off. He wanted to check out, and he meant to do it now.

Where the hell was Selena? After all she'd done for him while he recuperated from his injuries, he wasn't about to walk out without saying good-bye. Just once, though, he'd like it if this bed-and breakfast weren't as far removed in mood from the commercial meccas of central and south Florida as it was close in terms of time and miles. Frustrated now, Garrett searched his mind for places his daughter might have gone to hide.

Never mind that the doctors wanted him to nurse his wounds another month or two. His little girl had been missing more than thirty hours now, and the police hadn't found a trace of her. Crippled or not, he couldn't just sit around and wring his hands.

Now that Elaine had finally decided to let him know Leah had taken off, he had to join the search. After all, finding folks who didn't want to be found was his business. Garrett clenched his fists, tried hard not to picture what might happen, could already have happened...

When he approached Selena, she looked up and smiled. Garrett would miss Selena's kindness, her gentle voice that epitomized the slow, healing pace of life along the river. He'd miss the peace of this out-of-the-way place. Truth be known, he'd even miss the otherworldly sense of magic he didn't quite buy into. "I'm leaving today."

"Leaving? Why? You're booked for another month. Your leg needs more time to heal," she said, disappointment evident in her soft, sweet drawl.

"My daughter's run away. I've got to try to help find her."

Setting her basket on the ground, Selena took Garrett's hand. "The stones could help you," she told him, her delicate features sober as she met his gaze.

"I'll try just about anything."

He supposed his desperation showed, because he'd made no secret about his lack of faith in the stone-casting mumbo jumbo she did with some of the other guests.

She smiled. "I know you think their magic's hokey, but it can't hurt to give them a try. Come with me and I'll give you the strongest talismans I have."

Impatient to be on his way but unwilling to hurt her feelings, Garrett followed Selena to a weathered cabin at the far end of the garden and watched while she sorted through some rocks set in tiny boxes as though they were precious jewels.

"Take these. They're special. I've worked magic into the lattices of the crystal and raised cooperation in the obsidian. They will help you, if only you can believe."

She dropped two stones, one smooth and round and black as night, the other a multi-faceted clear quartz crystal, into Garrett's hand. When she closed his fist around them and pressed the stones into his palm, her small hands warmed his.

"Thanks," he said. "For everything."

"Love has a magic of its own. If you let it, love will lead you to your daughter. And Garrett, follow your instincts. You'll know what to do when the time comes. You and Elaine will find Leah. And the stones will help you."

As he hurtled down the Florida Turnpike, Garrett recalled what Selena had said. Maybe the woman did have some occult powers, because he didn't remember ever having spoken of Leah or Elaine by name. He'd tried to banish them from his mind. After all, Elaine had tossed him out before he'd left on the job that had put him out of commission for the past six months.

The stones he'd stashed in his pocket exuded a strange warmth that soothed his still-tender thigh.

* * * * *

Two hours later, Garrett pulled his vintage 'Vette into the driveway of the house on Fort Lauderdale Beach that used to be his home. He glanced in the carport at Elaine's Mercedes coupe and recalled the many times he'd come home when she was at work late and he and Leah had fended for themselves. His jaw clenched at the thought he might never see his daughter again.

Feeling every movement, he heaved himself out of the driver's seat, limped to the door, and rang the bell. As quickly if she'd been standing there waiting for him, Elaine let him in. "Thank God you've come."

"What did you expect? That I'd say, 'So what?' That I'd kick back with a cold brew and watch the sunset while my daughter's out there somewhere, in God only knows what sort of danger?" He ran his fingers through his hair as he shifted his weight to his good leg."Garrett, could we be civil?"

Despite the frantic look in her eyes, Elaine looked as put together as usual. Not a pale-blond hair out of place, or a wrinkle in her teal silk shirt or snug-fitting pants. He'd bet money the underwear she had on underneath it was a perfect color match.

That irritated Garrett about her. Always had. It was as if Elaine couldn't ever let down her barriers outside the bedroom, even with the man she used to swear she loved.

But he was here for Leah, not Elaine, so he guessed he could cut her some slack, especially when he saw her tremble and sensed chinks in her armor of self-containment. "Okay. Have you heard anything more from the police?"

"No. Nothing."

Tears welled in her eyes, threatened to spill down cheeks whose pallor she had almost managed to conceal with makeup. "The detective said they're looking for over fifty runaways in Broward County alone," she said, a catch in her voice. "Garrett, why would she have run away?"

"To get attention?" Between the divorce, Elaine's career, and his own injuries, Leah's needs might easily have gotten lost in the shuffle.

"Maybe. God, I'm so sorry—"

It was too damn late for empty recriminations. Garrett turned on his heel, swearing more at the fact he was taking so long to heal than that he'd forgotten to baby the injury. The barely-mended crushed bones and new hardware hurt like a sonuvabitch. But to hell with taking it easy. He had to do something. With every passing moment, the chances of finding his daughter unharmed diminished. Determined to ignore the shooting pain in his leg, he strode to the door.

Damn. He couldn't leave Elaine. For all her seeming calm, he could imagine her collapsing into a brittle heap the moment he walked out. "Come on," he told her. "The cops are overworked, that's for sure. We can't just stay here. Forward your phone to my cellular so we won't miss any calls, and let's go see if we can find her."

* * * * *

Four hours later dark had fallen and they'd learned nothing, found no clues. Not a sign of Leah in any of the local teenage haunts, nor a hint as to where she might have gone after she'd sneaked out a window and fled from the exclusive Sandy Hills School for Girls.

Elaine admired Garrett's outward calm as she watched him question bartenders and beach bums, preppy college kids on spring break, and shady characters she'd be afraid to rub against for fear their seamy lives would somehow taint hers.

He was one hunk of a man, big and muscular and so ruggedly attractive that he drew stares from teenage Lolitas and gray-haired grandmas alike. His rumpled shirt and faded jeans contributed to his dangerous look, a look accentuated by windblown dark-brown hair that was overdue for styling, and a heavy five-o'clock shadow.

But Garrett's injuries had sapped much of the physical endurance she remembered so well. As the night wore on, Elaine noticed his limp becoming more pronounced and the furrows etched on either side of his sensual mouth growing deeper. He had to be in pain, though she knew from experience he'd never admit to any weakness.

"Let's go home," she told him when he nearly stumbled over a curb. "We're not getting anywhere here." Leah wasn't here. If she were, Elaine was certain she would have sensed her child's presence.

He nodded after righting himself, holding onto her arm as if it were she who needed support. "All right. We've done about all we can tonight, anyhow," he said as he headed for the car.

Chapter Two

℘

Elaine had been telling herself nearly every day since she'd thrown him out that she was better off without Garrett than she would have been, agonizing over whether his next assignment would mean his death. Tonight, though, she needed his strength, his presence. She needed the warmth of his big body to remind her life went on, and that where there was life, there was hope.

He seemed to need her, too. Or perhaps it was only that he needed not to sleep alone with the frustration he couldn't mask. For whatever reason, he offered no resistance when she took his hand and led him to the bedroom they'd shared between his treks to God knew where, journeys from which she'd never known if or when he'd come home.

At the touch of her hand to his stubborn jaw, he shuddered. Then he gathered her to him in a gesture that clearly began in compassion but quickly ignited the sensual flame their bitter divorce had banked but never quite put out.

"We shouldn't be doing this," he mumbled against her shoulder while she ground herself hard against his crotch.

"I don't care." Reaching between them, she rubbed her hand along the hard ridge beneath his zipper. "Make love with me now, Garrett. Please."

"I don't have any protection for you," he said as he tried to pull away.

But his grunted protest paled by comparison with the way his penis surged against her hand. "I'm on the Pill. And I trust you to have been careful." She doubted he'd want to hear she'd had no lovers since him.

When he slid his big hands down and cupped her buttocks, she knew she'd won.

As if they'd never been apart, they undressed each other and lay across the king-size bed. Their exploration was new and exciting, yet familiar, too.

How his hands, so rough and callused, could stroke her so gently yet stoke the flames that lay hidden deep inside her, Elaine had never understood.

Those hands seemed smoother now, a reminder of his forced inactivity these past months. A reminder that her premonition about that last assignment he'd accepted hadn't been too far off the mark.

She traced a network of new scars on his back and leg and said a silent prayer of thanks that the nightmare she'd lived with since sending him away had been only partially prophetic.

But neither the scars nor the bitter memories they evoked could cool the heat that coursed through her body at every touch of his long thick fingers, each brush of his beard-roughened cheeks against her breasts, her belly.

Lips as soft as he was tough everywhere else sampled the tender skin of her earlobe, suckled her breasts, nipped at their tips as though he'd been starved far too long.

Then he spread her legs and lay between them, his jaw resting against her inner thigh. "You kept your pussy shaved," he said before spreading her outer lips and fastening his hot mouth onto her quivering flesh.

She'd shaved this afternoon after he'd told her he was coming home, but he didn't need to know that. But she couldn't stand much of this sensual torture. Not now. She'd been alone too long.

"Yes," she said when he ran a finger along her smooth, wet slit. "Garrett. Take me now."

He nibbled at her clitoris for a few minutes, and she couldn't help squirming at the delicious sensations. Then he slid up her body and claimed her mouth. The taste of her own juices on his tongue fueled the flame that was building fast in her lower belly and spreading through her body.

Groaning, he sank his huge hard sex inside her. First he stretched and filled her, and then he began the rhythmic thrusting that had always set her on fire. She wanted him closer, deeper, harder. As though by their own volition, her legs tightened around his waist, drew him in until she felt the blunt head of his penis nudging her womb.

"God. You feel good. So good. It's been so long. Too long." He sounded urgent, as though he was in pain.

Elaine opened her eyes and framed Garrett's rugged face between her hands. God, but she loved this impossible man. Always had. Always would, no matter what.

When he moved inside her, he touched her heart as well as her sex. Like no other man had ever done, he made her body come alive. And she loved the feeling, loved the feel of his hard muscles straining against her as he thrust and retreated, pushing her closer to the climax she'd missed so long—the climax she wanted him to give her now more than all the riches on earth.

How had she managed to drive him away, let her fear overcome the love that wouldn't die? "Don't hold back. I'm not," she whispered as she urged him with her hips to move faster, push them over the edge.

"Shit. I'm coming. Now," he ground out between ragged breaths.

She convulsed around him, the waves of pleasure coursing through her veins and taking her breath away. While the aftershocks had her tingling with pleasure, he slammed into her one last time and shuddered as he found his own satisfaction.

* * * * *

Their lovemaking lent a bittersweet edge to the night, and when Garrett gathered Elaine into his arms and held her, he dreaded going back to a life without her as much as he shared the fear for Leah that was a palpable presence between them.

They'd had so much—great sex, a child they both loved. Why couldn't they have resolved the differences that had made them end their fifteen-year marriage?

Through the night, until dawn tinged the sky with shades of rose and purple against clouds of brilliant white, her steady heartbeat reassured him, let him sleep fitfully despite his fear.

When he woke he noticed Selena's stones glittering in the morning light. Damn worthless things anyhow, he thought. They'd certainly been no help last night when he and Elaine had trekked all over the beach looking for Leah. Shaking his head at Selena's good-hearted foolishness, he picked them up off the bedside table and took a closer look.

All he saw were cold hunks of mineral. Nothing magical or even particularly attractive. It must have been his imagination working overtime when he'd thought the stupid rocks had beckoned him.

But suddenly he felt them growing warm against his palm.

The damn things *were* heating up. There was no mistaking it. When Elaine rolled onto her back, he reached over and caressed her satiny cunt. And the stones grew warmer still.

What the hell?

Could there really be something magic about these two hunks of rock? Garrett moved them away from Elaine, felt their heat begin to dissipate.

Puzzled, he moved his hand back toward her, laying the stones in the hollow between her hipbones and keeping his hand on them while they grew warm…warmer…hot.

He observed the clear crystal taking on a glow. They gave off a weird aura, something sexual yet spiritual.

His balls drew up close to his body and his cock began to stir, but he was in no hurry to appease that hunger.

Gently he bent and wakened Elaine with a kiss, stroking her teeth with his tongue while he traced circular patterns on her naked body with the stones.

Her breasts. Her belly.

The stones gave off a radiant heat, not unpleasant but mildly arousing, Elaine thought sleepily when Garrett enlarged the circles then narrowed them again over her crotch and thighs.

She liked the feeling of heat. Liked waking up with Garrett after a night of making love, inhaling the heady scent of him and her and sex. When he laid the stones down again on her belly and began to lick between her legs with long, slow strokes of his velvety tongue, the heat intensified.

His hot wet breath tickled and tantalized her, and she shifted restlessly against his mouth. But the stones remained where he'd put them, their warmth radiating to some place deep inside her belly where not even his huge, hot penis could reach.

It was strange how those stones gave off an aura. Very strange. The black stone glowed, while the crystal one reflected the orange rays of the early morning sun that streamed through the patio doors leading out to the beach.

The aura intensified as Garrett sucked her clitoris, brightening around his dark head like a warm, surrealistic halo when he inserted first one, then two more long fingers inside her.

"Oh, yesss." She clamped her thighs over his head, holding him to her as waves of incredible pleasure washed over her.

And before she closed her eyes and gave herself over completely to the magic he was working on her, she had a fleeting vision.

Of Leah, her arms outstretched, against the backdrop of a stormy sea.

But when Elaine came down from the orgasm that had taken her breath and rendered her practically unconscious, the vision had disappeared.

Garrett slid up her body, bracing his weight on arms bulging with muscles undamaged by his near-fatal accident. "I'm going to fuck you now," he whispered against her lips, joining their bodies in one smooth thrust while he mated their mouths. His kiss was rapacious, his penis throbbing and hot as fire. She still tingled all over from the force of her climax.

He pumped into her hard, fast, as though driven by some force he didn't understand. The stones lodged between them, their heat so intense it nearly took his breath away. And her pussy clenched his cock, drenched it in the slick, hot juices he still tasted on his lips and tongue.

She shuddered again, her composure swept away again on the wings of pleasure. And he let his eyelids drift shut, sank in her up to his balls, and let himself go.

He came for what seemed like hours, spurting again and again, so deep it had to be going straight into her womb.

When he finally rolled off her and opened his eyes, he noticed the stones glowing brightly on Elaine's belly, as if something had anchored them. Thinking they'd burn her if he left them there, Garrett lifted them and carried them out onto the patio that overlooked the beach.

So much for Selena's stones that by now had grown so hot he had to toss them from hand to hand. Heat or no heat, they hadn't given him the first hint of where they might find Leah. He'd trust his instincts any day over the witch-woman's hocus-pocus.

Frustrated, he tossed the stones onto the sandy patio.

It couldn't be. Garrett blinked, and when his vision cleared, he still saw Leah, plain as day. She wasn't on the patio, though. He didn't recognize the trees or buildings, or the stretch of aqua oceanfront in the background. "Talk to me, baby," he said, taking a step outside and reaching out to her.

"Come on, honey. Tell me where you are," he coaxed. "Mom and I are worried sick."

All he saw was a childish face, so like Elaine's that Garrett wanted to cry. Not a word, nor a hint of where they should search. He cursed the useless magic, but picked up the stones and took them back inside.

They'd cooled somewhat, but the things still scorched his palm. Maybe he should tell Elaine about them.

He wasn't about to raise her hopes, though, and common sense told him to write off what he'd just seen as a figment of his imagination.

* * * * *

During the morning, Garrett thought he "saw" Leah several times. Not wanting to give Elaine false hope, however, he didn't tell her.

Instead, he called Selena.

Trust your heart. That was all the white witch said.

It had been so long since Garrett had done that, he didn't know if he could. When he rubbed the stones together in his pocket, though, the vision came to him again. This time Garrett recognized the setting—a resort in the lower Florida Keys where he, Elaine, and Leah had spent their last vacation as a family several years ago.

Could a child have gone so far, so quickly? Logic said no. Still, the stones had shown him Leah on that beach, under a distinctively shaped pagoda where they'd picnicked and watched small sailboats bobbing in the nearby cove.

"Elaine, I think she's gone to Paradise Cove," he told her when she set down the phone and looked at him through tear-filled eyes.

"That's impossible. And that was Detective Delgado. They've got no news. Nothing."

"We'll find her. Don't lose hope. And I know it seems impossible, but..." Dare he tell her about the stones? Or the visions he'd had of Leah? "I saw her. In my mind. As plainly as if she'd been right here in front of me."

Elaine shot him a look he couldn't decipher. "You saw Leah? In a vision?" Very quietly, she explained that this morning she thought she'd seen their daughter briefly while they were making love.

"It's these stones." Garrett pulled them from his pocket, feeling them grow warm again when he held them. Could sex be the catalyst that caused the stones to produce these visions? When he thought about it, the idea didn't seem that farfetched. After all, if he accepted the idea that magic was tied to love the way Selena had implied, and since he knew damn well some kinds of love equated to sex, it hardly seemed impossible.

As if afraid, Elaine clasped her hands together when he'd have handed the stones to her. "What are they? And where did you get them?"

"The woman who runs the place where I've been staying to recuperate is a psychic or something. I'm not exactly sure what you'd call her, but she casts stones like these and sometimes sees things before they happen, or so she says. When I told her why I was leaving she gave these to me and said that if I believed, they'd lead me to Leah."

"And the stones are what you think let you 'see' Leah in the Keys? How on earth could she have gotten that far?"

"I don't know, but I'm going to fly down there to check it out. Are you coming?"

He watched her face turn pale. Elaine didn't fly in small planes. She hated the fact that he did, and that he'd kept a little Cessna since early in their marriage. Her nod was practically imperceptible.

"I'll pack a bag," she said as she got up from her place at the kitchen table.

While Elaine packed, Garrett called the airstrip where he kept his plane and arranged for it to be brought out of the hangar and gassed up. By the time he'd arranged to rent a car at Paradise Cove's private airstrip and informed the local police where they would be if any news came through about their daughter, Elaine had returned, his duffel bag and an overnight case in hand.

"I'm ready if you are," she told him, her smile brave even though she trembled when she spotted the dark clouds that had started rolling in over the Atlantic.

Chapter Three

༄

Elaine was obviously terrified. And she couldn't quit chattering about Selena's stones while they waited out the sudden thunderstorm in a deserted office at the airstrip.

Garrett rubbed the stones together, but no matter how hard she nagged or how hard he concentrated, he couldn't conjure up another vision of their daughter.

Finally his patience flew the coop when she ordered him to stop the thunder and lightning.

"Damn it, I'm not God. The fucking storm will quit when it gets good and ready. But it shouldn't be long. These afternoon squalls usually blow over pretty fast."

"My baby," she sobbed. "If Leah's out there in this weather, she's in danger. We could drive down there instead of waiting out the storm." Sobs caught in Elaine's throat, and he saw she was shaking uncontrollably.

She also was making no sense at all. If they drove, they'd be stuck in traffic jams on Highway One while a dozen storms played out.

Garrett shut her up the only way he knew how. In one quick motion he swooped down and claimed her mouth, thrusting his tongue inside while he burrowed his hand into her impeccable French twist and sent pins flying in all directions.

She whimpered against his mouth, but still her slender body shuddered beneath his hands.

Garrett knew just one way to distract her when she lost control like this. And he was ready and eager to fuck her so hard and so long that she'd lose sight of everything but how his cock damn near split her apart every time he slammed her pussy down on it.

With his other hand he swept her long skirt out of the way and ripped off her lacy thong when it got in between his hand and her cunt.

"Unzip my pants and let my cock loose if you want it," he muttered into her mouth, and when she freed him he lifted and impaled her.

Her breathy moan could have meant she liked it or she didn't. He chose to believe she liked having his cock rammed in her cunt as much as he liked to ram it there.

"Hold on tight," he said, helping her wrap her legs around his waist while he limped forward to the wall and braced her against it.

Pain shot through Garrett's bad leg, but it was nothing compared with the incredible pleasure of having his cock inside his wife's tight cunt. Thunder boomed in the distance, and lightning crackled in an eerie light show outside the smoke-stained window. Elaine's nails dug into his shoulders, and she rode him hard and fast, as though this would be their last fuck.

"Do it harder!"

She gasped when he slammed her down again so his cockhead made contact with her G-spot.

He clasped her around her slender waist, then did it again. "Like that, do you?"

"Oh, yesss. Make me come. Now."

His muscles bulging with the effort, he lifted her until his cock was nearly free, then pulled her down on him, hard, at the same time he locked his knees and ground his pelvis into her cunt. The slapping noise of wet naked flesh mating, the feel of her incredibly tight pussy fisting his throbbing flesh, and the sounds of her little screams mingling with the thunder nearly overwhelmed him.

"I'm coming, baby. Come with me."

"Again. Harder."

Once, twice, he pounded into her. The third time, when her slick juices bathed him and she sank her teeth into his earlobe, he let go and poured her full of cum. Then, out of breath and wrung out, he looked out the window and saw a brilliant rainbow peeking through the sheets of rain.

"Looks like we'll be able to leave soon," Garrett said as he gathered up hairpins and handed them to Elaine along with the ragged remains of her lacy underwear.

* * * * *

She looked pale beneath the gentle tan of her skin and the flush of lovemaking that still colored her cheeks an hour later.

Was Elaine reliving their last years together the way he was, now that they shared the silence of the Cessna's compact cabin? Garrett knew he was.

They'd fought over everything from his job and this airplane to Elaine's insistence that her job as a financial analyst could support them.

As if he would ever have let himself live off his wife's earnings.

Methodically following the flight plan he'd filed, he visually ticked off each familiar landmark along the Florida coast. As they moved south, the stones grew warmer against his thigh, sending a tingling sensation upward that settled in the pit of his stomach.

Garrett glanced at Elaine. Why the hell couldn't she relax, at least enough to let go the death grip she had on the armrests of the second seat?

If he'd had any idea what to say, he'd have done his best to comfort her. Trouble was, though, he was as terrified as she was, not of flying in the reliable little airplane, but of whether and how they'd manage to pick up the rubble that would remain of their lives if they lost Leah.

Paradise Cove lay there in the distance, serenely calm, its sapphire waters beckoning. As Garrett began his descent, the stones seemed to radiate not just the familiar heat but an energy of their own. He banked right and lined the Cessna up with the resort's well-kept airstrip.

"You okay?" he asked Elaine.

She bit her lip, the way she always had done when she was scared stiff. "I'll live. Garrett, what will we do if Leah isn't here?"

"Keep looking." What else could he say?

The stones rattled in his pocket when he climbed out of the plane and held a hand up to steady Elaine as she came down.

"What was that noise?" she asked.

Garrett pulled out the stones. "Our magic stones."

"Are they showing you something now?"

"I'm not sure." But Garrett felt a pull, almost irresistible, toward a deserted stretch of sand beach at the far end of the landing strip. "Come with me. I'm going to take a look down there."

Selena's gentle voice rang in Garrett's ears. *Love will lead you to your daughter. And the stones will help you find her.*

Suddenly he remembered something else Selena had said, one night when she'd cast a healing spell for a lonely guest. *Sex strengthens the magic.*

Garrett had no trouble buying into that. Hell, the stones got blistering hot every time he and Elaine had sex, and the visions of Leah had come after they'd fucked each other to mind-blowing orgasms.

* * * * *

Even with his injured leg, Garrett's long stride ate up the distance, making Elaine struggle to keep up. When he came to a halt at the edge of the beach and leaned against the trunk of a tall palm tree, his numb expression reminded her of how he'd looked just before he walked out of her life a year ago.

"She's not here." Garrett dug into his pocket, then hurled the magic stones toward the crystal clear water. "Damn it, I was so sure we'd find her here."

"Garrett?" Elaine backed away toward the water, pulled by some unseen, unheard force she couldn't deny.

"I saw her. I swear, Elaine, I saw our baby in the pagoda in front of the Paradise Cove Resort. Then, when I got off the plane, I saw her again, here on the beach. But she wasn't at the pagoda, and she's not here either. The damn stones lied."

His voice carried eerily on the strong breeze, called her back. But the force kept her moving, then dragged her to her knees.

There they were. Two stones, one black and smooth, one crystal clear and faceted as though by a master jeweler. She couldn't look away, for something about them held her in thrall, warmed her heart and soothed the terror she'd lived with since learning Leah had run away.

"Elaine?"

Garrett's voice came from somewhere far, far away, or so it seemed. The stones glowed in the sand, their aura surrounding Elaine. Leah's face appeared on the horizon, came closer, then stopped just outside her mother's reach.

She wants you both. Together.

It was as though the stones had spoken, yet they had no voice, no life. Was it Leah speaking? Elaine looked up, but Leah's image was fading away. "Garrett?"

He limped to her, knelt, encircled Elaine in a gentle embrace. "I'm sorry, love."

It had been forever since she'd heard him call her that, since he'd whispered gentle endearments whenever they had a moment to themselves.

"So am I." She was sorry for everything. For being too weak, too scared to live with Garrett's penchant for danger. For burying herself in her own work, thinking financial security would make her adventurous lover content to stay by home and hearth. For putting her own fears and needs above his—and Leah's. "Garrett, I saw her, too."

"Where?"

"In the stones." Her gaze locked on the crystal and the obsidian, glowing brightly, side by side.

Together. As we are.

The glow grew brighter, the aura stronger. Elaine leaned against Garrett's broad chest, felt his heart beat against her back.

"I want us to be together, too." Garrett spoke so softly she could barely make out the words, yet they were there, hanging between them.

"You and me?" Elaine squeezed Garrett's hand.

"Yes," he told her.

And me, too.

Was that Leah's voice she heard now, or merely a whisper on the wind? Elaine felt Garrett's muscles tighten, so he must have heard it, too.

The stones glowed brighter, compelling Elaine to pick them up. They warmed her palm while Garrett's big hands surrounded hers. A feeling of serenity and hope came over her.

And the beginnings of arousal stirred, growing stronger as if by magic.

A deep, spiritual arousal that transcended mere animal attraction. A melding of sex and magic—and something more.

It seemed the most natural thing in the world when he pulled her to the sand and knelt between her legs. The most beautiful moment since he'd handed her their newborn daughter when he bent and kissed her, his lips as soft on hers as his big body was tough and rugged. When he freed himself and joined their bodies it was as though they'd finally come home.

He was making her a silent promise of more than his body to ease their lust. A promise that she sensed was what their daughter had been seeking when she ran away. A vow as binding as the ones they'd once made and broken, she thought when he took her mouth with a soft, sure thrust of his tongue.

Anyone could see them from the cove or the beach. Yet for Elaine saw only herself and Garrett, and a curious seagull circling overhead. And she recalled the promises they'd foolishly tossed aside but never abandoned.

"Sex makes the magic stronger," he whispered as he rocked slowly, deeply inside her body, the slapping sounds they made mimicking the breaking of gentle waves against the sand.

He loved her gently, stroked away her tears with callused thumbs while he moved in her slowly, deeply, almost as though she were some pagan goddess burnished by the sun.

But of course Garrett had always sensed her sexual needs…fulfilled them…a lot more than she'd ever done for him. He gave and she took.

Before. Now she wrapped him in her arms, in the love that had faded but never died. Shifting beneath him, she flexed her hips, took all of him inside, and squeezed his throbbing penis as if she'd never let him go.

His anguished groan told her more than words that he liked it, so she contracted her inner muscles again.

He moved one hand between them and put gentle pressure on her clitoris. "Come for me, my love," he whispered. "Let's bring back the vision that has helped us find our way."

As quiet as their last mating had been volatile, this time brought Elaine to tears as the sensation of Garrett's seed spurting into her womb sent gentle waves of pleasure, overwhelming sensations no less intense than the wild waves that had overcome her hours earlier.

The vision came again, this time to Elaine. As clearly as an hour before when they'd walked by and found it empty, she saw the pagoda where they'd picnicked years ago before they let the pressures of living tear their lives apart. "Did you see it, too?" she asked, and Garrett nodded.

"Let's go there now," Elaine said, certain now that Leah would be there, and safe.

* * * * *

She was—and she was sound asleep. Garrett carried their daughter to the plane, and while he flew them home, Elaine held the magic stones.

Very disparate objects, they apparently were inert and silent by themselves yet powerful in tandem. Like her and Garrett, they were different in nearly every way, yet meant to be together.

Elaine thanked the fates that they'd recognized that in time to save their love—their marriage—and their beautiful, unhappy child.

* * * * *

Late that night after Leah had gone to bed, Garrett held Elaine close to his battered body. "Marry me again," he said, reminding her he'd never been one to waste unnecessary words.

Elaine had an equally simple answer. "Yes." No more needed saying.

"And let's keep Leah home with us instead of sending her back to boarding school. These old bones aren't up to any more of the kind of battering they took last time. I'll be flying charters, period. No more chasing fugitives all over the Caribbean." He sighed as he stretched his big body across the bed and held his arms out to her.

"All right," she said, her expression dreamy. "I'd like to spend our second honeymoon at that bed and breakfast where you went to heal and get to know the white witch who gave you these." She shifted so she and Garrett could both see the stones.

From the spot on the bedside table where she'd put them, she could see the stones had taken on a warm, contented glow. Were they trying to tell her they'd wrought this miracle, too?

She liked to think they'd played a part in Garrett's change of heart about his work. And she felt sure they'd helped her realize that for however long fate gave them, she wanted to spend it in his arms.

The stones beckoned her, and she touched first one and then the other.

"They're like us, you know," Garrett said, his deep voice as mesmerizing as it had been the first time they'd made love so long ago. "Black and white. Day and night. Separate, they're helpless, Selena told me, while together their power can know no bounds."

"Colors of magic," Elaine murmured, picking up the magic stones when she dimmed the light then nudged her lover's muscular thighs apart.

The stones grew warm in her hand, warmer when she rubbed them gently over the puckered scar tissue that marred his thigh and back. Perhaps, if she loved him enough she could help him heal the pain that clouded his dark eyes even now.

How she loved this man who always saw to her pleasure before taking his own!

Now it was his turn to be healed and loved the same unselfish way that he'd loved her through the years. Her gaze settled on his magnificent erection that seemed to lengthen and thicken as she looked at it and thought about all the joys it brought her.

Replacing the stones on the bedside table, Elaine lay between Garrett's legs, her cheek resting on his muscular thigh while she tangled her fingers in his dark pubic curls and weighed his heavy testicles in her palms.

"You're soft here. So soft," she said, blowing on his scrotum. "Not hard like here." With her tongue she traced the vein on the underside of his growing erection, then circled its crown before licking around the thick, blunt head of his penis like a mother cat might bathe her kittens.

She felt herself growing wet for him, but this was all for Garrett. From his low-pitched purr she guessed he liked what she was doing. A lot.

The pre-cum she noticed glistening in the slit at the tip of his penis tasted slick and salty, much like her own juices that she'd tasted on Garrett's lips and tongue so many times. Suddenly she wanted more.

She wanted him to let go and come in her mouth now. For the first time in her life she couldn't wait to take him deep in her throat and swallow. To pay him back in this small way for the pleasure he'd given her nearly every day of their marriage when he'd unselfishly sucked and tongued her until she shattered inside.

Though she'd done it, she'd often complained when he'd asked her to keep her pubic hair shaved clean for him. And she'd shrunk away from such intimate contact with the part of him that gave her so much pleasure.

Intimacy she'd never wanted before but that she wanted to share with her lover now.

"Garrett?" she asked softly before taking the throbbing head of his penis in her mouth and sucking in as much as she could, while wrapping one hand around the base of him and sliding it up and down.

"God, yes. Stuff your pretty mouth with my cock. Suck it. Hard. Yeah. Like that. Squeeze my balls, too. Baby, your mouth feels so good."

Her fingers tangled in the coarse hair around his cock. And it was obvious from the hesitant way she sucked him that she hadn't ever had much practice giving head.

But her mouth was warm and wet and welcoming, and he loved having her love him this way, the way she'd never done before except in his wildest dreams. He loved it so much he was going to come right now.

And there wasn't a thing he could do to hold it back. "Stop. Please. Oh, shit. I can't help it, baby. I'm coming." He cupped her cheeks with both hands, trying to get her to let go before—

Hot bursts of semen flooded her mouth, but she wouldn't let him go. Instead she took him deeper, swallowed his cock and his cum.

"You didn't have to do that, love," he said much later, after he'd returned the favor and brought her to a screaming climax with his tongue.

"I know. I wanted to. But if you like me giving you head, you'd better get yourself a haircut down here, too." She gave his pubic bush a playful tug that amazingly had his cock raring to go again.

Garrett chuckled. "I'm game for whatever turns you on."

Then he glanced over at the magic stones, thinking their glow had grown brighter, clearer. "Colors of magic, indeed," he murmured, drawing Elaine's warm, satiny body close and cupping her breasts in both his hands.

The stones had brought them back together, brought their daughter home. Tomorrow they'd deal with Leah and whatever other crises might occur. And they'd work out their problems together.

Like the magic stones, he and Elaine worked best in tandem.

But tonight was for them. For the lovers they'd always been, and the lovers they would always be.

Epilogue

Strange how he'd gone full circle in just three weeks.

Garrett stood at the window of the same room at Selena's Bed and Breakfast where he'd stayed before rushing home to find his little girl, only now he was looking out at her and Selena as they strolled along the riverbank.

It was a good thing Leah had hit it off with Selena right away, because all he'd been able to think about on the drive from Fort Lauderdale was that soon he was going to fuck Elaine for real in the old-fashioned canopy bed where he'd spent the first weeks of his stay. His cock swelled against the black silk pajama bottom he'd put on while waiting for his brand-new bride to join him.

The silk slid sensuously over his skin and tickled his clean-shaven balls. Fuck the stares he'd gotten at the gym where he'd kept up his therapy while he was home. He'd shave himself from head to toe if Elaine asked him to, just to feel her swallow his cock and taste his cum on her lips and tongue.

The afternoon sunlight filtered through moss-laden oak trees, making lacy patterns on the gauzy canopy that surrounded the king-size bed. And on Elaine, who'd just come in the room.

Shit. She'd gift-wrapped her sexy little cunt in a nightgown of see-through, clinging black silk. Her hair hung almost to her waist, long and pale and so soft he longed to wrap it around his cock and have her rub it all over his body while they fucked.

"You had this on before," he said, reaching out and cupping her beautiful breasts through the lace-trimmed bodice.

She lifted a shapely eyebrow. "Before?"

Of course she was bound to think he'd lost his fucking mind. "Before you called me. Baby, I dreamed you came to me just like you're doing now. Wearing a thing just like you've got on. I ripped it off you and tied you up with it," he told her, sliding his hands inside the low neck so he could roll her nipples between his thumb and forefinger. "I straddled your face and made you give me head while I went down on your sweet, hot cunt."

"Want to do it again?" she asked, her eyes sparkling when she looked up at him and licked her full red lips. "You won't have to tie me up this time. Whatever you want today, my husband and lover, it's yours. "

He bunched her gown in his hands and tugged it off her. "First I want you naked, so I can taste every inch of your gorgeous body before I ram my cock in your pussy and fill you full of cum. Then we'll play."

But she wasn't having that. On her knees now, in front of the window where anybody who looked could see what she was doing, she pulled out his cock and balls and sucked him off.

"Your turn," she told him after he'd licked the last of his cum off her lips and chin.

As though offering herself like a pagan sacrifice, she slid back the canopy and bent forward over the king-size bed.

Her pale pink cunt glistened, already wet and ready for whatever he had in mind, and his cock sprang back to life as though he hadn't already come moments earlier. Her little clit stuck out, ruby-red and inviting, and her sweet ass beckoned him. He nipped her plump ass cheeks one by one, using his teeth to gently mark his territory.

Rubbing her clit in slow circles with his thumb, he used the other hand to stroke her slick, hot slit and spread the copious juices he found there.

"Now, Garrett. Take me now. Please." She lifted her ass higher in the air, inviting him as surely with her action as with the fervent plea.

He circled the puckered rosebud of her anus with his finger. "This way?"

"Oh, yesss."

Reaching into the pocket of his PJs, Garrett took out the silver-and-black ben-wei balls he'd bought her a few days earlier. "I'm going to put these in your pussy first," he said as he reached up and rubbed the toys over her breasts and belly before spreading open the satiny lips of her cunt and inserting them high up in her hot, wet hole.

His balls tightened when he let down his pants, donned a condom, and smeared his sheathed cock with warm, slick lubricant. Guiding it with his hand, he positioned its swollen head at her rear entrance and pushed little by little until her sphincter muscle relaxed and let him in.

"Oooh," she murmured, lowering her head onto the bed and arching her back to take more of him.

"Want more cock?" He was in her only an inch or so, but her ass was tight. Incredibly tight.

Unbelievably erotic, the feeling of utter fullness. "I want it all," she said, and when he gave her another inch, then another, his movements set the balls he'd put inside her into motion.

The tension built as he gave her more. Pleasure mingled with the pain of being stretched and stuffed the way he'd done with her a few times before, when she'd been in heat this way.

"I'm coming. Oh, God, it hurts so good." Her eyelids closed as waves of ecstasy coursed through her veins. Vaguely she felt him withdraw and fish the ben-wei balls out, and when he rolled her onto her back and mounted her again, she realized he was still as hard as stone.

"I want to put my cum where it will do the most good," he told her, bending and suckling her nipples as though she were the baby they'd decided last week to try to have. "Squeeze my cock, baby. Make me give you my cum."

And she did. Again and again, during the two idyllic weeks they spent with their daughter in this quaint old-fashioned compound along the Suwannee River, learning the colors of magic—and of love.

Also by Ann Jacobs

☙

eBooks:

A Gift of Gold
A Mutual Favor
Awakenings
Black Gold: Another Love
Black Gold: Dallas Heat
Black Gold: Entrapped
Black Gold: Firestorm
Black Gold: Forever Enslaved
Black Gold: Love Slave
Club Rio Brava 1: Loving Control
Club Rio Brava 2: Switching Control
Club Rio Brava 3: Unexpected Control
Club Rio Brava 4: Learning Control
Colors of Love
Colors of Magic
Commitment
D'Argent Honor: Eternal Triangle
D'Argent Honor 1: Vampire Justice
D'Argent Honor 2: Eternally His
D'Argent Honor 3: Eternal Surrender
D'Argent Honor 4: Eternal Victory
Dark Side of the Moon
Gates of Hell

Gridiron Lovers: Hot for the Reunion
Gridiron Lovers 1: Naked Bootleg
Gridiron Lovers 2: Forward Pass
Gridiron Lovers 3: Hot in the Clutch
Gridiron Lovers 4: Coach Me
Haunted
He Calls Her Jasmine
Heart of the West 1: Roped
Heart of the West 2: Hitched
Heart of the West 3: Lassoed
Her Very Special Robot
Illusions
Lawyers in Love: Eye of the Storm
Lawyers in Love: Gettin' It On
Lawyers in Love 1: In His Own Defense
Lawyers in Love 2: Bittersweet Homecoming
Lawyers in Love 3: Mastered
Necessary Roughness 1: Sackmaster
Necessary Roughness 2: End Run
Out of Bounds
Pleasure Partners 1: His Pleasure Mistress
Pleasure Partners 2: Pleasure Slave
Storm Warnings *(anthology)*
Tip of the Iceberg
Topaz Dream
Wrong Place, Wrong Time?
Zayed's Gift

Print Books:
A Mutual Favor
A Shining Future *(anthology)*
Black Gold: Another Love
Black Gold: Dallas Heat
Black Gold: Firestorm
Black Gold: Sandstorms *(anthology)*
Bound by Love *(anthology)*
Club Rio Brava 1, 2, 3 & 4: Controlled by Love
D'Argent Honor 1, 3 & 4: Full Circle
D'Argent Honor 2: Eternally His
Forbidden Fantasies *(anthology)*
Gridiron Lovers 1 & 2: Home Field Advantage
Gridiron Lovers 3 & 4: Men in Motion
Haunted
Heart of the West *(anthology)*
Lawyers in Love: Enchained *(anthology)*
Lawyers in Love 1 & 2: The Defenders *(anthology)*
Lawyers in Love: The Prosecutors *(anthology)*
Lords of Pleasure *(anthology)*
Out of Bounds

About the Author
⍟

Ann Jacobs is a sucker for lusty Alpha heroes and happy endings, which makes Ellora's Cave an ideal publisher for her work. Romantica®, to her, is the perfect combination of sex, sensuality, deep emotional involvement and lifelong commitment—the elusive fantasy women often dream about but seldom achieve.

First published in 1996, Jacobs has sold over forty books and novellas, some of which have earned awards including the Passionate Plume (best novella, 2006), the Desert Rose (best hot and spicy romance, 2004) and More Than Magic (best erotic romance, 2004). She has been a double finalist in separate categories of the EPPIES and From the Heart RWA Chapter's contest. Three of her books have been translated and sold in several European countries.

A CPA and former hospital financial manager, Jacobs now writes full-time, with the help of Mr. Blue, the family cat who sometimes likes to perch on the back of her desk chair and lend his sage advice. He sometimes even contributes a few random letters when he decides he wants to try out the keyboard. She loves to hear from readers, and to put faces with names at signings and conventions.

The author welcomes comments from readers. You can find her website and email address on her author bio page at www.ellorascave.com.

Tell Us What You Think

We appreciate hearing reader opinions about our books. You can email us at Comments@EllorasCave.com.

Why an electronic book?

We live in the Information Age—an exciting time in the history of human civilization, in which technology rules supreme and continues to progress in leaps and bounds every minute of every day. For a multitude of reasons, more and more avid literary fans are opting to purchase e-books instead of paper books. The question from those not yet initiated into the world of electronic reading is simply: *Why?*

1. *Price.* An electronic title at Ellora's Cave Publishing and Cerridwen Press runs anywhere from 40% to 75% less than the cover price of the exact same title in paperback format. Why? Basic mathematics and cost. It is less expensive to publish an e-book (no paper and printing, no warehousing and shipping) than it is to publish a paperback, so the savings are passed along to the consumer.
2. *Space.* Running out of room in your house for your books? That is one worry you will never have with electronic books. For a low one-time cost, you can purchase a handheld device specifically designed for e-reading. Many e-readers have large, convenient screens for viewing. Better yet, hundreds of titles can be stored within your new library—on a single microchip. There are a variety of e-readers from different manufacturers. You can also read e-books on your PC or laptop computer. (Please note that Ellora's Cave does not endorse any specific brands.

You can check our websites at www.ellorascave.com or www.cerridwenpress.com for information we make available to new consumers.)
3. ***Mobility.*** Because your new e-library consists of only a microchip within a small, easily transportable e-reader, your entire cache of books can be taken with you wherever you go.
4. ***Personal Viewing Preferences.*** Are the words you are currently reading too small? Too large? Too… ANNOYING? Paperback books cannot be modified according to personal preferences, but e-books can.
5. ***Instant Gratification.*** Is it the middle of the night and all the bookstores near you are closed? Are you tired of waiting days, sometimes weeks, for bookstores to ship the novels you bought? Ellora's Cave Publishing sells instantaneous downloads twenty-four hours a day, seven days a week, every day of the year. Our webstore is never closed. Our e-book delivery system is 100% automated, meaning your order is filled as soon as you pay for it.

Those are a few of the top reasons why electronic books are replacing paperbacks for many avid readers.

As always, Ellora's Cave and Cerridwen Press welcome your questions and comments. We invite you to email us at Comments@ellorascave.com or write to us directly at Ellora's Cave Publishing Inc., 1056 Home Avenue, Akron, OH 44310-3502.

Discover for yourself why readers can't get enough of the multiple award-winning publisher Ellora's Cave.

Whether you prefer e-books or paperbacks,

be sure to visit EC on the web at www.ellorascave.com

for an erotic reading experience that will leave you breathless.

CPSIA information can be obtained at www.ICGtesting.com
230363LV00001B/29/P